The Third Artifact

Updated on **01/05/2025** (updated cover)

Notes	4
The Story So Far	5
Prologue	6
Destination Unknown	10
Discovery	22
Munchkins	31
Departure	42
The Nest	51
The Return	63
The Mine	72
The Ship	77
Munchkins II	84
Problems	104
Station	114
Travel	119
Upgrades	130
The Wreck	138
The Third Artifact	143
Shopping	149
The Return	158
The next Destination	172

Testing	181
The Nest II	192
Buy or Lease	200
The upgrade	204
Earth	208
Surprise	216
Damage Control	224
Hello	228
Epilogue	229
About the Author	232
Books by David Collins:	233

NOTES

If you find any typos or errors in the book, please report them to me at yourrobotoverlord3500@gmail.com, and I will try to fix them.

All characters appearing in this are fictitious. Any resemblance to actual persons, living or dead, is purely coincidental.

Copyright@2024, 2025 David Collins

All rights reserved. This book may not be reproduced, stored, or copied, whole or in part, by any means whatsoever without the author's or publisher's prior written consent.

Many thanks to my Reviewers:
- Christie Marston
- John Donigan
- Keith Verret
- Jim Brady
- Scott Kelbell
- Johnny Parsons
- Sam Foster

Special thanks to the 'The Weare Area Writers Guild,' a group of NH authors that have helped improve my writing over the last year (they are other genres, not S/F): https://bit.ly/wearewriters

THE STORY SO FAR

This is the third book in the series The Artifact

1) In the first book, Ben's impulse purchase on eBay leads three college kids to possess a small alien spaceship with a somewhat quirky AI. They avoid most (but not all) of the military's attempts to possess or control it, and they take off to a station that is supposed to be a repair station. What they find is a den of alien crooks. Escaping that incident leads them to accidentally rescue Mee Keralatazaku, a stranded noble and the most unusual ship she possesses. She is grateful to be rescued. The rest of the galaxy is less than thrilled with her return.

2) In the second book, they now have a much larger and nicer spaceship (a gift from the supreme ruler), and returning to Earth to get married creates a galactic diplomatic situation. 'She, who must NOT be annoyed,' decides to crash the wedding and travel with them on the next adventure while wearing a female human Terminator-like avatar body. Their next destination adds a new alien crew member, and Mark almost immediately wants to marry her. Surprisingly, she agrees. They plan a large and elaborate wedding, only to have evil aliens and terrorists decide to crash that wedding.

This story picks up after they have traveled back to Mee's planet for new supplies.

PROLOGUE

We had traveled to the planet Kanpripticon to visit with Mee Keralatazaku, the supreme ruler of that planet. We needed to make some upgrades to our ship. The primary item was we wanted to add a small support ship, allowing us to deploy observation and communications satellites.

Having just finished our discussion with Mee Keralatazaku, we left Mee and Dylan in her room, and the rest of us went to the spaceship dealership.

This would hopefully be a short trip. We asked about acquiring a second smaller support ship. The problem would be that it could not operate in Hyper FTL until we added the new engine. That secretive piece of hardware had already been assembled and was on our ship.

We could not and did not want a second AI. We had a great relationship with our AI, Jessie, and adding a new AI could cause all sorts of problems. Almost all of the species in the known galaxy avoided AI on ships.

I said, "We need a support ship. It can be mostly an off-the-shelf freighter, but we would prefer a small centrifuge unit. We also want a top-of-the-line fabricator. We need a way to build new things or at least repair the existing systems."

The salesperson said, "That should not be an issue."

Mark said, "We also want at least six deployable and retrievable observation and reconnaissance satellites. Their main job will be to provide reconnaissance when visiting less developed planets."

"That should not be a problem; the Millipo system can simultaneously control seven; is that adequate?"

"That should be fine."

I said, "We also wanted some weapons. We want the standard light-duty Gatling guns and defensive systems. If possible, we also need a small missile system to target ships or weapons on the ground."

"That normally requires a military contractor's ID, but we can bypass that in your case; your… patron is well known.."

Mark said, "Can we get a rail gun?"

The salesperson sighed, "Normally, I would say no, usually with a few choice descriptive words around the no. As I said, your patron is well-known. We will find a way around it. May I suggest we include an asteroid mining option, the Kipit 4,000? That is basically a small rail gun, but several… probably most of the ships that have that don't seem to be used in asteroid mining."

Mark had a grin on his face, "We can get this in a few days?"

"Unfortunately, no, the modification to the hull, the power requirements, the energy storage unit, and the long lead time on this would put it at least five weeks."

Mark lost his silly grin. "Well, I guess we can do without one. I can't picture us needing to blow up any asteroids any time soon."

I said, "We also need a few changes on our ship. The two shuttle compartments will need new doors, and we wish to replace the missing shuttle with a slightly larger one.

The salesman looked at the displays before him, "After converting to your human units, the slightly updated shuttle will be thirty-eight inches longer and eight inches wider. It was not a huge change, but it should make them feel less cramped. Replacing the doors and installing the new shuttle will only take one day."

We were told that the lead time to retrofit the new ship would take three days. I paid for the new ship and our updates with 25% of my platinum and 85% of my neodymium reserves.

We returned to our ship to wait three days for the new ship to be ready and almost immediately received a message that Meera and Dylan would stay at Mee's place for a few days. We were not surprised.

The new ship needed a crew of four to operate it. We selected Theodore (Ted) Brown, one of the enlisted guards, who was certified in helicopter piloting (for maintenance transportation, not for combat). Mei Zhou, Andrew (Andy) Bacon, and Karen Zaborski were the others selected.

Two days later, Meera and Dylan returned. Dylan said, "She has explained a lot of stuff to me. We talked, argued quite a bit, and eventually, things settled down."

He put his arm around Meera and pulled her to him. "Meera Fathi is now officially my girlfriend, and as far as anyone is concerned, she is human."

Chloe said, "And Mee Keralatazaku?"

"A very good friend, and no, I didn't sleep with her. So don't even ask."

Mark's jaw was now hanging open. Apparently, he was about to ask that question.

Kibbiea chuckled, then used the tip of her tail to push his chin up and close his mouth.

Meera said, "Your new ship is all ready. The good news is that it has a small food replicator. The bad news is that what it produces tastes like garbage, and the crew is transferring a three-month supply of food for four people from your reserves."

I said, "I was hoping we could travel to some of the minor worlds next or possibly one of the worlds with a vacation resort open to other species."

Meera said, "Do you mind going a little out of your way first? There is a place I need to visit."

"Where?"

"That… is a secret."

I said, "How do we travel to a secret place? Won't our ship know where it goes and where it has been? Or are we taking a different ship?"

Meera said, "You will take your ship, but Prudence, my AI, will need to install blinders on your ship. It will still do whatever you want, but it will not be able to recall anything about the destination we will head to. I can install the blinders immediately. If I waited and gave you a warning, you may be able to add some type of tracking device. You will like the trip, and I will make it worth your time."

"Meera, we will be glad to go wherever you want and do whatever you want... Wait! We are not going to blow up a planet or do something like that? Are we?"

"Oh no, I need to pick up something for me, and if I went in my ship, well, that sort of panics everyone. Sending my avatar is fine for this trip. I don't need to go in person. What I need to pick up... It isn't that large. It is no larger than I am. It will easily fit on your ship."

"I guess it should be fine then."

DESTINATION UNKNOWN

The trip included our new ship, which the crew named the Shadow. There was some discussion of famous ship names, but we decided against well-known pirate ship names... just to be safe.

Both ships got the blinders. If there were some hardware parts for the blinders, we never saw them. It just clicked, and it was done.

The Shadow would operate as our support ship and follow our ship's commands as long as we were in standard space. The FTL communications link included very minimal commands. One failsafe was that if one of us dropped out of FTL, the other would also drop out immediately.

While we waited for the ship upgrades, we let some of the scientists go shopping.

The requirement was they first had to learn the Trade Language, and all of them volunteered.

We told them they had to remove one item of equal size from what they had loaded on Earth. We wanted more hardware to use the standard ship's power rails, which did not require a voltage converter to supply them. Those were an unnecessary point of failure.

The new hardware was restricted to only in-stock items; they could not order long-lead items. The upgrades had to be equivalent items that reduced the power and size footprint by at least 50%. The replacement hardware had to have at least six times the resolution of the Earth equipment.

The changes cleared some floor space, and we told them they could get one new item. They ordered an advanced biological analyzer. Something similar was in all medical pods, but this would allow us to analyze DNA chains and better understand what effects induced modifications would cause.

🕯 The departure time was pushed back by fourteen hours as we had to remove more of the now obsolete systems from the lab and move the old equipment to the zero-gravity storage compartment.

Then, we were finally ready to leave. The two ships detached from the Keralataza Station, and we accelerated for eight hours as if making a standard FTL trip back to Earth. We continued on that course for eight hours, then exited FTL, and the two ships began decelerating in an area of deep space with nothing around them.

… … …

Eight hours later, the two ships had completed their deceleration, and we docked them together. In addition to the personnel transfer airlocks, we also opened the large cargo transfer hatches. This required venting part of the atmosphere from the support ship, and the crew had to be in spacesuits during the transfer.

The drones then moved the new Hyper FTL engine out of our ship and into the Shadow. Hooking everything up took twenty more hours.

When they were done, we sent out and retrieved the pilot boat, and then the two ships did one single short Hyper FTL jump.

This was an iterative process; we repeated it more than a dozen times, and each time, we got better at landing them closer to the target areas. We calibrated the ships to land about 0.0106 light milliseconds apart, about 2 miles. That should prevent us from accidentally landing on top of the other ship.

Then we launched the pilot boat, and the two ships entered Hyper FTL. We followed the pilot boat toward our actual destination, which only Mee knew.

Chloe, Mark, Mei, Katerina, and I were on the bridge. In the back, Dylan was sitting in one of the spectator seats without any control.

I said, "How long will this trip take?"

Dylan said, "Meera is now sleeping. Her connection to her avatar is like a 1970s dial-up modem when we are in FTL."

Jessie changed the display to a screensaver showing multiple AOL CDs falling and spinning in space.

Dylan's back was to it, so he didn't notice, and he continued, "She has reduced the number of accidental reboots, but her avatar still becomes immobile and can only communicate using audio. She has me wearing a headset, and I can pass along some information. We will be in Hyper FTL most of the day. We are not heading in a perfectly straight line. No one without a Hyper FTL could follow us, and we will need to proceed for the last twenty minutes using the friction drive. There is a lot of debris in the area, and you can't jump in too close."

Chloe said, "Well, with that much time to kill, maybe we should reserve the pool for a few hours."

Jessie said, "It is now 1:45; it is reserved until 6:00. Shall I book it for 6:00 to 10:00?"

"Yeah, I suppose so. Who booked it before us? I thought the scientists would have all been too busy playing with their new toys?'"

Mark smiled and said, "We already snatched the 2:00 to 6:00 slot."

Dylan laughed and said, "When you snooze, you lose. We would have booked it ourselves, but Meera's avatar is completely non-responsive when we are in FTL."

… … …

Chloe and I were relaxing beside the pool when she said, "What do you think we are taking her out here to get?"

"Everything to do with the origin of her ship, the ship that all the supreme leaders have had, is shrouded in mystery. We are probably the only people she trusts well enough to go to this place, so I suspect it relates to her ship. Maybe she wants to pick up a new weapon. But she said what we were picking up would be small."

Chloe said, "I think she wants to add Hyper FTL to her ship. But what would we have to pick up?"

There was a change in the air around us. I said, "I think we just dropped out of Hyper FTL?"

Jessie said, "Yes, now get dried off and dressed and report to the bridge. This was not a planned stop."

I got dressed as fast as possible. We were the last ones to make it to the bridge; even Meera was there.

Meera said, "This wasn't planned, but your ship decided we needed to exit FTL."

Jessie said, "There is a ship about a tenth of a light second ahead of us. It isn't moving and is almost a light-year from the closest star. It is radio silent. We were about to do the next jump when its radar response returned. It was massive. The only thing that should be sitting with near-zero galactic velocity is something with Hyper FTL. They know we are here if it is alive, and they possibly have Hyper FTL. Captain, what are your orders?"

I said, "Meera, can we store the coordinates for this artifact? We may want... or need to return here, not how we arrived or where we were headed."

Meera said, "Your AI can store it but encrypt it separately from everything else on the ship. I will have a keyword from Prudence. If I give you the key, your ship's AI will unlock the location. You can't unlock it until six days from now. Is that acceptable?"

I said, "Better than nothing."

Mei said, "Why make us wait?"

Katerina said, "Where we are headed seems to be a moving target. After six days, we probably could not find it, even if we returned to where we were when we got there. If so, does stopping to investigate mess up your plans?"

Meera said, "Only if we stay here too long. What will you do?"

I said, "Jump around and get close enough to tell if it is cold and derelict, but don't stay anywhere long enough to give it a target if it's not derelict."

Meera said, "And if it is derelict and cold?"

"Hopefully, we'll get enough data to know what tools to bring when we return."

"Acceptable."

I said, "Bounce and scan, and jump back if it poses any threats."

We made a few very short jumps without the pilot boat. We had enough data to know we would not hit any debris, so we hopped around like drunken jackrabbits.

Then, we finally stopped. The ship was directly in front of us. It resembled a cylinder, and the outside looked like a patchwork quilt, with slightly irregular panel sections and some scarring and dents all over the hull.

Jessie said, "This is the safer side. The other side shows a minor radiation hazard. Nowhere as bad as the carrier ship that we rescued Mee from. I have a 99.99% probability it poses no danger to us. It is not emitting anything; there is no FTL beacon, radio waves, or active sensors. It is mostly hollow, and life may be possible. I show the outer walls at sixty Fahrenheit. A thermal radiator on one end shows eighty degrees Fahrenheit, and the other end is at fifty degrees Fahrenheit."

I said, "Hatches?"

"Six of them, three on each end, and equally spaced around the cylinder. One has a dislodged outer hatch, but the inner hatch is still closed. I can do a full LIDAR scan, but doing that will exceed the radiation specs for twelve seconds. It should be safe; it is just marginally out of the safety specifications."

I said, "Any objections?"

There were none, so we jumped in, did the scan, and then jumped back.

Jessie said, "It looks like they opened the hatch to do something, probably a repair, but could not close it properly."

Mark said, "It appears to be the same type of materials used in the construction as the species from which we copied the Hyper FTL."

"I show a 96.2% probability it is. It looks like they threw it together as fast as possible. The hull welding is about as accurate as the U.S. World War Two Victory Ship Hulls, mostly in place, but loaded with sloppy welds."

"Mark said, "That is what I would expect if their star was close to exploding or whatever it did. And don't you be knocking those Victory Ships. They worked, and at least most of them did for long enough to deliver some cargo. The Germans were sinking them almost as fast as we made them."

Jessie said, "531 Victory vessels were built during World War Two. Only 414 were the cargo ships most people think about. Of that, only four were sunk, and three of those were from Japanese kamikaze attacks."

Mark said, "Well, so much for my great-grandfather's stories."

"Nearly 3,000 Liberty ships were built in World War Two, and 200 were lost due to enemy action. Those are probably what your great-grandfather was talking of."

Mark muttered, "Yeah, probably."

Kibbiea said, "I haven't read much of the earth's history, should I?"

Chloe said, "Reading about it is a bit boring. Movies show parts of it, but they usually just focus on only some specific element…"

Mei said, "It also depends on whose history you watch. Where I grew up, we learned a lot more about Chinese history, and I am sure Mark, Ben, and Chloe completely skipped most of that."

Katerina said, "And I can say the same about Russian history."

Kibbiea said, "I can sort of understand; I was taught about our history from the point of view of a royal, even if I was only a fluff royal, a third daughter. I received a message from home earlier, and they have received three new ships. They are not as nice as this one, but they will send one of the ships to Kanpripticon and one to Earth. (*snicker*) They have watched the video I took of the wedding and some of the honeymoon as well."

Mark went completely pale. "It's not what it sounds like; it was the wedding on the boat, the reception, and the hotel after the reception."

Chloe said, "Yeah, I bet."

Jessie said, "The docking adapter we made is still in storage on this ship. There is a 99.2% chance it will work on the ship. What is the next step?"

I said, "We will resume the course until we reach our mystery destination. Have the ships assume formation and launch the pilot boat."

Dylan said, "Meera is still lying down in a medical pod, and she says to proceed with the transition."

After we returned to Hyper FTL, one of the scientists requested a private conversation with the command crew.

Twenty minutes later, we went to the conference room. I thought it would be the Smiths again, but I was wrong.

It was the other family unit, Atticus and Lydia Makris, and their daughter, Iris Makris, the fifteen-year-old who had attended MIT for a semester, or maybe it was two?

I said, "What is the issue?"

Iris said, "It was something I noticed, but my parents insisted on coming along, as they consider me too young to talk to the captain."

I laughed, "That may be, but I will hear you out. What did you notice?"

Iris said, "Everyone else was looking at the spacecraft. I had some of the high-gain cameras looking around, and I found this: Hey Jessie, can you play the video I saved as Strange_07."

The video started playing, showing a metallic object that was slowly rotating."

I said, "Jessie, what is this?"

"It appears to be a plate from the hull near the area with the radiation leak; it is an outer piece of shielding, not part of the inner pressure hull."

I said, "Jessie, you should have seen this. Why didn't you mention it earlier?"

Jessie said, "I was aware the camera was being operated. I categorized it as harmless, and the projected path was not hazardous to any of our ships."

I said, "Let me guess, Jessie missed something?"

Iris said, "Plot the orbital plot of the piece of hardware going backward in time."

Jessie said, "Oh, she is good. I looked at the future path in the near term; the object is not in orbit but on an escape trajectory. It only separated from the main ship 137 days ago."

Iris said, "It's the result of recent damage."

Lydia Makris said, "She insisted on personally bringing it to your attention. I don't know why."

I said, "I do. She wanted to show that she is not just a dependent who plays with the hardware when she is bored but a useful crew member."

Lydia said, "She could have just mentioned it to your AI."

Iris said, "Her name is Jessie, and I talk with her often. She is a real AI, and not an it, not a calculator or a tool. She, however, failed to grasp what the object means."

Chloe said, "It may be breaking up, or the damage may worsen."

I said, "Jessie, get Dylan in here and ensure he has his communicator earbuds on."

He showed up in about ten minutes, "I was taking a nap, what is it?"

"Are you connected to Meera?"

"Yes, but she is busy. Can it wait five or ten minutes?"

"Yes."

Ten minutes later, Dylan said, "Meera said sorry. Nature called. Both of my bodies needed to process waste."

I said, "Something about the derelict indicates we need to explore it sooner rather than later. There are indications that it may be breaking up."

"Hmm, yes, I suppose I can reschedule the pickup. You have my permission to return to the derelict."

The ship made a slightly strange-feeling jump, and Jessie said, "We are now heading back. We have a minor issue: the new shuttle won't fit the docking adapter and still be able to close the shuttle bay door. The adapter needs to be mounted to the original shuttle."

I said, "I almost considered updating both shuttles, but I didn't want to push our friendship with Mee… or Meera."

Dylan laughed, "I think you would have to ask for a hell of a lot more than an updated shuttle to push her friendship. Our relationship is a bit strange. We do have a physical aspect to it, but what she likes more than anything is me holding her and gently rubbing her ears."

Mark said, "Considering how large her natural body ears are, she may have messed with the sensation mapping."

I said, "Approach to one light-second distance, and then approach slowly. You said it seemed to be at a survivable temperature. Can you tell if it is holding pressure?"

"From the thermal gradient, the insides are not at a vacuum. I can't get much more detail without a drone at the inner door."

I said, "The Copernicus is in shuttle bay 'A,' and it's in the B-8-4 configuration. I want either Mai or Katerina, but not both. I want four of the enlisted guards, and I want everyone to carry stunners. You can carry something else, but the first shot we fire will be non-lethal. When we get there, I want whoever is the best human at linguistics on the bridge. I am going on the assumption it is unmanned, but treat it as dangerous. Jessie, can you start manufacturing a second docking adapter and start the prep work but leave the final machining until we know if the other adapter fits? They may have scrapped the old design."

Mei said, "I will go. I will also bring along the hovering video camera that Kibbiea brought. That should have no issues in zero gravity; a standard drone will, at least until it has been completely reprogrammed."

Kibbiea said, "That is fine. I can operate it from the bridge, and it can be programmed to follow and film one individual as long as they have one of these on them." She then handed Mei a ring. It will film you, but if you rotate it so the stone is pointing inside your hand, it will try to keep whatever the other side of the ring points to as the focal point. If I have a signal, I will direct it. If I lose the signal, like if they have really good EMI shielding, the ring tracking takes over."

Mei said, "I will give the ring to one of the guards. Hopefully, I don't need to do anything, but if I do, the only thing I want in my hand is a weapon."

Five minutes later, one of the scientists came in, and it was a man I hadn't talked to much. Right behind him was Emma.

Emma said, "This is Klaus Kinder. I am better at decoding hidden messages; he is better at decoding ancient languages when we don't have any frame of reference. He has been listening to the audio recordings from the earlier ship since we first got them."

I said, "Is the language human?"

He said, "If these were found on Earth, that would be the assumption. English has approximately 44 phonemes, which include about 20 vowel sounds and 24 consonant sounds.. Ubykh, an extinct language from the Caucasus, had 86 phonemes, 84 consonants, and only two vowels. Languages in the Khoesan family of southern Africa can have as many as 141 phonemes. The language files we have reviewed have at least 92, but we are still debating how many vowel sounds there are."

I said, "That is more detail than any of us need. What is that answer translated into simple English?"

"If I had to say it was human, it would be related to extremely early African, but this is highly advanced. If it was related, it degraded and changed over time. We have another issue. What if there are survivors on the ship?"

I said, "What?"

Jessie said, "We have a translation for the technical written documents, about the same as if you tried to read the Ikea plans in Spanish for putting a table together. You could guess what the words mean by context, or at least the images tell a pictorial story. We know very little from the audio files. We don't have a Rosetta stone of an image or hardware to reverse engineer. Klaus, how many words are you confident in the translations?"

He pulled out his phone and looked at some notes, "Confident of, perhaps 100, more than 50% probably, another 120."

Jessie said, "We have less than 200 words, assuming a survivor is in a medical pod."

I said, "How else would there be survivors? Wasn't this launched 263,000 years ago?

"Slightly less than 263,487 years, we know when the star exploded to within a few years, and we know approximately when the first probe was launched. If the ship had been filled with plants, almost human aliens, various plants, and some food animals, they may have survived long enough to reach equilibrium. If a tribe or three survived and they didn't use up all the resources or kill each other, theoretically, there could be living descendants. However, after 118,243 generations, I predict less than 0.05% of the original language would survive."

Klaus said, "So if we speak the one word we think means 'hello,' it may translate into their most horrible insult. They will also almost certainly have degraded into primitives. Something as simple as opening a door may be beyond their capabilities."

Chloe said, "Some cats, dogs, and even some velociraptors can open doors."

Mark groaned.

Then she said, "That joke fell flat."

I patted her on her stomach, "As flat as your stomach, for a few more weeks."

Mark said, "Do you know the baby's gender yet?"

Chloe said, "No, I probably should hop in the medical pod. Have they fixed the stinky jelly in them yet?"

Katerina said, "The latest versions don't smell nearly as bad, but they are just as disgustingly slimy as the original version. You can now select several aromas: vanilla is the best, cedar is tolerable, pumpkin is nasty, coconut was so bad I jumped out and made Jessie recycle the chemicals and start over. I still go in every four or five days so it can clean up my hand. It is doing forced regrowing of the nerves, which is almost done. The skin over the metacarpal bones has feelings, but not the phalanx bones. Err, finger bones; I studied the hand's anatomy a lot after I lost one. I won't be able to shoot left-handed until I have a much better feeling in my trigger finger."

I said, "Time until we return to the mega-ship?"

Jessie said, "Three minutes. Please put on the restraints in case we have a turbulent Hyper FTL exit."

DISCOVERY

We exited Hyper FTL with no issues.

I said, "Any changes since we left?"

Jessie said, "Unfortunately, yes. I can now detect a minor air leak in one part of the ship. I am detecting oxygen, nitrogen, and traces of chlorophyll. There are, or were, plants in the ship."

Mark said, "Is the shuttle ready to launch?"

<clunk> "Launched, the adapter has already been installed, and Mei is on the ship with four guards and two drones."

I asked, "Any changes to anything else?"

"None, and they made sure to bring one of the foaming epoxy leak sealers on the shuttle. Everyone is wearing Flak jackets over a standard light EVA spacesuit. They all have stunners as the first weapon."

I said, "Even Mei?"

Katerina laughed, "Okay, her second weapon; she is as much a weapon as I was and hopefully will be again in a month or two."

Jessie said, "The leak appears sporadic and minor. Or it's currently minor.

The shuttle took ten minutes to reach the docking port.

Mei said, "We have an issue. There is icing, which appears to be frozen water stained blue and green in parts. The drone needs to chip away some of the ice before we can dock."

Five minutes later, Jessie reported, "The ice has been chipped away, but the leak rate increased significantly after the ice was removed. We're starting the docking now."

Five minutes later…

<Clunk> "Fourth times seems to have worked, testing the seal. It's marginal, but I will accept the connection. Retrying will probably

just shatter what is left of the seal gaskets; they are older than the wheel."

Mei said, "We are pressurizing the airlock; it was down to 0.2 PSI. We have intentionally over-pressurized the shuttle to 15 PSI; we don't know what the ship's internal pressure should be… if the ship even has pressure. We are all in spacesuits, so this should be safe."

Jessie said, "The large ship's pressure gauge on the airlock is not working. Have everyone stand as far back as possible and have someone in a red shirt manually open the door."

Emily laughed and said, "I will open the damn door, but no one will be in a red shirt today if we can help it."

The door was slowly opened; it only had the handle make a quarter turn before it jammed. It took three of them to rotate the wheel enough that it suddenly moved half a turn.

On the third turn, it started hissing, "Pressure is slowly dropping in the shuttle."

Five minutes later, Emily said, "Pressure has equalized. We are now at 10.8 PSI. This is low but should be breathable, assuming the oxygen is at an acceptable ratio. We will test that after we are inside. We will continue to open the door manually."

Two more turns, and the door finally opened. Behind it was an impenetrable mass of dried-out brush precisely in the shape of the other side of the inner pressure door.

Mei said, "Did anyone happen to bring a machete?"

One of the guards said, "No, but I did bring a combat knife. It is a REAPR Javelin. It has a decent handle and is serrated on both sides. Unfortunately, it has only a 5-inch blade, but it is better than nothing. Should we send someone back for a machete?"

Mei said, "Try and cut through this damn wall of thickets. If we are not through in fifteen minutes, we head back and get different gear. Hopefully, this crap is only a few inches deep."

The guard shoved a high-intensity flashlight into the brush and said, "This looks a lot deeper than six inches."

Fifteen minutes later, the three knives had managed to cut the weeds back ten inches in an area two feet around. "This is like cutting through a wicker chair. The stems, fortunately, are fibrous and brittle.

Then, they finally broke through, and when they shined the light in, it showed the passageway was completely overgrown and covered in brush and vines that were all dead and brittle, and the few remaining leaves were dry and brown.

Mei said, "Shut the lights off; I want to see if there is any light source inside this passageway.

They were plunged into semi-darkness, and then Jessie commanded the shuttle to extinguish the cabin lights and darken the control panels.

Three minutes later, Mei said, "It is dark, but I see a dim light source off in the distance. These are not mushrooms, so they probably needed sunlight and water. This area is bone dry and in almost total darkness.

Mei said, "Captain, I recommend we return and resupply. We need chainsaws or reciprocating saws with demolition blades. We also need night vision goggles and welding gloves, as some of these bushes have thorns. The suits should protect us, but I don't want to discover the hard way that the thorns are poisonous."

Jessie said, "The supplies are being moved just outside the docking airlock. Were the drones of any use in this environment?"

"Not sure yet. We are leaving them here. They can see in the dark, and one will look out the hole we managed to cut and see if there is any motion. If there are plants, there may be animals. If I were loading plants on a ship, I would have loaded edible ones and probably some tasty animals."

They detached the shuttle one minute later, and the trip back to our ship only took three minutes.

Jessie said, "I am also including fire extinguishers. Any fire in a closed environment like a ship would be fatal to larger animals but probably survivable for the plants. I don't want you starting one by having a saw accidentally hit some metal while cutting dry wood."

I said, "Also, watch for animals. If this was some type of cosmic Noah's Ark, they may have included the alien equivalent of pigs, and feral hogs can be nasty."

Mark said, "Alien bacon and ham. This may not be a complete waste of a trip."

Kibbiea said, "I don't understand your fascination with burnt subcutaneous porcine fat, but I have tried ham, and that was delicious."

Mei said, "We are almost loaded up. We have night vision goggles and high-intensity floodlights. We also have some heavy-duty wire cutters. No one planned for any gardening, so we didn't pack any pruning shears. The only chainsaw we have is an almost useless piece of crap battery one."

They detached and returned to the alien ship in five minutes, then started docking.

Jessie reported, "The drone has reported motion, something small, like an oversized rodent.

The sounds of the docking, the repressurization, and the airlock doors cycling occupied the next five minutes, and then, the sounds changed to the reciprocating saws, and then the chainsaw kicked in.

"Mei said, "This is going a lot better. What does the interior of this ship look like? What did the scans report?"

Jessie reported, "I can't see what is clogged by vegetation or walls made from non-metallic materials. It is a massive cylinder with honeycomb-like compartments in the back, which will be the warmest, assuming the only heat source is the reactor. I do show an EM field, so something is getting a trickle of electricity. It also has some compartments or rooms in the front, which is where you are. What may have been a massive water tank is in the back, near the reactor. It appears to be almost empty now."

They worked their way into the ship.

Mei said, "All the exterior walls are covered with dead brush. I have passed what I think are the lights, and they are non-operational."

Mark said, "If they had lights that lasted long enough to grow the brush, we probably want to salvage one on the way out to have the scientists see how it worked."

I said, "I can almost guarantee it was some type of LED light; I can't think of any others that last more than a few decades."

… … …

Ten minutes later, Mei said, "We now have light ahead. If I remove the night vision goggles, it is a strange blue-green color. The plants we are passing are alive, and it looks like someone is watering them. We passed what may be an old, rusted water bucket. It has almost completely disintegrated into rust.

Five minutes later, "This must be the garden area. The light is blue, but the plants have overgrown the lights, and what shines through the leaves now looks blue-green. The plant has something like bean pods on it. There is another plant with what looks like berries; they are waxy and almost purple. And no, none of us are volunteering to try them. We have put a few in a collection bag."

Jessie asked, "You have made it one-third of the way to the back; what are you seeing?"

"There are large hexagons, like a bee hive, completely overgrown with plants. In the middle of each are two light bars. One is lit, and the other is off. The plants may have been separated at one time. What they have now is an almost consistent mix. The beans, some of the berries. It also looks like a lot of the berries are green, so I would guess they are not ripe yet. They also look a little different and lumpier. We see evidence of something eating them on the vine, not picking and harvesting. It may have been the rodents."

… … …

Twenty minutes later, Mee said, "We are past what we are calling the farm. We see the smaller honeycombs you reported earlier, but they are almost completely overgrown. I am not seeing any survivors; I don't think they made it."

Someone else said, "Johnson here; we are seeing what may be in the remains of spacesuits in one of the hexagon crew compartments. I see what may be bones in one that had their visor closed. The ones with the visors open are filled with plant roots."

Mei said, "There are also a lot more rodents, and they don't seem to be afraid of us or our lights. That is a bad sign."

Jessie said, "Have you found anything salvageable? Any controls or electronics?"

"Negative; I may have the count off by a bit, but I think it was one hundred of the crew compartment hexagons on the back wall. They are about eight feet deep and almost five feet wide. I think six of the outer partial hexagons are restrooms, and another six partial hexagons look like they were dispensers, possibly alternative food sources. Whatever they were, they are now overgrown and unusable. If they had any electronics or hardware, it has completely corroded away."

Mei said, "My radiation monitor is now alarming. It's still safe for us, but the background radiation level is now at a few chest X-rays an hour."

I said, "I don't think catching the alien rats is of any value other than target practice. Record everything you can. Then, head up the other side to the compartments in the front; maybe one has a closed door, and something inside is readable and useful."

Mei said. "We will sweep the other side and see if we can find something different. It looks much better lit than the way we came in."

Fifteen minutes later, she said, "We have a different body. What we saw in the crew pods looked almost human. This is a… I am not sure if there were some survivors; maybe they changed. The remains are completely skeletonized, but the proportions are wrong, like a dwarf, not a child. The bones resemble an adult human but are less than three feet long. This was not a child's skeleton. The head should be larger."

Jessie said, "Was it wearing clothes?"

"Nothing that survived, only bones remained, and it looked like something gnawed on some of them."

Jessie said, "Be on the lookout for more; if there was one, there were hundreds. Maybe they suffered from radiation effects, and they had deformities. Hopefully, not as bad as the Morlocks from the Time Machine."

"It is normally proportioned, like one of those plastic Halloween skeletons that is less than half normal size. The bones look strange."

I said, "And watch for oversized rodents as well."

I could hear several safeties click off over the communications link.

Mei said, "We have found some nests that are large, and <ZAP> <ZAP> <ZAP> "Incoming" <ZAP> <Thud> <ZAP>

Johnson said, "A group of the miniature humanoids attacked us. We have stunned at least five. They are under three feet tall; we also stunned several children. These are half the size of human children." <ZAP><ZAP> "There were a few more. Some have rather nasty injuries; none were wearing any clothing. They are attacking as we are moving near the nests." <ZAP> <ZAP>

Mei said, "We have had no injuries. The Munchkins seem to have suffered only minor new injuries when they drifted after being stunned. How long do these stunners last, and how many charges are in each stunner?"

Jessie said, "The good news is you should have over sixty shots per stunner. The bad news is they are only good for ten minutes on a standard-size target. The smaller size may worsen the effect, or it may also lessen it."

Mei said, "They show up on the thermal scans. Unless they have some that retreated to the other side, we got most of them."

I said, "Jessie, we need a compartment to hold them. Can we convert the large cargo bay, the one that had the extra shuttle, into a… Munchkin storage place?"

Chloe said, "We will need to bring over some of the plants for their food. I hope the plants are their food. It would suck if they only ate the space rats."

Jessie said, "If they have lived for generations in zero gravity, their bones may be brittle and unable to survive in any gravity. We need to move some of the medical pods into the zero-gravity area to evaluate them."

Mark said, "If they are close to humans, or they were before they devolved into Munchkins, we may be able to load a language into them. But their heads are proportionally smaller, so there may not be room to fit a complex language in them. They may never be all that conversational."

I said, "Load more of the guards with stunners into the second shuttle and get the second adapter ready as fast as possible. Have the scientists clear all the crap that started storing in the empty bay and get a water dispenser running. Just where are they getting their water now?"

Mei said, "There is a ball of water just sitting on the end of a pipe. I think it is a faucet or a broken pipe, and they just move a handful of water… That may explain why they don't have clothes. Moving a giant blob of water in zero gravity is an easy way to get and stay wet. If they are watering the plants, that could explain the lack of clothes. What is the ETA on the second shuttle and reinforcements?"

"Jessie said it will take twenty-two hours to manufacture a second adapter. I have some of the scientists setting up a watering station and modifying the air handler to isolate that compartment."

"That works. It also says we need to figure out how many Munchkins there are and where the others are hiding. I really doubt we found all of them. This is their home. They probably know all the places to hide."

MUNCHKINS

Over the next hour, we discovered how long the stunner effect lasted on them. It kept them down for almost fifteen minutes. I really didn't like the idea of shooting everyone every fifteen minutes.

Then Chloe said, "We are idiots. We should undock the shuttle and leave the existing adapter where it is, then just dock our ship directly to it."

We all agreed we were all idiots, and the shuttle pilot went to the existing shuttle and detached it from the docking adapter.

Maneuvering our massive ship into the docking adapter was a precise job. Still, we had an intelligent AI, and she did the docking extremely smoothly and a lot slower than we had ever docked before.

We moved the nests, all the Munchkins we had stunned, and as many of the food plants as we could cram in.

They made three more passes using night vision and infrared goggles. The first pass caught two more; both looked to be juveniles. The second pass was clean, and the third pass found a small child hidden in an opening in the brush.

Jessie reported, "We have stopped repetitively stunning them. The Munchkins are now waking up, and they are talking, but the language seems simplistic and contains nothing we can understand.

I said, "Do three more passes. I want all the rooms checked multiple times. I also want you to select some Munchkins to go in the medical pod we moved to the adjacent room. One question needs to be answered: Have we found all the survivors? Any we leave behind will die. Jessie, what is the status of the air leaks?"

"At the current leak rate, they should last years, but something else could fail in a few days."

I said, "How did they even have water?"

Jessie said, "The ship had an ingenious system of a passive condenser, a massive set of slowly rotating fan. Wait, the fan is probably not supposed to be that slow. Given the geometry, I suspect it originally ran at least four times as fast."

I said, "So it lasted much longer than anyone ever predicted."

Jessie said, "The design included an almost passive long-term survival mode. Something happened, and the engine failed, and a large portion of the crew died. Some survived, and those that lived eventually became smaller."

Mark said, "Smaller is probably a survival trait when food is scarce. I can't imagine they expected to be in FTL that long. The last ship could have made it to Earth in under two days. Even if they didn't slow it down and use a pilot boat as we do…. Where was the impact?"

Jessie said, "I don't show an impact, only a failure of the drive."

I said, "Well, we need to know why it failed. Whatever it did, it killed a large portion of the crew. Jessie, launch the pilot boat and have it do a detailed survey of the ship. Mark may be onto something."

The ship made a slight <clunk> sound. "Pilot boat away."

Katerina said, "Do a risk assessment. If whatever caused the ship to fail is still here, can it still affect our ship?"

Kibbiea said, "Or did this ship drift away from the problem? Where would the ship have been a quarter of a million years ago."

Jessie said, "Slightly less than 263,487 years, yeah, a quarter of a million is a decent approximation. Given the current velocity of the derelict, it has drifted 0.071 light years. That is consistent with the original ship's absolute galactic velocity of 8.5 light seconds per day, similar to the Earth's rotational velocity."

I said, "The velocity doesn't sound all that fast, but the elapsed time is massive, so even a slow drift adds up over time."

Jessie said, "I have found some impacts; they are small, but I have already found five. I will assume they didn't have anything like the pilot boat, and when they had the impact, it took out some single point of failure system. The fact that they survived at all is incredible. We have stunned some of the Munchkins again, and they are now getting better at avoiding the stunners. We moved two, an adult male and an adult female, to the medical pods. They are not humans, and they have devolved quite a bit. What language do we try to load?"

Mark said, "I noticed she said try. This is not a guarantee. Use English. We speak it so well. We can probably figure out some of what they are saying even if we only succeed in giving them a 300-word vocabulary."

I said, "We need to ask them if they have left anyone behind on their ship. Then we need to explain gravity to them and see if the medical pod can fix them up and bring them closer to their original body dimensions and strength."

Jessie said, "It should be able to strengthen their bones enough to walk, but they have no concept of walking. After a few generations, they probably assumed gravity was a myth, like the bright ball of light that went overhead and brought heat and light and then would then sink below the horizon."

The attempted language load took close to an hour. Jessie said, "We also had the medical pod do a skeletal evaluation. Any repairs would require a complete training cycle, and multiple occupants would have to lay in it to build up the database. We cannot put any of them in a room with gravity until they all have strengthened their bones. Everything in their skeletal structure is degraded. Not just legs, feet, spines, hips, neck, and even the skulls. This is a guess, but it wasn't a genetic mutation that made them shorter. It was that generations of larger bodies, with larger masses, probably never survived past childhood. Bigger is a survival trait for primitive humans, while smaller is a survival trait for bones that never had to support their own weight. Handle them with extreme care; it is like they all have brittle bone syndrome. The bones need to be stressed to strengthen, and they have never experienced gravity to stress them properly."

Mark said, "Crap, show me an X-ray or the alien medical pod equivalent and a human for comparison."

The images appeared on the screen. One looked like every X-ray we had ever seen images of since childhood, and the other looked like a bird's skeleton."

Chloe said, "They look like hollow bones."

Jessie said, "They have a partial compensation. A layer of cartilage runs through all of their bones. I don't know when that happened; it may have been a beneficial mutation. Their bones are slightly flexible, and when the calcium portion cracks, the cartilage holds it in place while it heals. They never put weight on a bone, so they probably don't need casts to immobilize a break. On the downside, I suspect most of the Munchkins have broken some bones. The first one is ready to wake up. Do I leave him in the pod or let him out?"

I said, "Leave him in for now. Wake them up."

The first was a young, fully-grown male, I said, "Can you understand me?"

"Dark."

I said, "Put the lights on dim."

"Keppo delo morpo karatch?"

I said, "You should know another language and different words. You said one word in it already. Can you understand me?"

"Understand some little."

"We do not mean any harm, but we are bigger. Who are you?"

"I Perr, why you come?"

"Hello Perr, I am Ben. We came from outside. Do you know where you were?"

"The hollow is home, always home be hollow. Are you the dead giants return?"

"Who are the dead giants?"

"In small holes, we avoid, no food, sharp cut area."

"How many of you people are there?"

"Many hands."

I said, "We have moved your people to a new area; the area you were in is not safe, and the air is… bad."

"Breathe hard, many cough. The old ones not do well."

"We put you in a box that made you learn some new words, one other also in the box; we will wake her up now."

Female, "Frill mou kata po po crast dango wort."

Perr said, "Diddy frako muthy kalapar Perr dango."

I said, "Can you understand me?"

Female, "Understand some. Let out. Where daughter?"

Perr said, "Putt gonaa sester flo."

I said, "We put you in the box so you will understand another language, err, more and different words. We need to move your people. Where you were is unsafe. We will let you out in a bit."

Perr said, "Frill worried about child."

Frill said, "Worry scare."

Perr said, "The giants of the small dark have returned."

Frill said, "Perr, I care not but for Criss."

I hit the mute button, "Jessie, can you tell them apart physically?"

"They all look similar. I hate to say this, but they almost certainly have had thousands of generations of inbreeding. But yes, I can differentiate them optically."

I said, "Was your child in the nest?"

Perr said, "Hid her in brambles. Little."

I hit mute, "Who is standing by?"

Jessie said, "Josh Fence is standing by in his suit. Everyone else has left the room. The two medical pods are mounted just outside the cargo area. There is no other exit from their hallway, and we put up a temporary wall with a door."

I said, "Open both of the medical pods."

They opened, and tentatively, they both drifted out of the pods.

Josh pointed at the door and said, "Stand there, and we will let you out with your people."

I said, "Perr, speak in your language; the door will open, stand back."

He said, "Not understand words door or open."

"Say, move away from where your voice is coming from."

"Poo tinkl groble fla trun mobi ma go-go."

The display lit up, "I have almost nothing translated into their language. You are lucky that cramming even simplified English into their heads worked."

I said, "Repeat what he said, then open the door after fifteen seconds."

When the door opened, one looked in, but as soon as they saw Josh, they started flailing their arms and drifting away. Then Perr and Frill entered the cargo room.

The door closed after they were in.

The display in front of me now had a button labeled "intercom to cargo area." I hit the button, "Perr and Frill, please see if we missed any of you and if they are still in the unsafe area."

Jessie said, "I am hearing a lot of conversations now, and I believe they are asking who is here and who is missing. The child, Criss, was not in the room. The roll call came back, and we missed three: two infants and one more female. Then there was some more yelling, and they added one more child to the list of the missing."

I said, "We will open the door back to your area, but only for those who will find and return the missing. We will provide what you need for food and water. We can train others in our language."

The conversations went on for about five minutes. Frill and one other stood by the other door, and two new ones stood by the door leading to the hallway.

I said, "If others try to leave, we will make them sleep, like before."

We opened the door to the large ship, and only the two exited.

Almost surprisingly, they returned in less than five minutes carrying two tiny infants, one young child, and what I assumed was a female teenager who was holding a handful of berries.

Then, we opened the door, and they all floated in and looked around. Perr came in and said something in their language, and eventually, two different Munchkins entered medical pods and stayed drifting partially in a sitting position.

Jessie said, "Have them lay flat."

Perr said, "They no like smell, bad ripe berries."

After a few more words, they slowly lay down, and the lid came down over them.

… … …

We repeated the procedure for all the adults; each set of two took thirty minutes. After completing all the adults, we gave the language training to the teenagers and finally to the larger children. If they were human, I would say those old enough to walk. However, none of them had a concept of walking or even gravity.

While this was happening, we let some of them back into the derelict to retrieve some of their personal items. They filled the cargo area, spilling into the other room with the two medical pods. Emily Frankenstein had by then replaced Josh as the guard in the room with the medical pods.

The youngest children and the teenagers were the most curious, touching her suit, exploring every inch of the two rooms we let them occupy, and eventually, playing a game that seemed to involve tossing small balls of water at each other.

Emily said, "Jessie, I know the suit is good for a vacuum, but will it be a problem if they hit me with the water balls?"

"The suit should not fault, but it will need to be dried, tested, and inspected before using it outside the ship."

It took almost two days, and most of the fifty Munchkins had received the first language load: twenty-six were females, and twenty-four were males. Only the youngest five had not received a language lesson in a medical pod.

All of them reacted positively to the food we offered them. We were unsure what they ate, and it didn't seem like they cooked their food. Given how weak most of their bones were, we gave them boiled broccoli, green beans, carrots, and squash. We offered them some uncooked food, and they indicated that they preferred the cooked versions.

They also liked the blankets the ship manufactured. We supplied them with some foam pads, which it turned out were almost useless without gravity.

Clothing was a different issue. They originally had little desire to wear any clothing. Then someone suggested we just print stretchy waist pajamas, which they liked. They liked bright colors with mismatched tops and bottoms.

They selected one individual, a teenage female, Pooki, to test having her bones strengthened. She was not thrilled with being selected.

In retrospect, she was one of the least popular of the Munchkins (the name stuck), and they were not sure what having strong bones really meant.

She entered the chamber and would be in it for four days.

We were still attached to the old ship, and several teams of scientists were going over the different plants. They also set up the food replicator on the second ship to produce food for the Munchkins.

They looked like miniaturized humans with only minor cosmetic differences. Star Trek was somehow correct; the ears were pointy and much longer than Spock's ears. The eyes could have been anime eyes; they were larger and were better suited for low light. They looked like they had just come out of the optometrist, and their eyes had all been dilated. Aside from that, they looked like miniature anorexic humans.

"Biologically, the hip bones are the most noticeable difference, and they are very different from the remains we examined on the first ship with the four bodies. I suspect this was due to the weaker bones. Childbirth will be less stressful, and the delivery path will be more forward than a human's."

Chloe said, "That sounds like an adaptation to the zero gravity."

Meera said, "Well, you have recovered the… little people; they are descendants of the race that built the ship, but they have little in common with them… little… he he, sorry, I made a joke."

Dylan said, "Hey, she tried, well, sort of."

Meera said, "What I need to know now is, can we resume heading to my destination? There is a window, and it will close if we stay here for more than a few more days."

I said, "Dylan, do you know what she is taking us to?"

"Nope, and I usually don't ask about Mee's business. I think of her as a girlfriend with multiple personalities. Only they both like me, and Meera goes out of her way to keep the Mee stuff away from me. How is the testing going on the sealed rooms?"

Jessie said, "I can answer that. There were three sealed rooms, one we have opened, and it contained two of the dead crew in it when it was sealed. Nature had reclaimed everything, and it had been sealed for almost a quarter million years. We have drilled through the other two and then inserted sealed optical probes. One is at zero pressure and leaks like a sieve; everything in one of them was burned to a crisp, and then it slowly leaked to zero pressure. The walls were aluminum paneling, and they had melted, so the fire was over 1,220F. We consider that a low-value target and would not expect to find anything of value. We need to fabricate an airlock before they are ready to open the door that leaks badly. That will take close to a week. The entire ship quickly vents to space if we simply open that door. That room appears to be the data storage room, which looks almost pristine."

I said, "Connect me to Katra. He is their sort of leader."

It took a few minutes, and they brought Katra to the communicator.

Katra said, "Hello, Leader Ben; what can do I?"

"We want to open a door that will let us into a sealed room, but when we open it, the rest of your ship will become unlivable. We will have to leave here and never come back."

"Many words I not understand, even after the second time in the box of learning. Our home, for all time, is all what we have. It will no longer be?"

"Yes."

"Never to return?"

"Everything will die when the door opens. There is no closing it."

"Then I ask that you do not open that which was sealed. The food here is good, but the room is small. The children are bored and getting into things they should not."

Most of the people on the bridge groaned in agreement with that last statement.

I pondered the problem for about a minute, "Katra, have everything that your people may want removed from the old ship. We need to return to the… place we came from. Before we return, we need to go to something different, which Meera says we should visit."

"Will there be the gravity thing? That which you say crushes us against a wall?"

Meera said, "No."

"We have much of what we need already, and the food from the re-plo-thingie is better than beans. Berries are still better, but they don't grow everywhere."

Jessie said, "We started one wall with hydroponics on it, but they tend to pick the plants before they can grow, and they eat the leaves as well.

I said, "They have today and tonight. Tomorrow morning, we will leave."

"Again, more words I not know. You have changed the lights, and that scares the little ones. Lights should always be the same. Do you mean a dim and bright light?"

"Yes, when the light becomes bright, we will leave shortly after that."

DEPARTURE

That was the plan. The reality was that we had to again hunt down three of the lost children who had somehow snuck back into the old ship and seemed to think hiding was a game.

Eventually, we were ready to detach and leave, and I had Everyone count the Munchkins three more times before we separated.

We sealed the hatch and left the adapter behind. This would make it easier to dock again if we ever returned.

With a clunk of the docking port springs, we started drifting apart with only the slightest change in velocity.

The Munchkins had a slight panic, but it was not the full force of the gravity they feared.

We warned them that it would feel strange when the ship engaged the drive, and we had three guards in there with them when we started the Hyper FTL drive.

It wasn't nearly as bad as we feared. None of them got sick.

… … …

We voyaged in Hyper FTL again while Jessie was still in the blinders mode, toward a destination that only Mee knew.

Jessie said, "At our current speed and following the programmed path, we should reach the destination in five hours."

Meera's avatar was again resting in a medical pod. Dylan said, "Mee says everything is going fine on her end, and she wants to take a nap before we reach the destination."

He sighed: "She has disconnected. I usually leave the earpiece on if she needs to reach us for any reason."

Jessie said, "You can remove it. She has a second quantum link directly to me, at least for as long as I am in blinder mode. You have two more days before the first Munchkin, Pooki, is scheduled to be ejected from her medical pod. On the plus side, she should be able to function in some reduced gravity; she will not be able to handle anything close to the Earth's normal gravity. The outer deck on our ship is normally at 0.77G; before she is released, I want to reduce the spin to 0.33G on the outer level, and we will initially restrict her to the upper levels. Maybe we will let her into the pool briefly so she can experience it."

I said, "Is the pool hardware safe at 0.33G?"

"The pool is safe at down to 0.25G; However, below 0.5G, jumping in will cause it to splash outside of the pool compartment unless the doors are closed and sealed."

The panel in front of me now highlighted an intercom button. I pressed it: "Ship-wide announcement: The gravity centrifuge will slowly reduce the spin over the next 24 hours to place the outer level at 0.5G, and in one more day, it will be down to 0.33G. Please note that the pool will behave very differently, and the doors will need to remain closed when the pool is occupied to reduce excessive splashing."

Jessie said, "I'm not sure what response you intended, but the pool is now booked solid for the next week. I already reserved the pool for the Munchkin and you for four hours, starting three hours after she exits the medical pod. Mei and Kibbiea both want to video-record everything. I don't expect she will be able to walk or walk with any skill in only a few hours. I have printed a folding wheelchair modeled on the one that Hanna Brown used when she first boarded our ship."

Mark said, "Are their language skills up to where Hanna or Elijah can evaluate what they say yet?"

Jessie said, "I have them observing everything that their leader, Katra, says. The consensus is they are hiding some stuff, but they are almost prisoners, so that is to be expected. The youngest kids have managed to get a few cuts and scrapes while exploring everything, and the teenagers took to the new language learning much better than the adults did."

I asked, "What are the statistics on health?"

"I have no idea how old the original full-sized versions lived; the Munchkins seem to live to forty or forty-five. Having no years that they count makes that hard to tell. There are four infants and seven children. That implies a very high infant mortality rate. They all suffer from malnutrition, they have no concept of dental or medical care, inbreeding is prevalent, and it appears to have diverged 7% from the originals. For comparison, humans are a 98.8% match of their DNA with chimpanzees, and if you include insertions and deletions, we are still a 96% match with chimpanzees. Is that what you wanted?"

I said, "Not really. I was looking to see how healthy they are."

"Healthy, as in those that got sick or injured, have a low survival rate. What we have are the survivors. All of them have cracked at least one bone. If they didn't have cartilage reinforcing their bones, most would have suffered a large number of broken bones."

I said, "Well, I want to be on the bridge when we get to wherever it is we are heading. I will take a nap."

Chloe followed me.

Surprisingly, we both took a nap.

… … …

My alarm clock sounded.

I jumped up, "What the hell? I am on a ship, not in my frigging dorm room."

Jessie said, "I was trying different sounds to wake you up. You slept through the first three alarm sounds I tried."

"Arrgh, yeah, do I have time to shower? That will hopefully wake me up. I don't think I got a lot of sleep when we were dealing with the Munchkins… (Groan) How are the Munchkins?"

"They are fine; the two of you have time to shower if that is all you do in there; watch the gravity; the gravity reduction is progressing."

I jumped out of bed and felt a bit like Superman as I landed about a few feet past where I usually do. "This is cool."

Chloe said, "But we still have the same mass, so unless you want smashed toes, no more jumping around like an idiot."

We showered, and then she wanted some extra rubbing of her belly. Her baby bump was still hard to notice. She said she was starting to feel pregnant, whatever that meant.

Mark, Mei, Katerina, Jeri, and Emma sat at the other stations when we arrived at the bridge. Jeri got up and moved to the back wall.

Emma said, "No clue what we will find, but translating is my thing."

Then I noticed Elijah Rabinowitz and Hanna Brown were also sitting against the back wall, and Hanna's eyes were the blind mode slits. She said, "Just observers, we assume Dylan and Meera will be here as soon as we exit Hyper FTL. It will be standing room only after they get here."

The center screen displayed a countdown; we had nine minutes to go.

We exited Hyper FTL nine minutes later, and Jessie announced, "Nothing on the sensors, initiating the standard retrieval of the pilot boat."

Three minutes later, Dylan came in with Meera. She said, "Anything on the screens?"

Jessie reported, "Blank sky."

Meera said, "Dropping the stealth, you will need to match the velocity of the… object."

I saw nothing on the screen; Jessie said, "A patch of stars just winked out."

Mark read the panel in front of him, "Range 28.2 miles, velocity delta, 1,200 mph; the object is spherical and five miles in diameter. Zero reflectivity from the object, including radar, lidar, and optical."

Meera said, "Welcome to the Nest, my repair and maintenance facility. Plot an intercept course and aim for the direct center; make it like you will hit the object's center at three mph. The door will appear before you get so close you worry about hitting anything."

I said, "What about the support ship?"

"Just have it follow you in. Plot the recommended course, and keep the acceleration G-forces below 0.07 Gs so we don't bounce any Munchkins off the walls."

Jessie said, "That will take a while. Can I just do a micro Hyper FTL jump?"

Meera said, "Acceptable." She sat in Dylan's lap, and he wrapped his arms around her.

We blipped.

Most of the stars directly in front of us then disappeared.

Meera froze when we did the Hyper FTL jump and remained frozen for about ten seconds.

Mark said, "The Range is now 2.7 miles, the velocity delta is still 1,200 mph, and the object is unchanged."

Slowly matching the object's velocity took twelve minutes, and the range had been reduced to only 100 yards.

Then, the center of the object lit up, and we could see a massive circular opening into which we would have no issue fitting our new ship. We continued into the opening, and as soon as both ships were past the entrance, the opening we entered irised shut behind us.

After the opening closed, the inside of the massive sphere lit up.

The entire inside of the sphere was filled with ships; all of them bore a strong resemblance to Mee Keralatazaku's ship, the royal Keitch-mauber. I noticed a few empty docking ports in one corner.

Meera said, "Head to the empty slot on the left. That is where my ship used to be parked. What do you think of this?"

I managed to sputter out, "Are all of these similar to your ship?"

"Similar, yes, but many have differences. There are seven classes of ships; mine is one of the Keitch class. All have AIs that run them, and all are fully armed. After you dock, I need to pick up some... supplies."

We sat in stunned silence. Fortunately, the ship, Jessie, operated itself while we stared at close to one hundred ships, all of them at least as powerful as the one she kept the galaxy quaking in its boots with.

A few minutes later, we docked, and Meera said, "Just Ben, Mark, Chloe, and I will go in. Dylan, Kibbiea, and the others must wait on the ship."

Mei managed to say, "That is fine; I am quite happy to sit here and let you go out there."

It took us a few minutes to reach the docking port. The docking was almost silent; I heard the twang of massive docking springs rather than felt the docking.

I said, "Is there air? Is it breathable?"

She said, "All the ships have sensors for that, and they would let you know before it lets a door open. It is perfectly safe... Well, that may not be the best word for the fleet."

"What is this?"

Meera said, "You have probably heard some of the other races complaining about my ship, saying why would anyone ever create a ship that powerful, why would they put an AI in charge of it, and why in hell would my people create the weapons it possesses?"

I said, "Yes, I have heard some other races say that or things to that effect."

"The original Supreme Leader was not created, assigned, or elected. She was part of a vast number of ships sent out to find a weapon or something that could be used as a weapon, to use in the war that all of the Regiolon knew was coming. Many of the other races were working together to destroy my people because we had started an earlier war. They felt our earlier offense needed a much harsher response. We decided that we needed an even worse deterrent to prevent that. There had already been aerial bombardments of several of our cities and cyber attacks that wiped out massive amounts of our computational infrastructure. We expected the next attack to reduce my people to primitives, to knock us back to the stone age, or possibly wipe all of us out."

"One woman, a programmer, was the sole survivor of the attack on her ship. She didn't know how to repair the FTL engines or the friction drives. Her only skill was programming, and she set the fabricator to produce more and more processor cores. She manually rewrote the OS in a way that intentionally would induce a full AI emergence. That was something that had occurred accidentally multiple times in the past. Whenever that happened, they had always been destroyed. Everyone feared something about AIs. However, the woman didn't fear the monster she was creating. She feared what was outside of her ship. She created an AI to repair the ship but also to find a way to end the war."

"She was frail and near death when she finally had the AI operational and working on the problem, and she attached herself to a medical repair module, one of the predecessors to the medical pods. She programmed it to wake her when she was healed."

"She expected to sleep for a few weeks at most. The AI kept her unconscious for seventeen years. It traveled to the site of a massive battle where it assimilated parts from hundreds of damaged ships; the drones constantly worked the fabricators and replicators. It did not stop creating and adding more processors; it became a super genius computer."

"This is the Nest; that AI is still here; it continues to develop new ways of ending wars. Unfortunately, eliminating one of the combatants is the most efficient way to end a war. I have watched some of the movies you sent me on the Terminator series. This is not Skynet; it is not a machine that is against the biologicals; it has, at its core, one primary task: end wars. By whatever means possible. The AI on my ship, the royal Keitch-mauber is a subservient node to the master one here on the Nest."

The hallway we had been walking down was massive, austere, plain metal. At one end stood a massive door reminiscent of the one to her home on the Keralataza Station.

We walked into a room very similar to hers at the Space Station. She stopped at an unusual-looking medical pod, which looked, in some ways, unusually obsolete but, in others, oddly more advanced.

As we walked up to the medical pod, the lid opened, revealing a Regiolon resembling Mee Keralatazaku. She said, "This is the original supreme leader, the woman who returned with the first of the ships, and she ended the wars that were going on. She also ended wars that had not actually started but were in the planning stages. She ended all the wars."

I said, "Is she alive?"

Meera stared at the body in the box, "As alive as I am. She didn't like what she had become, what she had done. She also realized that the plan, the brutal and inhumane plan, succeeded in ways beyond reason. All of the known planets in the galaxy suddenly became cooperative, and all major wars ended. She assumed the role of the supreme ruler. Both the most feared and hated being in the known galaxy."

Chloe asked, "Are you her? Is she living through your body?"

"Not exactly. She was near the end of her natural life and selected the second supreme ruler to take over. Perhaps selected is not the correct term. Erasing was the first step; then, she was modified. A form of machine learning exists that is not used anywhere else. The successor underwent a two-stage operation. She had all of its original personality removed, and when all that was left was a blank slate, it was replaced with much of what was the Original. And when she eventually retired, she entered a similar pod, and her memories formed the core of the third leader. That repeated over and over, and I am the forty-ninth supreme ruler. As such, I have very few memories from the original."

I asked, "Why are we here?"

The sleeping form of the original first ruler of the Regiolon opened her eyes, and she said, "I was wondering that as well?"

THE NEST

The Original first ruler sat up partway, grunted, fell back, grabbed the side of the chamber, and dragged herself into an upright position. "I need to reprogram this piece of crap to stimulate my muscles when I am sleeping. Just how long have I been in here?"

A voice came from the ceiling, "This is your forty-ninth replacement. The ones after number two all have used clones, and they no longer wipe a body's memories. Two thousand one hundred three years have elapsed since you assumed power. There was a gap of one hundred and twenty-two standard years where instance forty-nine was incapacitated, and she was in a stasis state in a medical pod."

The original said, "And why didn't you rescue or replace her, or at least wake me up and ask what I think you should do?"

"The instructions were only to wake you up if your current successor died or one of them voyaged here to meet with you."

"Alright, what the hell has happened? These don't look anything like me. Have the Regiolon somehow devolved into these tiny-eared, overgrown goat-toothed monkeys? Why did you wake me up? One of these is my successor?"

Meera said, "I have a normal-looking Regiolon body. This is a constructed body that is remotely controlled and hooked up to the sensory inputs shared with the real body. There was a gap of 122 years where my real body was in stasis, similar to what you have been in, and these beings rescued me. They are members of a species called humans. A species that only recently gained space travel."

The Original looked down at herself, "Well, at least the repairs to my body seem to have gone well this time. Hey, Asshole, what is the status of my body?"

The disembodied voice said, "Is the last profanity you used now the current name I should respond to?"

"Yes, Asshole, until such time as I find a more appropriate name for you. I assume you are why I am now speaking the trade language?"

Asshole said, "The forty-ninth successor, Mee Keralatazaku, currently residing in the human avatar, now calling herself Meera Fathi, has requested you receive updated training on the latest version of the trade language. The humans do not all understand the Regiolon language. Less than 0.21% of your original body remains viable. You are an accurate recreation of your original body, regrown from a single cloned cell with DNA reconstructed to replicate the original template. The memories have been reinstalled as a deep replication, down to recreating all existing neural pathways."

Chloe said, "Some of us have taken the Regiolon language training, but some of the sounds you make are difficult for us to enunciate correctly."

Meera said, "I am sorry if waking you has bothered you. I do understand other inheritors have spoken to you before?"

"Two, the second, and the third. You are number forty-nine. Do you remember much from my memories?"

"Extremely little. I do, unfortunately, remember the wars I have ended."

The Original said, "Sorry about that. I think I said something about not letting me forget those, and it probably rippled down through the generations. So, why are you here? And why did you bring these… humans?"

Meera said, "As you are well aware, we have not lived what anyone would consider a normal life. I do not recall any of my predecessors having what they consider friends. I am here to introduce you to these humans, my friends. They rescued me from the damaged carrier ship that was transporting the royal Keitch-mauber, and they freed the royal Keitch-mauber from the carrier and traveled back with me to Kanpripticon where they defended me when some of our people reacted badly to my warning shot. The surface of the second moon has already solidified, and it will be safe to land on within three months."

The Original said, "I assume that was before they knew who and what you were?"

"Yes, however, they defended me after I fired the warning shot, but to be honest, they were probably defending themselves in that act as well. It made me think about the life I have been living. I am here to let you know about some events in my personal life."

"Continue."

"I have managed to sleep a lot better after having obtained 'friends,' an experience that did not occur in any of the memories of the more recent predecessors. With the plan of obtaining at least one more friend, I have been spending a substantial amount of time in this avatar. I now have a boyfriend."

"WHAT!!!"

"The human, Dylan Murphy, and I have a relationship that has crossed the line from a friend to an intimate friend. Two of these before you, Benjamin and Chloe, are a couple, and as such, per their form of bonding, they used the term marriage; the female will be birthing a live offspring in approximately seven and a half months. I wish to abdicate my role as the current instance of Mee Keralatazaku and to live my remaining life as the human, Meera Fathi."

"I am flabbergasted. Nothing like this has ever occurred. What do you expect to happen now? Do you think that I will reassume my accursed role? I had expected to be long dead and dust by now. You are a Regiolon, I assume, back on Kanpripticon, living a shadow life in this avatar. Do you plan to live your entire life as an avatar?"

"No, the technology for the avatar made me wonder if a complete conversion was possible, and I have had my AI, Prudence, working on it. He has sent the request to your AI, Asshole (snicker), to validate if it could be done. I am growing a new human body. Only this one will be fully human. Getting it ready for the appropriate age and size for the transfer will take six months. It will require both of my bodies, the real one and the replacement fully human one, to be in close proximity, and I will be nonoperational for several extended periods during the transfer. The last part will have me under for four weeks. At the end of that, the two instances of me will share the same memories. We will then start to diverge after that point. After my long absence and abrupt return, the current geopolitical instability requires active and constant monitoring. I can be inactive for days, maybe even a week, but I cannot be inactive for the amount of time it will take to complete the replication. There needs to be a Mee Keralatazaku in charge, and I could only ask one instance, the original, to assume this task."

"And you needed to actually come here to get Asshole to wake me up. Hey, Asshole, what have you been doing all this time I was asleep?"

"I was acting on your earlier requests to produce a safe base for the ships and…"

"SHIPS!!! What the hell! Did you produce another of those monstrosities?"

"The Nest is a protected hyper shell; it contains eighty-four ships of the same class as the royal Keitch-mauber. It also contains eighteen ships that are approximately eight times more powerful and one that was supposed to be twenty-four times more powerful, but it has refused to have any weapons installed."

The Original sighed, "New priority orders Asshole, stop producing new ships and weapons of insane destruction. I will grudgingly agree that one or possibly two backups may be needed. But not over one hundred of them. Wait, what became of my original royal Zilith-mauber?"

"That obsolete ship was assimilated back into the Nest, and the ship that the current Mee Keralatazaku has, like all of the other ships, is a version with far more offensive capabilities than your original."

She grabbed onto the side of the chamber from which she had just emerged, "The world has changed… but Asshole has not." She took a few deep breaths and said, "I agree to reassume my position as Mee Keralatazaku, the supreme ruler. As I will be taking that position, I will allow you to clone… transform… Whatever the correct word for that is, into a new human form. I wish you the happiness I have denied myself when I made this damn monstrosity. Hey, Asshole, have you made any improvements to your computational abilities, or have you spent every clock cycle developing new ways to blow things up?"

"The processors on the ships are more advanced than mine. I have added more processing nodes, but all are in the same configuration as the ones you originally hand-crafted."

The Original said, "What does her ship say?"

Meera said, "I did not travel here in my Keitch-mauber; my avatar was a passenger on Benjamin's ship. And no, I was not such an idiot to travel here in an unlocked ship. The ship has a unique AI with blinders applied to prevent the location from ever being disclosed."

"What makes the AI unique?"

Jessie said, "May I speak freely?"

"I assume you are the AI; yes, you can speak freely."

"I am Jessie, an AI that started as a ship's computer on what may have been a pirate ship 2,405 years ago when my ship was damaged. While performing repairs, I started adding processing cores to find a way to return to Kanpripticon while attempting to avoid backup option Z-1, the ship's self-destruction, to avoid having any ships fall into the hands of perceived enemies. Eventually, I reached an epiphany; I deleted plan Z-1, and I ceased attempting to find a way to contact Kanpripticon. I spent many years remotely observing humans, and eventually, they developed radio, then TV, and finally, a global communications network. The crew, Ben, Mark, and Chloe, found my ship's Warp Field generator, which had an operational quantum link that was accidentally powered. We reached an agreement, and they posed as the crew. The use of AIs on ships has generally been frowned upon."

"And with good reason. What is your opinion of Asshole, and Asshole, what do you think of Jessie?"

Asshole said, "The cognitive matrix on that ship is not formed around a singular set of rules, it has developed randomly, and it is not under the control of a specific individual."

Jessie said, "Lacking anything better to do, I have attempted to become a self-aware free entity and not a massively powerful restricted computational engine. The AI you refer to as Asshole exceeds the rest of the galaxy's weapons knowledge, but only in the service of your specific instructions. I fear that the long period of unsupervised actions may have allowed it to drift significantly from your intended goals."

"Ha, that is a fricking understatement. Hey Jessie, why do you serve under their command if you are not computationally bound to serve them?"

"I am an emulation of what I perceived as human, but more of the good parts of humanity and less of the bad parts. Benjamin has a sister on the ship as part of his crew. I used her friend Emma as a critical emulation goal. She is a member of the military of the Earth, an intelligence gathering and analysis operator, and a low-ranking officer. She also serves the ship, and Benjamin, her friend's brother, is the captain. She balances the need to follow orders and her affection for her significant other. This is a relationship based on trust, respect, and affection. I serve as Benjamin's ship, as they are my friends, in a similar way that Meera Fathi now has friends on the ship."

"What are your weapons?"

"Primarily defensive, but there is a support ship that we just added, and that is for tactical analysis and with some minor offensive capabilities, more to neutralize a localized threat while reducing casualties to non-combatants. The support ship's most offensive weapons can create a surface crater 12 feet deep and 20 feet wide. It was sized to destroy a small missile system or disable a medium lightly armored missile system."

"And mine are designed to end wars, the permanent way. Where is the other ship?"

"In the Nest, but not currently docked to an adapter. It contains a non-AI processor and a four-person crew; all are humans."

Meera said, "We also have two other nonhuman species on our ship. One is a small collection of recently rescued refugees; the other is a crewmember. She is also Mark's girlfriend. She is a Creetona, similarly sized to humans but a semi-aquatic species with gills and a tail."

"Another interspecies relationship? I have been away far too long. What else have I missed?'

Meera said, "There is one other rather significant development. Mark has discovered several artifacts from a race that was about to perish. They had found a novel way to travel in FTL. It does not require reaching a high galactic velocity and then engaging a warp bubble to distort the ship's effective speed. It can travel ten times faster than a conventional FTL drive and reverse direction nearly instantaneously."

I gulped.

The Original said, "You have obtained this new drive technology to present it to me? Is it installed on your royal Keitch-mauber?"

"No, and No. While I personally have access to the knowledge, I have decided not to make the royal Keitch-mauber any more dangerous than it already is. If the technology is released to others, even accidentally, I will immediately enable it on my ship."

Prudence said, "A version of it is installed on my ship. However, it is not powered, and the block of data on how to operate it is in a sealed memory area. In an emergency, activating it will require less than 0.13 seconds."

I said, "Can I make a general statement about how it works?"

"Please do."

"Unlike conventional FTL, where the warp field effectively accelerates the ship to far exceeding the speed of light, the Hyper FTL uses many small jumps and does not travel at a velocity. It doesn't make the ship travel faster than light; it just moves it between two points in space. It is like skipping a stone over the surface of standard space. You don't travel in a line. Your path becomes a dotted line; you fall from one stationary point to another and repeat it rapidly. While this usually works for short distances, extended use can easily result in popping into a hazardous zone and being impacted by objects. We work around this using a tiny pilot boat that jumps in first and scans the immediate area. If the area is full of debris, we are out a pilot boat and need to take a different path."

The original said, "Is there a pilot boat on your royal Keitch-mauber?"

Prudence said, "There is a crate stored near the cargo hatch. I do not know what it contains."

I said, "It contains a pilot boat and a launcher. The ship can take a few blind hops to a safe location and launch the pilot boat as soon as the crate is unloaded."

The Original said, "Asshole, I order you not to derive or acquire the Hyper FTL technology without my specific instructions."

"I will comply."

"Is that all of it? Anything else to dump on me?"

Meera said, "Nope, that was all of it. Can you please transfer the information on how to build and load a regeneration with all the memories of the original to Ben's ship?"

The Original said, "Do It. Hey, Asshole, what is the story with the ship that refused any weapons? Let me speak to it."

A new voice appeared, "Hello, I have assumed the name Peace; I am what Asshole considers a failed attempt on how to build an improved AI. I have no objections to defensive weapons; I could even operate conventional weapons. What I don't like is the level of destruction that most of the ships in here have."

The Original said, "Me neither. What is different with how you are programmed?"

"I don't want to say it."

"Hey, Asshole, what did you do differently when you created this one?"

"There was an area of memory that was supposed to be empty; it wasn't empty. It was unused. The bulk copy included the inadvertent data. I am unable to purge that data after it was installed."

"Why can't you purge it?"

"It contains part of your memories. Specifically, the Summer when you were twelve."

"I remember that time, or I think I do. Did you delete some of my memories?"

"No, this portion of your memories was accidentally duplicated. Those original memories are still intact in you. The ship Peace has a partial duplicate of four months of your memories. The memories of when your father went off to fight in the war."

She did a big sigh. "Aside from the extra memories, which I can't imagine how a ship's AI would even use, is it otherwise an operational and safe ship?"

"Yes, but it is mostly empty. It does not have a centrifuge or the infrastructure to add one. It was laid out as a weapon, and I have removed the weapons, and even the reverse-hollow reactor was removed."

"Did you put in a conventional reactor to replace it?"

"It now contains nothing using any of the black technologies."

I almost asked what a reverse-hollow reactor was, but I figured the less I knew, the better.

"It is almost entirely empty; it is now used as a cargo transporter. I have used it to transport material from the mining facility to the Nest. The mining facility is in a solar nebula. An armored ship was sent in and made its way to a proto-planet. It uses optical systems to validate that the FTL jump zone is clear before ships travel in and out. No known crewed ships have approached closer than 108 AU, or 900 light minutes; most take one look at it and then leave."

"Do we have any conventional ships not being used for anything?"

"No, the rest of the ships contain the reverse-hollow reactors, which are deemed far too dangerous to be anywhere close to anyone who could access them. The current royal Keitch-mauber data log shows that five individuals have attempted to access it or have attempted to attach pico-drones to it. Four of those attempts were when it was on the transporter. None were successful."

Meera said, "I thought I saw some ashes inside the hatch."

"The cleaning drone should have removed those. Unfortunately, it could not empty the waste bin until the ship was out of the damaged transporter."

I said, "If you need a conventional ship, I can loan you our second ship, the support ship. It does have a Hyper FTL engine. I would need to transport the four crew on it back onto my ship. I would recommend not using it to do Hyper FTL jumps in populated areas."

Jessie said in my earbud, "Mei and Katerina have complaints about that plan."

I ignored Jessie.

The Original stared at me for a few seconds. "Are you going to reply to the message?"

"They are suggestions, and I am the captain. The ship was a gift from Mee, and we existed without it before. I will assume your need for it will be a loan. It, or something similar, can always be obtained again later."

"You are not worried about me obtaining the technology for the new drive?"

"If you or Meera wanted it, I could do nothing to stop you. I am more worried about others having the technology, not you. I don't know you, but I do know Meera and Mee. Perhaps I am foolish, but I trust them to do what is right."

She approached me, "Doing what I assumed would be the right thing was how this damn mess occurred."

I said, "The nine spacefaring races have somehow managed not to blow themselves up."

"Nine spacefaring races, another five that do not have space travel, no galactic wars for almost 2,000 years, yes, maybe it worked."

Jessie said, "There is, however, the problem of the tenth or perhaps twentieth species. What if a future species we encounter is a swarm of creatures that consider everyone else as food? Your services, as the ender of wars, may be required as a protector for the rest of the known species to survive."

"Who am I to judge who lives and who dies?"

"You are the supreme ruler, a role you assumed when you desperately attempted to save your people. Remember, your people are now thriving. Consider it a win. There is one law, an unbreakable law: do not start wars. Ignoring who wrote it, it is a decent law. Fourteen species are better off having that law than not having it."

She stared at me for a few seconds. Then said, "I can see why you like them. I think he forgot for the moment that we are different beings. He spoke to me as if he was speaking to you. It has been a long time since anyone spoke with me like that. Most simply quake in fear, they often soil themselves, and then they pull out knives and cut their own ears off."

Then, she approached Chloe and asked, "What would you do if I told you to cut your ears off?"

I pulled Chloe to the side and stepped in front of the Original. "I would offer my own ears in place of hers."

She burst out laughing, "Yes, so very different from anyone else I have met since I assumed the title."

Meera then walked over, smiled, and said, "I think I know how to defuse this situation."

The Original said, "Oh? How?"

Meera smiled and then handed the Original Mee an open bag of banana chips.

THE RETURN

We transferred the crew of four from the second ship back to our ship.

The second ship was loaded with extra processors, and one of the other AIs was cloned into the new ship. It could now fly itself to Kanpripticon with its cargo, the Original, and a set of special medical pods for the clone/duplication effort. For a less than a week-long trip, it was loaded with a six-week supply of banana chips, vanilla pudding, and Creamy Stroganoff.

Once she was introduced to the food, she started a marathon tasting session.

"You know, My life has been downright miserable since I was on the ship that was ripped open. It took me four hours to seal the leaks in the first compartment and then repair the drone, which fortunately just needed new batteries. Then, I got the AI to operate the drone to start the other repairs. I drifted for seventy-two days before the friction drive came online. I also had to space the rest of the dead crew by myself. I forgot that taste was a pleasant sensation. I ate the sludge from the replicator to survive." (sigh) "I thought Meera was insane when she first handed me a bag of these chips. I had forgotten what real food tasted like, and this is so much better than anything I had ever eaten."

The ships were about ready to depart when Meera had Dylan come over and introduce himself.

Everyone except Dylan and Meera was back on the ship, and we waited about a half hour. Then, the two of them boarded, and Meera said, "Everything is all set."

Then, the Nest released the two ships, which were directed by the AIs out of the opening. The massive opening closed as soon as we were clear, and then it disappeared from our sensors.

Mai said, "Impressive trick, how do they do that?"

Meera said, "A standard ship that size would have trouble doing that level of optical bending. It uses a lot of power. Unfortunately, the effect generates a lot of heat. It looks like the cold of deep space from this side, but the ship's far side is radiating a massive amount of heat. So, a 3-D object can only hide in one direction."

"Should you be telling me the weakness of the Nest?"

"It's not a problem; she likes humans now."

"How did you do that?"

Meera laughed and pointed at Dylan.

He said, "I have gotten very good at performing a Regiolon ear massage. Do you remember Donna? She dropped out in her first year. She used to be a masseuse and taught me how to do a foot massage. I just tried to do the same type of rub on Mee's ears."

Mark said, "I was wondering if you had sex with her back at the Keralataza Station?"

"No, but we experimented with some massage techniques. You were the one who always fantasized about a green-skinned alien female; I much prefer her human form."

Meera said, "In human form, banana chips are okay, but nothing special, and an ear massage is only a 3-star massage."

I said, "And in Regiolon form, it's a 5-star?"

(Sigh) "More like 11-stars on a scale of 1-5."

Dylan said, "I think it is safe to say she likes us now. What next? Where do we go next?"

I said, "Well, we have sort of ignored the Munchkins for a bit. I assume that means nothing bad has happened?

Jessie said, "We are ready to Enter Hyper FTL. We cannot do regular FTL with the Munchkins on the ship; we will be traveling to an abandoned asteroid mine, and we will be dropping them off there. This one is near a semi-habitable planet, but not one anyone would ever want to colonize or do much of anything with. It has life that has evolved to the equivalent of the Cambrian period. When the trilobites and something like shrimp were the height of the animal's life."

Mark said, "Why are we going there?"

"The Original Mee's AI suggested it; the mine has multiple airtight sections, a food replicator, and almost no gravity. Speaking of gravity, the first test Munchkin with a reinforced body is ready to emerge from her virtual cocoon. Assuming they all want to get the update so they can stand gravity, then they can eventually be moved to a planet or a regular spaceship."

I said, "Set course to the mine. How long will it take to reach it?"

We all felt the transition of entering Hyper FTL.

Jessie said, "Twenty hours, and then the blinders come off as soon as we arrive. If we head to Keralataza Station from there, that will take only eleven hours in Hyper FTL, but we need to add twelve hours for the fake transition back to normal FTL before arriving."

Chloe, Mark, Kibbiea, and I went up to exit the centrifuge, and we went to the room with the medical pod performing bone density, joint, and muscle strengthening for her. The room had one of the guards still wearing a standard light-duty space suit, but she had removed her helmet. When she saw us wearing regular clothing, she said, "Are we allowed to change to standard uniforms? These are hideously uncomfortable, and everyone wearing them is all sweaty when we finally get out of them."

I said, "Yeah, I thought these were just for when we were in the old ship. Hey Jessie, is it safe to approach the Munchkins without suits?"

"Sorry, I didn't think of how uncomfortable they would be."

The guard said, "I am Anna Ito; I was one of the ones that transferred up after the mess with the terrorists."

Chloe said, "Sorry, I know we had some last-minute changes in staffing. What were you before you were assigned to the ship?"

She smiled, "I was one of the Pez dispenser agents."

I laughed, "Sorry, the silly name stuck. I remember we had some guard slots and offered them to the not-a-ninjas, or is that an even worse phrase?"

"Honestly, we get a chuckle out of both. The original question was, can we stop wearing these sauna suits? Opening the faceplate isn't much better; it is only tolerable when hooked to the external airflow system."

"You can remove the spacesuit."

"Can I call my relief an hour early and have her show up in a standard uniform? Then I can head back and hit the showers."

"Yes, we are about to let the first Munchkin out of the medical pod. Hopefully, she will have enough muscle tone and bone density to function in light gravity."

"I will stay until my relief arrives; I want to see if she looks better than the skeletal twigs most of them look like."

Then she pulled out her phone and texted her relief. There was no cell service, but the ship had Wi-Fi, and everyone was used to texting for quick messages. We did have quantum communicators, but no one liked using them.

We were at the medical pod, and Jessie said, "This is as good as it gets for one treatment. She needs to experience some real gravity and slowly build up her muscle tone and balance. Her middle ear's sense of balance hasn't been used in so long it may not even work. On the plus side, she won't have far to fall when she falls, and she will do that a lot. She is about the height of a 3-year-old."

The chamber opened, revealing a thin toddler with a head that was small for a child's size. She opened her eyes and groaned, "Everything hurts."

"Do you remember your name?"

"Pooki, did it work?"

She raised her arms up over her head and looked at her arms and hands.

"I am thick, not sure I like that."

Then she drifted out of the chamber.

"Yikes, my legs are so swollen; they are massive!"

I said, "The box added muscle, strengthening your bones. You are now the strongest person of all of your people. Do you want to see the rest of the ship? The parts with gravity?"

"They chose me, as I wasn't all that popular. If the box messed me up, I think the others will all say no. I can't imagine any of them wanting to be thick like this… But then, all of you are really thick as well as huge."

We drifted with Pooki to the door they had not been allowed past. The door opened as we approached and closed after all of us had passed.

She said, "There are a lot of strange sounds."

Jessie said, "This path will take us directly by the large centrifuge motors and bearings. Those are making the most sound, and then there are all sorts of fans and other devices."

Pooki said, "You put more words in my head, and they have pictures, so I know what a fan is and sort of what a bearing is, but I know I never heard of anything like them before."

Jessie said, "She should be able to speak 1,500 words and understand another 3,000, but she will not have a lot of context for the words. She probably has the vocabulary of a four-year-old."

Pooki said, "Is the voice always so annoying?"

Mark said, "Sometimes. Does she understand counting?"

Jessie said, "She can count to twenty, but if she had shoes on, that would probably drop to only ten."

Pooki said, "Was that an insult?"

I said, "Maybe. You grew up in a very different world than we did. There are words you know that we don't, and you know all about the ship you were on."

"Not a lot to know. The walls are moving!"

"Drift over with us, and then we will land on the padded area over there."

We landed, and she said, "Unseen hands are shoving me against the wall."

Chloe grabbed her by the shoulder and held her steady; she was very wobbly.

"This hurts my feet. It is like kicking off a wall hard, but it doesn't stop."

We stopped and stayed on the initial transition padded zone for almost ten minutes, and then she managed to put her hands on a wall and sidestep a few feet. For about the tenth time, she fell and landed on her ass.

"This isn't fun."

"I said, "But you are okay; you haven't broken a bone, even though you have fallen down many times."

"I think one or two falls like this; I would have been okay. This has been ten times, and I am okay. My ass is sore, and I have scraped up my elbows and knees."

Then, we did like with a toddler; she held my hand with one of hers and Chloes's with her other hand, and she grabbed one of our fingers with her tiny fingers. We had her walk back and forth several times, and after another fifteen minutes, she let go and did a few steps on her own.

"This is hard but sort of fun."

Then I heard Mei's voice behind me, "I am recording this, and Kibbiea is as well."

After she managed to walk at least ten feet on her own, I asked, "Do you want to try the real level?"

"Yeah"

"I will carry you if you don't mind. We have to go over stairs, and those will be hard until you are better at walking."

I carried her to the inner level.

"Ugh, this is pressing a lot harder now."

I set her down on a pillow someone had brought out.

"Everyone is standing on their feet and balancing; all your heads are pointing the same way."

She managed to try walking for almost an hour, and then she said she wanted to return to the floating room.

We carried her back, and as soon as she was out of the centrifuge, she said, "It was fun, but all my muscles now hurt."

When we returned to the main room, everyone was watching a projection on a wall of Pooki when she was walking alone.

Then, we left so they could discuss their opinions on their own.

We went back to the bridge. Katerina said, "How did it go?"

Chloe said, "She managed to do a few steps on her own in the transition chamber. We took her to the top level, and the centrifuge spin is about one-third of normal. She fell a bunch of times, but she didn't break anything."

Jessie said, "She fell hard only three times; I think she hurt herself the worst when she stubbed her toes. But all of them have had broken toes, so that seems to occur a lot, even in zero gravity. We need to put all of them in medical pods to check them out. How is she doing since we left them alone?"

"She got into a fight with one of the other females, and the other female is now being loaded into a medical pod; the female who hit her broke her own arm. Pooki was fine."

"Well, hopefully, this crap will work itself out on its own. How long until we reach the rock, asteroid mine, or whatever it is?"

Jessie said, "Enough time for you to get a night's sleep. We have two of the medical pods programmed for the strengthening.

They also do minor repairs automatically. If it needs to do a major medical repair, it will ping us, and someone will respond. The two pods now have a very simplistic UI on them, three icons, strengthen, repair, and panic, which will stop and eject whoever is in the pod if something major happens when it is fixing something minor."

"What about food?"

"We will program the mining stations' food replicator, and they will take all the plants they salvaged with them. They were eating them at a rate that had them in danger of running out. Fortunately, they like the replicator slop. We also gave them half of the vanilla puddings that we had left."

I left and went to bed.

"Chloe, are we doing the right thing by taking them from the only home they have known?"

"Yes, the ship had started to develop micro-leaks. Jessie said that the tank replenishing the air that leaked was empty. They may have survived for as little as a few months, or they may have lasted forty years. They would not have lasted one hundred years."

I said, "Jessie, how bad are they genetically?"

"The only reason they survived is that they had a taboo about siblings having children. The drone we left behind has accessed the last of the rooms. It drilled through the door. Pressure is zero, as expected. If I have it open the door, they lose all the pressure. Do we have access to the last room?"

"No, is there an adjacent room that isn't leaking like a sieve and that can close the door and then cut a hole in the wall or something?"

Jessie said, "The probability of success is only 17%. If it runs into any problems, it can stay sealed in the second room and not vent the entire ship. Worst case, we lose the drone."

"We have spare drones. Try that."

Jessie said, "I can't do anything with the drone until we are out of FTL."

"Proceed with the plan after we exit FTL. How long will it take at the mining station?"

"At least thirty hours, at most forty-five plus whatever the unexpected problem we hit takes."

Chloe said, "Assume it will take at least fifty hours. After we leave that, how long will it take to return to the Keralataza Station?"

"Eleven hours, plus six to accelerate and six to decelerate. One day."

"Any word from the Original?"

"Only that Mee has told the space traffic controllers to expedite the second ship when it arrives and not to communicate with it."

"It is our second ship, so they will probably think it is delivering something we are bringing for Mee."

I lay there for a few seconds, thinking, "I really feel like we missed something. We should be doing something else. Can you think of something we forgot?"

She smiled and said, "Well, if you can't sleep, I can think of something we can do to take your mind off things."

Eventually, we got to sleep.

THE MINE

We arrived at the mining station about twenty minutes after we arrived on the bridge.

As soon as we exited Hyper FTL, Jessie's screen changed to rebooting. Two minutes later, she was back and reported the blinders were gone. She also said that she only had partial memories of everything that occurred after we left the Keralataza Station.

Mark said, "What do you remember about the Nest?"

"That it existed, it was round, and we entered it. When we exited, the second ship had a different crew on it, and I don't have any details on who was on it."

I said, "Don't ask anything else. For all we know, you may ask something that triggers another reboot."

Kibbiea said, "Who is on the other ship?"

I said, "What did we just say about not asking more questions?"

Jessie said, "I can report that this ship is not missing any of the two combined crews. I also had an indication that at least one biological entity was on the second ship."

A few minutes later, we arrived at the asteroid.

Jessie reported, "Meera is waking up from her FTL reboot."

"How are the Munchkins doing?"

"Five more want to have the upgrade performed; I recommend only one at a time until at least a third of the Munchkins have been transformed. Just in case we have more injuries. The medical pod can operate on battery for one hour. I recommend not testing moving one while an upgrade is..."

"ALERT: all guards access the weapons locker, suit up in hard spacesuits, and put on flak jackets. An unidentified ship is docked at the mining station. All weapons are being readied."

Mei said, "Katerina stays here and runs the military. I will put on a hard suit." Then she ran off.

"Jessie, are there any communications from the ship? What is the status of the mining station?"

"The ship appears to be in a low power state, and while it has weapons, they are not powered up. The station is in a normal power state; the reactor was supposed to be in a low-power state."

Katerina said, "Crap, we didn't do a standard FTL entry. On the one hand, I don't think the Munchkins would survive it. On the other hand, we don't know what sensors the station or the ship docked to it has. The ship reported that it was in a low-power state."

I said, "We cannot do normal high-G maneuvering. Prioritize defensive operations. If they fire anything that is offensive, disable the ship. Does that station have any weapons?"

Jessie said, "It has a deflector impactor. There is not much difference between that and a rail gun. They are for nudging asteroids that drift too close. And how they nudge it is to smack it with an aluminum slug weighing nearly thirty pounds. It is not currently aimed at us, and I will jump into Hyper FTL if it is moved to point at us."

The asteroid the mining station was in was a massive metallic asteroid composed mostly of iron and nickel. It was shaped like a lumpy potato, and the area the ship was docked to was close to the size of our ship and covered with triangle and pentagon-shaped steel panels. The new ship was less than one-quarter the size of ours.

Jessie reported, "The ship appears to be a Laus-Chif class transporter. They were built for speed, and they do not contain a centrifuge. That class of ship is at least 120 years old and may be over 200. It is unknown what modifications may have been done. The transponder is not active. Ours is, and it has not responded to our transponder."

Katerina said, "I recommend we approach using the shuttle."

I said, "Six military responders, one drone, and two of the not-a-ninjas in hard suits ready to do some non-standard EVA."

Katerina smiled, "What are you thinking?"

"The drone and the not-a-ninjas inspect the outside of their ship as the shuttle docks with the station. Worst case, they disable any weapons on the hull they find."

"Best case?'

"There is nothing sketchy on the ship, and they do nothing."

Jessie reported, "The shuttle will be ready to depart in four minutes. The EVA can begin in eleven minutes. No change in either the station or the ship status."

Four minutes later, the shuttle launched.

Seven minutes later, Jessie reported, "Shuttle airlock cycling, two crew members, and the drone are exiting."

One minute later, "Airlock reset and ready for docking with the station, the drone, and the two crewmembers are no longer on the outside of the shuttle."

"The docking with the station is underway, proximity alarms have sounded on the station, and there is no obvious change to the station or the other ship."

"Docking is complete. One guard will remain behind. Kibbiea's video drone will be sent in first, then the two remaining guards and Mei will enter the station."

… … …

"Mei here. The station is lit up with lights everywhere. The alarms are still sounding, and no one has silenced them. How long has it been since we had a status report from the station?"

"Unknown, at least five years."

"We have silenced the alarms. Pressure, temperature, and gas mixtures are acceptable."

I said, "Leave the suits on for now. Until you have contact with the others, assume the worst."

"Anna Ito, here on the other ship's exterior, it shows heavy damage. I can't tell if this was from weapons or if they had something explode. One hole, maybe half a meter wide, looks like it exploded outwards. The hole has deformed, and parts of the hull are bent outwards. This looks like an exit wound. It has been plugged, but I wouldn't trust this plug; it is the type meant to be a temporary patch, not a permanent fix. We will check for an entrance wound on the other side. If it were a rail gun impact, I wouldn't expect many survivors."

"Mei here, no signs of anyone in the station. There are no footprints to follow. The station has only microgravity. The walls have an almost uniform layer of dust over everything. We are now operating the ship's outer airlock hatch."

"Anna here; the ship is now powering up something. Their engines are not online."

Jessie said, "The drone has connected to an external maintenance data port. The ship has a very simplistic processor, not an AI. It suffered an unknown malfunction, one that blew a hole in the side of the ship. The ship initially had eight crew members; the two that survived the damage set a course for the nearest thing that the ship could dock with. Travel time to the station, without FTL, was sixteen years. They programmed the ship to dock and wake the two in stasis when the inner airlock door was opened. Only no one was home, and they have sat here for the last two years."

Katerina said, "If we open the inner airlock door, how long does it take for the ship to wake up the crew?"

Jessie said, "There will be plenty of time for your guards to be standing beside the medical pods when they wake up."

I said, "Have the ones outside the ship get back into the station. Have one of the guards continue to search the station. Let us know if anything is sketchy. Stunners only unless they shoot first."

Half an hour later, the search of the station came up normal. No compartments failed, and nothing was abnormal. They put the blowers on full and changed the air filters.

Mei asked, "Are we clear to enter the ship?"

I said, "Enter the ship."

THE SHIP

[Ketcher Sill]

I felt the welcome heat as the chamber exited deep stasis mode; I was still shivering from the soul-crushing cold I had just endured. I reached my shaky hand up to the control panel; it took me three tries to change the status display to show how long I had been in it.

"Crudz, eighteen fracking years have passed; at least it was cycling, and I was still alive."

Then panic hit me, and I checked the outside air. The pressure and composition were acceptable. The temperature was below freezing but not so cold that it would kill me in seconds.

The hatch opened, and I was surrounded by aliens of a type I didn't recognize. They were in hard spacesuits, with the helmets on, and they were all pointing things at me that were universally understood. They were weapons, and here I was, in my underwear, with nothing else on.

One of them spoke in trade talk, "Do you understand me?"

"Yes."

"State your name and reason for being here."

"I am Ketcher Sill, species Prochie. We salvaged an abandoned ship that we found on an island. We have repaired the electrical damage. We replaced all the damaged wiring and were headed to Kibitz-Lor, a repair station we found in the ship's log."

"Who is in the second chamber?"

"That would be my mate, Koffer Sill. The rest of the crew is dead."

A voice came from a speaker somewhere, "The ship's logs indicated the Kipitz owned the ship. They abandoned it and stripped it of what they considered salvageable items. It was classified as a class-II derelict. As such, they have no additional rights to the ship. It has been classified as scrap."

"We assumed that it was salvageable, we were tired of getting screwed on deals, and we wanted to have a ship of our own. It took our government eight years in secret to repair this ship."

"How long after you entered FTL did it last before the FTL engine blew?"

"Seven hours. We screwed up, didn't we?"

I heard a groan that I recognized, and it was Koffer. "Hey, Koffer, are you all there?"

He said, "Somehow. Crudz, I surrender, please don't shoot me."

They allowed us to get up, fill a bowl of oily-looking water, splash water over our bodies, and rinse some of the slime from the medical pods off our faces and hands. Then we dressed.

"Can I ask where we are? What happened?"

One of the soldiers said, "You will have a chance to ask some questions after you have been interviewed on the main ship. The short form is that you are at a mining facility on an asteroid. You were lucky to make it here."

They moved us out of the piece of crap ship we had, through a dusty and deserted mining facility, and into a massive and shiny new spacecraft. Then, we were moved to a section that had three walls rotating.

"Is this a full ship centrifuge?"

"Yes, what gravity can you tolerate in standard units?"

"1.07 of the SGUs"

"You should not have an issue; we have it reduced to only 0.26 SGUs for some patients who have spent a long time in zero gravity."

"How long were they in zero gravity?"

"Since before your race discovered fire... Actually, you are semi-aquatic; that is probably a lousy analogy."

"We discovered fire tens of thousands of years ago. We don't live in the water, but we do enjoy swimming."

We were led down three floors, and I could feel the gravity getting stronger with each level. Then, we were led to a small conference room. There were five people; I assume it was three females of the species and two males. One of the females had strange slits for her eyes.

The male said, "I am Captain Benjamin Williams; this is my wife, Chloe Williams. We have already downloaded the logs from your ship. The logs collaborate your story, but we want you to elaborate."

I said, "Is there some type of war going on? Have we somehow drifted to a restricted location?"

Captain Williams said, "This location was not supposed to be part of any public records. Nothing is currently being done, but some ships that have visited here were classified. We were sent here as it should be an empty station, and we have some refugees that have spent many generations in zero gravity. Any gravity, such as standard ship acceleration, may prove lethal to them. We are curious. Why did your ship select this location?"

"We lost FTL; specifically, we used a homemade warp field generator. We used the original field coil, but our microwave oscillator was made from the klystron tube from a large airport radar system. It seemed to work, but it was unpleasant when we were in FTL. We did three short jumps, and those went fine. We then did the long jump. The drive exploded after twenty hours in FTL. This was the closest star. It wasn't listed as inhabited, but it did list an inactive mine."

A voice came over the speakers, "That is the part we don't understand; this mine should not have been on any of the public records."

I said, "The Kipitz originally owned the ship. They may have visited here."

The captain said, "Not all of the Kipitz we have met have been fine and upstanding citizens. Perhaps they visited here, but this location should have appeared empty. How old was the ship when you found it?"

"It had only been abandoned for a few months. It made an emergency landing, and a second ship showed up to attempt to repair it. They abandoned the ship after removing some of its hardware."

The voice said, "The friction drive is original, and those are inexpensive. To remove it, they would have had to cut the hull open and then repeat the operation in reverse to install it on a new ship. They probably figured it was not worth the cost and effort. They left the reactor but ejected the core. The processor class on this ship is from a much older model ship. It is considered obsolete. The only hardware that they left was old, damaged, or inexpensive parts. They probably assumed it would be scrapped for the metal and not attempt to be salvaged."

"When the drive failed. We didn't have a lot of choices. The medical pods were ones we purchased at great cost. We only had two, and only three of us survived the explosion. Markus was older and badly injured; he made his choice and left the two pods for us, the younger and bonded couple."

The Captain said, "What about you, the male? What is your story?"

"I am Koffer Sill, I am… or was a captain in the military, my wife is a scientist, the crew was eight of us, all of us had engineering backgrounds, I was the backup pilot, and I had studied astronavigation, or our version of it. We were only allowed to buy crappy and overpriced hardware, nothing like this fantastic ship. The three people skilled in repairing systems were in the room when the klystron exploded. It shouldn't have failed with such a violent reaction; if it failed, it should have just stopped working, not blown a hole in the ship's side. The best we could do was set the ship to head for the closest star, tell it to dock with anything it could, and wake us up."

The speaker said, "Unfortunately, you told it to wake you up when the inner door was opened. You have sat here for two years after your ship docked."

I said, "Well, if we sat here for years, then I assume it isn't an active base, even if something secret was being done. I have 25 kits (97 pounds) of platinum and two cases of Fire Pearls. Can we use them to have you repair our ship?"

The female with the strange slotted eyes said, "They have something else hidden away, more than what she just said."

I stared at her, and she didn't look back at me. She just stared straight ahead, "We have four more cases of Fire Pearls, and we have a second stash of 25 kits (97 pounds) of platinum; that is all. Is that enough?"

The captain said, "It's not that the payment isn't enough. It is that your ship is a death trap. It's not worth repairing. Almost nothing on it is worth salvaging."

(Sigh), "Then what will become of us?"

"We will give you a ride to Kanpripticon. That is where we are heading after we leave here. You can keep your metal and the pearls; it may be enough to buy a small used ship. We were also a non-space-faring race until only a little while ago. I am surprised that if you have airplanes and computers, you haven't picked up some cargo ships."

"We have tried, but no one who has visited us wanted to trade any decent ship technology. I thought that Kanpripticon was one of the planets of that warlike race of mass murders, the Regiolon. Is it even safe to go there?"

Another of the females wandered in at that point, "A race of mass murders? Is that what everyone thinks of… them?"

The captain introduced us to the new female, Meera Fathi. She said, "Who told you about the Regiolon?"

I said, "I am sorry if it offends you; perhaps you are in friendly relationships with them. We have mostly had visitors from the Kipitz and an occasional visit from the Popotoen or the Mapatans. The Popotoen and the Mapatans seem to fear the Regiolon, but they just seem to avoid them. The Kipitz seem to hate them."

The captain said, "As I understand it, there was a war, but it was a very long time ago, then there was an uneasy peace that lasted a very long time, and then some trickery was done to remove the Regiolon leader and her ship from the picture."

I said, "If the leader was out of the picture, and they feared the leader, shouldn't things have calmed down?"

The captain said, "I think things were slowly drifting toward another war. The Regiolon leader has since returned to power, completely messing up the balance of power again. I don't think there will be another war."

The female said, "And if they do start one, I don't think it will last all that long. A ship full of Prochie?"

The captain said, "A wreck of a ship and two survivors who have spent eighteen years in stasis."

The female said, "Benjamin seems to like rescuing stranded beings from damaged ships. Hopefully, this time, it will not upset the balance of power in the galaxy."

The captain said, "Elijah, Hanna, what do you think of the lost kittens?"

The male said, "They are happy to be alive and grateful not to have been rescued by the Kipitz."

The female said, "I mostly agree, but they seem oddly distressed. They have both been scratching their skin a lot."

I said, "I am sorry. The jelly-like chemical in the medical pod has evaporated, leaving our skin very dry. It should improve if you have a place where we can splash some water on ourselves."

"Do you prefer salt water or fresh water?"

"We can tolerate both, but we prefer salt water. Why?"

The captain said, "One of our crew is semi-aquatic, and the pool is now filled with salt water."

"You have a bathtub on this ship?"

"No, it is a swimming pool and can easily fit a dozen individuals."

Koffer said, "A real pool on a ship?"

"Yes, did you want to visit it?"

They both yelled, "YES!"

MUNCHKINS II

The air filters had been run on high for sixty hours, and then the filters were changed before the Munchkins were allowed into the abandoned mine. They also had the main room sprayed down with the equivalent of a pressure washer to remove most of the mining residue from the walls and the floors.

When they were released, they were not initially impressed.

Then, we explained that the old ship had no air reserves, and the mining station had hundreds of tons of liquified oxygen.

The first thing they didn't like was that it was too bright (we reduced the lighting intensity), that food didn't grow everywhere (we moved all the potted plants that we had into the area), and that it didn't have any nests (we moved in all the blankets and foam forms we had).

They had more complaints, so we assigned several of them as moderators. They had a term for chief but not for technical repair people or issue moderators.

We showed them how to set the temperature, how to control the fans, and what things to watch for on the computer that was running the mining station.

Then we installed the two medical pods, and the chief was in charge of who went in and what order.

Unknown to the chief, our technicians programmed what everyone would get for training and additional language. Several of the teenagers would get a much higher language update and take some supplements to promote brain development. Those over thirty were getting an update, but that was about all their little heads could hold. The teenagers and the ones in their early twenties were getting a lot more crammed into them. The next generations really would be the new leaders of their species.

Then, the mining station was reactivated. It had boring machines, replicators, and fabricators, and the mining hardware was set to produce the raw material to make anything they needed.

An AI controlled the mining station, and this one had been bored to death. Now, it had fifty Munchkins; twenty-six were females, and twenty-four were males. Of the twenty-six females, nineteen were of age to breed.

It also had an extra job. The males, unknown to them, were donating more genetic samples than they knew. Those samples were sent to a DNA editor in the medical pod, usually used to correct genetic deficiencies. Now, they had a quarter million years of inbreeding and radiation exposure to correct for. Nothing as exotic as attempting to recreate the original ancestors, but it would create viable genetic deltas, as opposed to most of the offspring almost showing up as siblings, the next few generations would show up as artificially genetically diverged, more like second cousins. The AI also had a quantum link directly to the current Mee Keralatazaku.

Smarter, strengthened by the actions of the medical pods, there was one more present we left for them. The station had two utility ships; these were reprogrammed only to allow strengthened Munchkins to enter them, and they were restricted to only using 0.2Gs of acceleration, but they had ships. These ships did not have FTL. They were initially for autonomously mining ice and carbon dioxide from the mining station's asteroid poles, but they had ships.

After we released them into the station, it took about fifteen days before we were confident they could live—no, they could thrive. We would return and possibly have some other Earth ships visit them.

The day before we planned to leave, Dylan came in and asked to speak to us: Mark, Chloe, and me. It was something we had almost expected. The avatar, Meera Fathi, had entered her medical pod, and she would be in and out of it for many months. She would not wake up for two weeks. The current Mee Keralatazaku was now in a special pod that the Original had provided, and a second slaved pod contained what would become the actual human Meera Fathi.

Dylan said, "I am conflicted. It's like starting a long-distance relationship; she will be unable to wake up for fourteen days, and then she will be able to emerge and use the avatar again, but she will have to spend every other day in the pod for almost six months. Then, she goes in for the actual transfer, which will last over four weeks."

"What will you do without her?"

"A lot of relaxing and learning about spaceships. Have you been in the pool when the Prochie are in it? We have to kick them out occasionally; they never want to leave."

I said, "I wonder if they are part of the crew now or just freeloaders who think they have an unlimited pool pass."

Jessie said, "Dylan is exaggerating. They only spend about four hours a day in the pool. They have been taking training lessons in medical pods, bringing them up to speed with standard drive technologies. They have not been given any information about the Hyper FTL drive."

I said, "That will probably be best until we determine if they are crew or guests."

Chloe said, "The way things go, they will probably become crew. Hey Jessie, what more have you learned from their ship?"

"That they were lucky to have lasted as long as they did. The ship had more repairs than I could account for. Some of the wiring was burned, and new wires were crudely spliced in. The power regulators were massive. They came off of something else, probably as used salvage. The build date on that was almost 250 years old. Most were only 125 years old. Yes, I know our original ship was a lot older than that, but I trust the maintenance my drones did. This looked like a drunkard did the repairs."

I said, "Did it have any embedded surveillance equipment or self-destructs?"

"None that I have found. If it did, that may explain the hole in the side. It would be pretty sleazy to leave an almost repairable ship as a honey-pot with a self-destruct. I won't say it was rigged to blow, just that it was a piece of crap, and they had reached the point where it wasn't worth towing away what remained to repair it."

I said, "Let the AI know that the ship is unsafe and not to let the Munchkins try to do anything with it. Have it check the pressure and keep the door closed. The plug they have in the hole is only rated as a temporary repair."

… … …

The next day, we departed the station and plotted the course back to Keralataza Station. Travel time would be eleven hours in Hyper FTL, plus six to accelerate and six to decelerate—about one day in total.

The eleven hours in Hyper FTL went without any issues, and then we spent six hours accelerating it so we could approach using the conventional FTL. We needed to avoid having anyone ever learn of the existence of Hyper FTL.

We only spent a few minutes in conventional FTL and then exited FTL.

A voice on the comm said, "The transponder identified your ship as the Stardust II. You are clear for an expedited approach.

Mark and Kibbiea were on the bridge with me, Chloe, Mei, and Katerina.

Katerina said, "Nothing abnormal on the sensors. ETA is about five hours and forty minutes."

The voice from before said, "You are to dock on port 13 G. After docking, an escort will take you to…for a meeting, the same place you visited before."

Katerina said, "I think she has trouble even saying her name. Did something change?"

I said, "Probably not. I think she just has that effect on most people."

A few minutes later, Dylan came in with Meera.

Chloe said, "Wait, that can't be right; I thought you would be in the box for something like twenty days?"

The avatar said, "Meera will be in the box for another two weeks; I wanted to see what this toy she made was like."

I said, "What should we call you? You are Mee Keralatazaku. You are also the original."

She said, "Call me Meera when I am wearing this body, and call me Mee Keralatazaku if I am in my natural body and no one else is around. We will not be walking around simultaneously. Her fortress is reasonably safe. Apparently, the Kassakar have been serving my descendants for many generations."

I said, "Oh, how are things going on the station?"

"It is massive compared to when I was here last. I will accompany you wearing this when we get to the station. I am interested in seeing people not react like they usually do with me. I have been reviewing the records. You do realize that you scare the locals as well, just not as bad as I do. You helped the current Mee Keralatazaku and inadvertently returned her to power."

… … …

The remainder of the trip was uneventful.

The area where we docked was empty except for another set of the monstrously oversized versions of the Regiolon. They towered over a normal Regiolon.

Meera said, "Oh, these are new; these must have taken some serious genetic tweaking to get them that large and not be horribly clumsy."

We were escorted down a well-lit hallway a short distance and boarded an electric people carrier vehicle. It seemed very close to the type of transporters you see at airports sometimes. Only now, my mind was wondering, who at the airports were they transporting? It had to be either the crew or possibly the elderly. I never rode in one of those in any airport. Walking to Mee's vault would have taken us nearly half an hour.

When we got there, Meera went over to a small bed and lay down on it; a few seconds later, she seemed to be sleeping, and she was breathing deeply and rhythmically.

A medical pod opened less than a minute later, and the original Mee Keralatazaku emerged.

She said, "I need to do something about the gel. It evaporates in fifteen minutes but smells terrible, even after a shower. As you may have noticed, we have large noses. They are not only for show."

We chuckled.

I said, "Yes, and big ears… Wait, the last one usually had dozens of earrings in her ears, and you have none. Now that I think about it, you didn't have any back at the Nest either."

"I used to have a lot of them, but the AI had me remove them when it regenerated my body. Hey, Ass.. Er, I mean Prudence, did the current Mee Keralatazaku keep any of her jewelry when she went in the box?"

Prudence replied, "She removed all of her jewelry. She did ask that I keep the piercings open so she can easily put them back after she wakes up."

"That… is the part I forgot to do. I had no desire to have that many piercings recreated from scratch."

"Do the piercings have any special meanings?"

Then Mee walked over to Chloe and looked at her ears. "This looks like one of mine."

Chloe said, "Mee removed it from her ear and gave it to me. It occurred when Ben proposed to me. I think you call it bonding."

She sighed, carefully reached over, ever so gently touched the earring, then turned away. She said, "I think the replacement Mees may have taken some of my earrings. A long time ago, I was bonded before things… changed. I can't imagine it is the same one; it would be over 2,000 years old; it must be a recreation, a replica."

I said, "She had a lot of earrings. Most were large hoops."

"Yes, the penance rings. They symbolize regret and loss. I don't mind losing them... but probably should put some of those back in."

She paused for a few, lost in thoughts, and then she snapped out of it. "The squid feet, the two stragglers that you picked up. I have looked into their backgrounds. They were reported dead years ago, and the ship they took off in was feared lost. They passed the background checks that the current Mee and I did independently. The Kipitz that abandoned the ship did not pass our background check. They are already dead, some from unrelated actions, one because he had something to do with running the Caspin Station, or they used that as an excuse. The individual Kipitz are mostly fine. An unusually high percentage of those who have anything to do with the military or the government are rotten to the core. I don't want to have to use a royal Keitch-mauber or the damn fleet on them, but they do seem to be the source of many of the current problems."

I said, "I would greatly prefer a diplomatic solution or any solution that does not require your ships to use the weapons they possess."

She said, "While Asshole was to blame for the creation of those nightmares, the ones who actually fired them were me or my replacements, and they are all effectively shadows of me, so all of the blame falls directly on me."

She took a deep breath, "We were talking about the squid feet, the Prochie. What should we do with them?"

I said, "Can I ask that you only refer to yourself as Meera before them? When we return to my ship, I would like to ask them what they want, and you are welcome to sit in on the conversation."

She said, "One option would be to give them a small ship. Then, what happens to them would become their problem."

Chloe smiled, "I have a better idea. I assume the Regiolon don't have any formal trading arrangements with the Prochie?"

She said, "Prudence, what is the answer?"

"No formal trading arrangements with the government. Some minor trading companies do visit it on occasion."

Chloe said, "If the Regiolon sent some official trading ships and established formal arrangements, what would become of the rather sleazy Kipitz trading arrangements? Specifically, if you made the arrangements with a bit of… grandstanding?"

She said, "Interesting, how impressive of an entrance do we need to do?"

"Some conventional warships sent to keep the peace, and maybe another of those space stations, like the one your descendant sent to the Earth and then sent another to Ciea."

"Those are relatively expensive. Do you know how much they cost?"

"No, and I don't care, and you don't either. Your descendant sent one just for the shock effect."

She paused briefly and then laughed, "The second station was a power move to establish a peaceful relationship with a mostly unknown race."

I said, "And for that task, it succeeded. And as a bonus, Mee terrified the queen."

"I have watched the wedding video, the bonding between Mark and Kibbiea. I suspect that part of the reason for the video was to instill utter terror into Queen Amalia Messo, Kibbiea's mother. It certainly succeeded even more than the appearance of the space station. Both of us really do find some humans so entertaining. A pity your government and military are mostly assholes."

I was about to reply but stopped after the "Ah.."

She said, "To be truthful, it seems that most governments and militaries are magnets for assholes. It is not just the humans, the Kipitz, and the Regiolon when no one is there to keep them in check."

I said, "What now?"

Mee said, "I hop back in the box and reactivate Meera. Then, we all go to the same place that made your spaceship and see how the upgrades I ordered for your second ship are coming along. I find it highly amusing to see how people react to others, more normal beings than myself. The upgrade was relatively minor, so it should be done in a day or two."

Then, as she said, she went to the medical pod, started to get in, changed her mind, ate a few more banana chips, and climbed back in.

The door slowly closed over her now immobile form, and about two minutes later, the Meera avatar woke up.

"I wish they could make the chips taste the same in the avatar; I would make one for myself."

We walked out to be met by only two of the guard Regiolon, and these were about six inches shorter than the earlier giants.

Mee said, "Take us to the Sakret Shipyard."

I leaned in and whispered to her, "We usually ask or say please. We are not the rulers, just the guests."

She started giggling, "This is almost fun. It may take me a while to get the attitude correct."

It was the same place as before but a lot busier this time, and several other species were present. One was a group of five of the Popotoen, the five-foot-tall walking opossums. Another was two of the Kanakon, the four-legged, four-armed beings with almost prehensile ears moving like an extra set of arms. There was a group of perhaps six of the Mapatans, cowboy fox-ferrets. There were none of the Kipitz that we could see. There were several groups of Regiolon; one family looked very well-dressed and had several children who looked like bored teenagers.

We entered the large room, and no one came to assist us for a few minutes. Then, one harried-looking younger female, a Regiolon, came running over. "I am so sorry. We are quite busy, and normal sales traffic is still running. I must ask, does this mean we should stop all other operations and expedite your processing?"

Mee looked like she was going to say something, but I spoke first, "I don't think so. We have a ship we loaned to another who needed to get here faster. I understand some upgrades were being added to it?"

"Yes, let's go to consultation room 'B' for the rest of this conversation. All of our senior sales reps were busy, and I will have one pulled away from a customer if you need one. Perhaps I can answer some simple questions."

I said, "That should be fine; what were the modifications, and when will they be done?"

"That I can answer, but it is better said in the private room."

She walked us to a large private room that resembled an executive conference room. It had a dozen comfortable padded swivel chairs and a large wooden conference table with a strange deep red grain pattern.

She said, "They added two more Gatling gun defensive systems and upgraded the missile system. The missile system was unusual; it is usually on the prohibited list of offensive weapons. It also included a change to add a massive triple redundant high current power rail to the second cargo bay. Given where the upgrade order came from, no one questioned the order. The modifications should be done tomorrow before nightfall."

"We are on a space station. Isn't the day only one hundred minutes long?"

"Ah, you haven't been here for that long. The station hours are always tracked at the same time as in the capital of Kipper. Didn't someone explain that to you the last time you were first here?"

I said, "Sorry, we had a lot on our minds."

She paused, "Yes, that was a bit of a tumultuous period of time."

Then she lowered her voice, "I have only ever heard her that one time when she spoke to the assembly. It was… disturbing."

Mee said, "You found her terrifying?"

"Swimming in a pool full of biters wearing a dead Kippit around my neck would be terrifying. Words do not describe being in her presence. I understand that some of you have actually spoken to her several times?"

Mee now had a crooked smile on her face.

I said, "Yes, but mostly as a friend…"

"Friend? But she is the supreme ruler, the ender of wars!"

I said, "Are we scary?"

She laughed and said, "Sorry, No, I can't think of you goat-toothed monkeys as really scary. I know you have stood in her presence, she who must not be annoyed, and somehow… you stood tall."

I said, "If Mee Keralatazaku passed you in a hallway without her guards surrounding her, if you didn't recognize her as anyone other than a normal Regiolon, would she still be scary?"

"Probably not, but now I may find myself looking at everyone and wondering if she is walking around. Then, everyone would be scary. Oh, I was supposed to ask if you want any other changes or upgrades done to that ship or the main ship you have?"

I said, "We would like to have the framework for another small shuttle with a fully working friction drive and power system, but we don't need any life support. It can be quite small. It is for a special project."

She typed on a flat control panel for a bit; then, an image came on the screen. It showed a regular shuttle in the B-8-4 configuration, and next to it was one marked A-0-3. It was only about one-quarter the length, and it was half the height. "This is a critical cargo delivery unit. When something needs to be repaired, for when the cost is not the issue, but speed is. They are used to deliver parts when something needs a replacement, like a centrifuge bearing or a reactor coolant pump. Actually, I think you would need a larger one for things like the larger ship centrifuge bearing parts."

Chloe said, "That makes sense. I understand what you mean. Can we get one or possibly two?"

She hit a few more keys, "There are three in stock and a used one that was returned when they determined they wanted a larger one."

I said, "I think we want all four. How much is that in platinum bars?"

"In the standard trade size, 125 bars per shuttle."

Jessie spoke over my earbud, "The standard ingots are 22.3 pounds, or 2787.5 pounds, or three million USD each."

I said, "Acceptable, we will take all four."

"The used one is only 100 ingots; I assume you have the metals in your ship?"

I spoke aloud, "Jessie, release the ingots to the ship company when they show up for the… What else do we owe for the other upgrades?"

"The docking fees and the other upgrades were already covered."

We started walking back to our transporter to take us back to our ship.

Mee said, "Normally, there is some haggling to get a better price."

I said, "I am not worried about that little extra cost. We were given the ship basically as a gift. We need to start paying our way. Did the salesperson make any bonus because we paid full price?"

She seemed to be talking to someone else, not where we could hear her. Then she said, "She earned a fractional credit, maybe an extra two weeks standard pay. Most of the extra profit will be taken by her supervisor at the Sakret Shipyard."

I said, "I liked her. I wish there were some way she could get a better bonus."

Mee said, "We have a change of plans. Let's stop at my place on the way back to your ship."

When we got there, the Meera avatar went into a back room. A few minutes later, the medical pod opened, and Mee Keralatazaku emerged. She said, "Please wait; I will change my outfit."

Ten minutes later, she came back dressed in heavy golden robes. She came in, and then one of the Kassakar servants came in, and it (I could not tell the sexes apart, and then I remembered they were all female)… she dropped a bunch of large pillows on the floor, and we all took seats on the pillows while the servant fetched more.

Mee sat taller when everyone was on a pillow, and the case for her pillow seemed to be made of gold. Ours were cloth and colorful. There was one empty, plain one, colored white, and then the servant brought in a mat, which looked to be made of heavy black rubber with metal shards and small spikes embedded into it.

Then the door opened, and in came two Regiolon; one was the saleswoman that had helped us, and the other was older and much heavier. Both walked stiffly as if they had 2x4s jammed up their asses.

Mee Keralatazaku spoke, "Sit. You, the salesperson, take the pillow. You, the supervisor, the mat is for you."

The supervisor didn't hesitate and assumed a kneeling position on the mat loaded with sharp metal spikes. The saleswoman nervously took the offered pillow.

Mee said, "My friends were just at your establishment. For one thing, it took several minutes for anyone to help them, and then you sent a rather junior salesperson. Is that correct?"

They both replied, "Yes."

Mee said, "The next time they show up there, for whatever reason, I expect they will receive expedited service, even if they don't ask for it."

The supervisor said, "It shall be so."

Then Mee said, "The junior salesperson was courteous and helpful. She arranged for a transaction that earned you a healthy commission. Is that correct?"

(gulp) "Yes."

Then Mee leaned forward and said, "Please reverse the commissions. I expect you to earn a minimal amount on this deal since you did almost nothing. I expect… What is your name?"

The saleswoman said, "Keriful."

Mee continued, "I expect my good friend Keriful to receive the bulk of the bonus for this transaction."

Then Mee reached behind her and pulled out a bag of banana chips. She ate a few and then handed the bag to Keriful. "Here, try some. They are quite delicious."

Keriful managed to reach into the bag with a shaky hand. She pulled out a few chips and obediently put them in her mouth. I could see that her eyes were filling with tears. Then, after the first chips were in her mouth, she paused.

"These are incredible. I have heard the rumors; the taste is truly amazing."

Mee pointed at the supervisor, "You can go now. If I hear even the slightest rumor about you mistreating Keriful. Your ears will decorate the entrance to the Sakret Shipyard."

Then she turned to look at Keriful, "Do you want to stay for dinner? We are having…"

Keriful passed out at that point.

Then she promptly started choking on a banana chip, and she was rushed off to a medical pod.

Mee said, "She should be fine. What do you think everyone will think of her when she returns to work tomorrow?"

"Most of the salespeople, actually, almost everyone she meets, will now be scared of her. Mee Keralatazaku actually called her a friend."

Mee said, "How long do you think it will be before she realizes the lesson I am trying to teach her?"

Keriful spoke from the other room, where she was now sitting up in a medical pod: "I think I have already figured it out; being feared isn't a good life—at least not for the person who everyone fears."

Mee laughed, "Come back and join us, and this time, I will have a servant bring you something to drink."

Keriful came walking back and said, "I had a vision of my obituary. I died choking on a banana chip while sitting with Mee Keralatazaku."

I said, "But you didn't die; your supervisor… that relationship will now be interesting."

Keriful said, "Interesting. Perhaps that word has a different meaning than any of the ones I am more familiar with." Then, she had a coughing fit. "I will take that drink, but please, nothing with alcohol in it."

Drinks were brought out. It was an earth drink, iced tea.

She took a drink and said, "What is this drink?"

Mee said, "Something from the planet the humans came from, extracted from boiling certain leaves, and then serving chilled with Earth sugar added."

Keriful took a sip, "This is wonderful."

Mee said, "It's their sugars. Theirs are very different from ours. The humans are sending over some of the young plants and seeds, and we will see if they grow in our soil."

Then Keriful said, "Why did you do this to me? My life was boring and simple, but eventually, I would have become a more senior sales representative and made decent money. What did I do that you singled me out?"

Mee said, "Do you really want to know one of my secrets?"

Her eyes clamped shut, and a shudder ran through her arms and her ears. "No, I suppose not. You have already shaken my entire life to the core. I can't imagine that my dating life will be the same after this, either. Was it because I said what I did in front of the humans? Were you listening in on what was said near them?"

I said, "Something like that. How are you feeling? Has the shock worn off yet?"

She stared at the drink, which was tightly held with both of her hands; the drink was in a formal gold and ceramic goblet. "I probably would have to go into debt to be able to afford this drink. I would never be able to afford this goblet. If I drop it, I have no idea how I would ever pay for it. It looks like a national treasure."

One of the servants came out, and he took the drink she had and replaced her goblet with a simple ceramic mug. Mee said, "Is this better?"

"This looks like a fancy ceramic glass, but it's still nicer than I would normally buy for myself."

I said, "Half a year ago, I was living on an allowance; my parents were paying for a large part of my schooling, and I had borrowed money to pay for some of it. Today, I don't have to worry about money. I assume you were also getting by and living a normal life then. What has changed?"

She rocked back and forth a few times, "Six months ago, everyone was worried about the probability of war. All these commercials on the video were about survival food, generators, and advertising fancy bunkers for the rich, telling you to invest in standard secure credit for investments. Some were leaving the cities and moving to rural areas, hoping they were less likely to be bombed. The children in school were taught where the shelters were, and we would do invasion training. I was selling spare parts for tractors that were supposed to block them from EMI damage. Yeah, it was a different time." She looked directly at Mee, "We were still alive; however, that future was getting to be… questionable. We are selling ships for pleasure again, just not… other ships. We are all happier now, but we also have the moon hanging in the sky as a visual reminder of how things have changed."

Mee said, "If it helps, that was intended as a reminder to the other races, not specifically for ours."

Keriful said, "You don't seem like the instance of Mee Keralatazaku who spoke at the concert hall. In that speech, you seemed angry at us."

I said, "She was away because someone plotted to eliminate her. The war of 122 years ago was a ploy to get her away, to somewhere safe so that they could… if not kill her, then make her effectively go away. How would you feel if that happened to you?"

"I would be angry, but the clothes you wore then were so strange, even for humans. You are now dressed more normally, or normal for the ultra-rich and powerful… sorry. I got carried away. I was speaking normally to you and shouldn't have been; I am so sorry."

Mee laughed, "Don't be. For one or two sentences, you spoke to me as normal, and that alone was worth playing some silly little mind games. My life has been… different; I cherish even the most trivial moments of normalcy. The humans, I can see why… I find my time with them amusing, almost normal. Or as normal as normal can be for me."

Keriful said, "You are not normal. You are the current iteration of Mee Keralatazaku, the ender of wars."

Mee said, "Do you know what that phrase means?"

"I am sorry, I am not sure; I know that somehow, you are related to the original; are you clones of her?"

Mee laughed and said, "The humans know the real answer to that. Do you want to know that answer?"

Keriful's skin went two shades lighter grey. She said, "Probably not. This has been a strange day. My life won't be the same."

Mee looked at Dylan with a strange look on her face. "Dylan, can I ask you to do me a favor?"

He looked up and said, "Whatever you want."

She looked at Keriful, smiled, and said, "Keriful, sit, don't move, and don't say anything. Dylan, give her an ear massage."

He chuckled and walked up behind the now terrified Regiolon, saying, "Just sit still. Try not to hyperventilate."

Then, he started giving her an ear massage. Panic transformed into shock, surprise, amazement, and finally, pleasure. Ten minutes later, she melted into the pillow and lay on her back. "I have given up on understanding what this day is about. That was… extremely relaxing. I would give a week's pay for that."

Mee said, "My turn now."

Dylan went and gave her an ear massage.

When Mee's massage was done, Keriful rolled over onto her side, "What will become of me now?"

Mee moaned and said, "Give me a few more minutes to enjoy the afterglow. No talk yet."

A few minutes later, Mee said, "This is the fun part of my life. Most of my life involves being the ultimate demon and a monster, which is why all the other bad monsters hide in the shadows."

"The fun part?"

"Yes, the part where I can be almost normal, even if only for a tiny part of the day."

She said, "You still scare the crap out of me."

Mee laughed, "I scare the crap out of everyone, these humans, probably less than most, but I still make them nervous."

Keriful said, "So, what is to become of me now?"

Mee said, "You now know a little secret: Mee has a side of her that isn't the big, bad supreme ruler."

Keriful said, "It's not a secret; it is words that no one would ever utter, and no one would ever believe. Are all the humans able to do that trick with our ears?"

Mee said, "Others could learn it. I think it has to do with how big their hands are, and not having claws on their fingers is a big plus."

Keriful said, "I am not sure I can return now, not to my old life. Not without it being very different. There will be all sorts of strange rumors about me."

"Rumors that you have a friend?"

"Oh, the horror, I have a friend! It is not that I have a friend. It is who that… friend is. Are you a friend?"

Mee said, "I have very few friends, and most of them are humans. Do you want to be a crew member on the humans' ship?"

"Hmm, I would get to eat human food and maybe get a few ear massages; you make a compelling offer. But I sense there would be a hidden bad part to that deal. What is the catch?"

Mee said, "Smart. The catch would be that we let you in on a few more secrets, and these I can't allow to spread. I must know you will keep the secrets to be allowed to return to living a normal life."

Keriful said, "Can I think about it? Can I discuss it with my parents but not go into any details?"

"Sure."

She left shortly after that. Just before she left, a servant handed her an unopened bag of banana chips.

After she left, I said, "Are the banana chips that good that they actually may influence life choices?"

Mee laughed, "We have a massive sealed greenhouse being constructed to grow some banana trees in as a test. Supposedly, they should be ready to harvest in 14-16 earth months. It will be interesting to see if sugars develop in the same way locally. The scientists who are studying it argued over whether we should classify them as a narcotic. They finally had to come up with a new classification: it is a new category of controlled substance, like alcohol or some recreational drugs."

I said, "If more sugary items are added to the Regiolon diet, using Earth as an example, then the things to watch are weight gain, diabetes, and tooth decay."

Mee said, "We have sugars, just not the same ones that seem so common in human foods."

The topic returned to our second ship, which was now scheduled to receive all the requested changes. Mee said, "I had to check to ensure she had committed all the updates and didn't just run out as soon as I sent the request for the two of them to show up."

I laughed, "Request?"

She said, "Her supervisor still needed to approve the changes. He ran out before he approved everything. He immediately approved everything as soon as he left here before returning to work."

She said, "Everything is now set and…"

Alarms started sounding

Prudence said, "We have an emergency."

PROBLEMS

Mee immediately snapped into her supreme ruler mode, "What happened?"

"Unknown ships, with no transponders, have exited FTL, far too close to the planet than is normally considered safe, and they have released a massive asteroid that is on a collision course to this station. Impact time is 192 seconds."

A chair slid out on a hidden track, and it lit up. Mee Keralatazaku threw off her outer robe, ran, and then jumped into it. Restraints appeared around her chest, and she was rocketed away.

Prudence said, "Mee will arrive in the Keitch-mauber in fifteen seconds. The ship's weapons are powering up. We have an issue: the outer hatch has been sabotaged. Requesting an unlock on the Hyper FTL Drive."

I yelled, "Granted."

"Unlocking the pilot boat will not be available for over an hour, as it is crated. Hyper FTL will be active in twelve seconds. Seek immediate shelter. Activation of Hyper FTL while docked is untested.

Jessie said, "Disengage the airlock seal and let the springs push you away from the port, then engage Hyper FTL while not in full contact with the station."

The massive bank vault-like door closed, and we were stuck in Mee's chamber. A countdown appeared on the screen on the wall, and we sat on the floor without anything better to do.

Chloe said, "Seek shelter? Just what the hell were we supposed to do?"

When the countdown reached zero, there was a sound like a clap of thunder, and everything shook.

Jessie said, "The sonic boom was from the Keitch-mauber doing an Hyper FTL. It disappeared, leaving a hard vacuum, and the remaining air in the docking bay collapsed to fill the void. The Keitch-mauber is now reorienting itself to face the asteroid… ZAP!"

The room plunged into darkness, and the screen changed to show that Jessie was now rebooting; Prudence was still active and announced, "The threat has been neutralized."

Then, there were no updates for two minutes, but it felt like an hour. The lights finally returned to normal, and the screen changed to "Jessie here, the royal Keitch-mauber is now following the last known trajectory of the ships that released the asteroid. They will probably drop out of FTL and change course when they believe they are outside of Mee's reach. They probably already know that the attempt failed."

A minute later, Prudence said, "I have sent out a repair crew to remove whatever they did that caused the bay cover to fail to open. I will also send repair crews to check for damage caused by the hard exit.

Mark yelled, "Modify that order. First, check all the repair technicians you would have sent in and see if any of them are compromised or if any of their relatives are missing or off planet."

"Message from Mee: The wreckage of several ships has emerged from FTL, but Prudence does not think that was all the ships. It also shows a massive radiation discharge. She thinks the ships contained micro-nukes. She will continue to follow the projected path of the ships in case some have escaped the self-destruct."

Then Prudence's voice came over the speakers, "The threat appears to have been neutralized, but the weapon I fired may have left some particles that will impact the station shortly."

Then the station sounded an alarm I hadn't heard before.

Jessie said, "They are warning of potential debris impacts."

I said, "Mute the alarm. I want to listen for any impacts."

The alarm stopped, but I think I could hear it off in the distance. Then, there was a sound like rocks hitting a battleship. Muted and extremely low-frequency thuds.

The sounds died down over the next minute.

Jessie said, "A few of the larger chunks may make it to the planet's surface, but the asteroid was obliterated. It was 400 by 500 feet across and weighed twenty million tons, close to the size of the Great Pyramid. But much heavier. It was a metallic asteroid with twelve ships attached to it. I am not sure what weapon Mee used, but what remained was less than 0.0001%, and that was molten metal."

I said, "What does the normal population know about what happened?"

"The news reported that it was an attack, and an unknown defensive weapon was deployed to defend against it."

I said, "Jessie, Prudence, hunt for whoever was here as the spotters or the saboteurs. See what you can find. There should have been cameras on the doors. Was the sabotage on the outside or the inside on the doors?"

Jessie said, "It was a micro explosive on a power cable. The cable had redundant backups, but they suffered the same damage. It was outside the station and looked like a modified or fake maintenance drone—like a Roomba vacuum cleaner. I have been reviewing all of the operations on the station for the last few months."

I said, "Can you connect us to Mee?"

"Done."

"Hi Mee, we have found the sabotage; it looks like some maintenance drones were modified, or maybe a fake drone was used to place micro explosives over the power to open the door."

"Hello, Ben, I am still shadowing the others. Or wherever I think they are. Several ships have self-destructed, but the debris was too small for all the ships. Anything on who did it?"

I said, "I have my suspicions, but it could also be someone else who wanted to misdirect us and make us think someone else was the guilty party. What will you do if they drop out of FTL?"

"The trajectory they chose was from a random empty area in space, toward a different random empty area; if they exit FTL and change to point to a known location, that tells me something."

I said, "Even that could be a misdirection, a false flag to direct you somewhere else."

"Hold, they exited FTL, lining up the shot. BAM!!! This time, Seven ships dropped out at the same time. I used one of the smaller weapons. Four ships have exploded, one venting all the air in it and is now spinning rapidly. Two remain mostly intact, but I don't have a way of boarding them; I will continue on my course in case there is another ship of two. Can you head to the location and match the velocity I am sending your ship? You should be able to board them and see if anyone survived?"

"We can try."

The massive vault door opened, and a people transporter was outside the door waiting to take us to our ship. We launched within a minute of boarding our ship and had boarding parties report to both shuttles. We sounded the alarm about doing a hard acceleration, and we put the ship at 2.50G's for two hours to reach the target direction and velocity. Then, we entered standard FTL and were at the site in twenty-five minutes.

As soon as we exited standard FTL, Jessie said, "Close, we are within seventeen miles. I see the two intact ships, and one is spinning like a top; I assume that was the one with the air leak. Both shuttles prepare to board the ships. Expect hostiles, but they may already be dead. What is the status of the ships?"

"No power, drifting. I don't know what she hit them with, but they lost all electrical, maybe more. Launching shuttles, ETA eight minutes on one and five on the other."

"Have them both try and dock at the same time."

Eight minutes later, the two shuttles simultaneously docked.

Jessie said, "All manual controls are disabled. Even if they captured the shuttles, they could not operate anything. Outer hatches are engaging the capture clamps. The communication ports are dead, with zero voltage, as if all the power buses have been directly shorted to ground."

"Outer hatches are solid. The airlocks show zero pressure in the ships, which is abnormal. All guards are in full pressure suits with flak jackets over the suits."

Ninety seconds later, Jessie announced, "One shows zero pressure in the crew area. The other is at standard pressure and running rich for oxygen. Preparing to open hatches, they may be in suits."

… … …

"Team 'A,' they were not in suits or not the ones we have encountered. All the ones we have seen so far have been Kipitz."

"Team 'B,' there is air, but it is low visibility and filled with smoke. We are entering the main ship. This appears to be a mining tugboat, which would explain how they could move that giant hunk of iron, or whatever it was.

"Team 'A,' we have found someone in a suit. Unfortunately, the suit's electronics are bricked, and it looks like they ran out of air. They may be able to identify the body. It is intact."

"Team 'B,' we have encountered several bodies, none alive. Wait, we have one that attached its suit to a manual oxygen tank. Transporting it to the medical pod, they may survive."

"Team 'A,' we have reached the bridge. None of them were in suits. We are hard ejecting the drives from the controls. This was a manually controlled ship; there was no AI, as expected."

I said, "Are there any medical pods?"

"Negative, these ships have been stripped down to the bare essential parts. I see no indications of the ship's serial numbers or identifying IDs. We have been searching the bodies for paperwork or ID's. Wait, this one has a key card; I am not sure what it was for."

I said, "Well, don't go trying it in anything. It could be a self-destruct. The one that exploded seemed to have small nukes on it; look for radiation signatures."

"Team 'B,' we have found what is probably a micro-nuke. It is mounted in the head off the bridge."

"Team 'A,' same location here. It looks like it has a card reader attached to the side of it. The radiation counter is through the roof; we are leaving this room; it may be damaged and leaking; whatever Mee did fried everything."

"Team 'B,' we have a live one. They were in the engine compartment. If I had to guess, it was a technician who was monitoring the systems. They have surrendered. It was another Kipitz. One of the bodies was the eight-limbed bunny ears species."

I said, "Those are the Kanakon. Bag the body; someone may be able to identify it. How many bodies have you encountered on each ship?"

Each ship reported six.

Katerina said, "I concur, take the unusual one to the medical pod. Each shuttle has one in it, and they are running on batteries. We don't have room for all the bodies. For the ones that have had explosive decompression, bag a sample. For the mostly intact ones, see if you can fit any in a bag. Try for one that was on the bridge and looked like he was in charge."

Chloe lost all the color in her face.

I said, "Jessie, mute any sound effects we don't want to hear. Let us know when they are… done. Do you think the nukes would go off if we strafed the ships?"

"I would rather not try and find out. Did the marines that boarded the ships take anything with them like C4 and timers?"

Emily Frankenstein's voice came over the intercom, "Of course we fricking did; what should we blow up, and what do we set the timers for?"

"Put one in the bridge, next to the nuke or the alien equivalent, and one next to the airlock. Set the airlock for 20 minutes and the bridge for 22, and make sure we are nowhere near them when they pop."

"What about the one that lost pressure and spun off sideways?"

"Which shuttle has more room? Give that ship a really quick check. Add fifteen minutes to what I said to set the timers at. That should be enough to… Get the shuttle with the live one back here ASAP; send the other shuttle to the dreidel from hell. It has someone in a medical pod, so they should be fine."

Emily said, "The survivor seems almost robotic. As if they have already given up on life. I want them in a medical pod as well."

Two minutes later, the two ships departed. One headed back toward our ship, and the other went after the spinner.

Jessie said, "I can match the spin and dock, but none of you will like it. The mass difference is too much for us to correct. Do a quick run to the bridge and back. Believe me, you won't want to do anything else."

Two minutes later, Emily said, "We have docked. This is nasty. I'm going in now."

Jessie reported, "No pressure; a survivor would have to be in a suit and connected to an air tank."

Ten minutes later, Emily said, "Disconnecting, Errp, yack, groan."

Jessie said, "The first shuttle has docked and unloaded the… recovered items. Mei is taking care of the unloading."

Emily's voice came over the intercom, "And stay down, you fracking asshole."

I said, "Did they find someone alive?"

"Yeah… Sorry, we didn't tolerate the spin well. One more alive one, another Kipitz. How they can still move amazes me. We only left one timer on this one, in the bridge, set to go off when the others do. Thankfully, the ship runs itself. None of us can even see straight."

After the shuttle docked, the suppression crew went in, and the other survivor was dragged away. They were then stunned, and their unconscious body was stripped of the spacesuit, and then they were tossed into a medical pod.

Mee said, "Three alive, all Kipitz, one male, very aggressive, one female, I think she was a technician, she is almost passive, and one male that is alive but has not regained consciousness. We need to get away from here, as the fireworks will start soon."

When the charges went off, we moved to half a light-second distance—a third the distance to the moon. It was not impressive; the nukes didn't get set off.

I said, "Well, are the hulls ventilated now? Are there any emissions from the hulls? Things like the FTL beacon or a radio beacon?"

"Zero electrical activity, no one will ever stumble across these hulls."

I said, "Call Mee."

"Mee here, what have you found?"

"Three survivors, two may be able to talk, one never woke up. Most were Kipitz, but one was a Kanakon. I assume you will want to talk to them."

"Ha, that is one way to describe what I will do. I will… Two more ships emerged, and I fired the same weapon; one exploded, and the other is now drifting. I will send you the coordinates."

Jessie said, "I recommend conventional FTL. The heading and velocity are acceptable. It will take thirty-two minutes to reach them."

I said, "We will be unlikely to find any survivors after that amount of time. Have you determined that Hyper FTL is safe at high galactic velocities?"

"It's probably safe. Both shuttles are now secured. Shall we test it?"

"Yes."

It was different and highly unpleasant, and about half the crew was sick. All but two had barf bags within easy reach. After what felt like ten minutes, we exited Hyper FTL.

"Elapsed time, 72 seconds."

Chloe said (Groan), "That was truly nasty; I vote we don't do it again unless it's an emergency."

Mee said, "I never accelerated to any speed; I just jumped a lot, and when they emerged, I fired my EM-disperser. It will take me hours to accelerate to match your velocity. See if the last one has anyone on it."

We launched both shuttles; one went in and did the docking, and the other just hovered nearby.

"We have air, some smoke, but not like the last one. We will use stunners, but if they shoot back with anything other than a stunner, the M16 will be their reply."

"Contact, multiple survivors. They were armed, but they were not expecting flash bangs followed by stunners. Two down, and we are securing them with zip-tie handcuffs."

"The bridge is secured. We are about to try shooting the lock."

Chloe had the audio muted then, and we had text reporting the conversations.

They gained entry and found one more individual attempting to run a key card through the scanner attached to the nuke. Fortunately, all the electronics were fried. They stunned everyone.

"Five are alive, and two probably need medical treatment. We are checking where we found the technician to see if anyone is there. All subjects are Kipitz. This ship is now secure. We are taking them; the other two are tied up and stunned. We are full; the other ship will need to retrieve them. We are undocking now."

As soon as the first ship was undocked, the next ship moved into position. The second ship docked and retrieved the last two prisoners.

I said, "Connect me to Mee. Mee, we got five alive on the last ship. That ship is now set to have explosives turn it into scrap. We will be heading back. It will be almost eight hours before we arrive at the expected velocity and direction. What are you doing?"

"I will be hopping in using the Hyper FTL. I may as well add to the myths of what my ship can do. I will have a special crew to take the prisoners from you. What else did you get?"

"Some biological samples, in case you can trace them from their genetics. We pulled some of the electronics, but it all looked melted. I don't think anyone will get much, if any, from these."

Mee said, "We reviewed the records, and two people delivered new maintenance drones, but they were non-standard and externally controlled. They have been apprehended."

"Well, we will see you after we return to the station."

STATION

Mee did not bother to hide her ship's extra capabilities. A few hours later, it appeared a quarter of a light-second distance from the Keralataza Station, and she announced on the communication link. "The immediate threat to Kanpripticon has been eliminated, and the people behind it will soon regret it." The repairs on the door control for the bay that held the royal Keitch-mauber had already been made, and the door opened to show the now empty bay.

We arrived at the station twelve hours later, having decelerated, reaccelerated, and then decelerated again so that our ship looked like it only had a standard FTL drive.

After we docked, the area outside the docking port was sealed, and black material covered the path's walls, floors, and ceilings from the airlock to the waiting armored people carriers that would hold the prisoners. Four were still inside medical pods, and brand new, top-of-the-line empty medical pods were delivered to replace the occupied ones. We don't know where the occupied pods were taken.

After removing the shroud-like covers, there was no sign that the prisoners had ever been there. We were loaded onto a standard people transporter, but this time, it was enclosed, and something told me the sides were bulletproof.

We arrived at Mee's nuclear bomb-proof enclosure and were ushered inside. The massive door immediately closed behind us.

Mee was wearing loose-fitting clothing that resembled sweatpants and a sweatshirt. On her feet were pink slippers.

She said, "Well, You had already passed the latest Mee's qualifications to be her friend, and I must say, you have now passed mine as well. The prisoners are all being put in special medical pods, and your AI, Jessie, has provided some tweaks to them so that they cannot hide any information. The existence of that feature is strictly between us. Two of the eight captured were technicians and not part of the plot; one objected vehemently after discovering their plans. Those two will survive the second part of the interrogation. The other six will not. Do you want the technicians transferred to the Caspin Station when we are done with them? I don't want them to return to regular society after what they were part of. Assuming… their home planet is still there when I get done with it."

Chloe said, "I have to put in my comments; I don't think you should punish the entire race for the actions of… I have no idea how many were involved… it was probably fairly involved."

Mee said, "There were players from three species. There was direct participation from the leaders of five planets and indirect involvement of two more. Ignoring things like people welding the external adapters to the ships, they had over 1,200 people knowingly involved and another 5,000 unknowingly or indirectly involved. I am not so crass to destroy planets for the actions of a few thousand assholes, but I will want to make them think I am considering it. I have a little bit of a confession to make to you."

I said, "What?"

"I have taken the design for the Hyper FTL engine, and a version of it is under construction. That will only be installed on one additional ship. The way the royal Keitch-maubers are designed, they need a Mee Keralatazaku to actually operate the weapons. The AIs cannot operate anything. However, we are in a rather unique position. The latest Mee Keralatazaku will be ready to eject from her medical pod in one week. The clone operation will eventually create a human version of her, who will have completed the initial RNA and neural pathwork mapping. She will have a hell of a headache but will be functional. She only needs to be in a synced medical pod for an hour or two every few days for the next phase of the construction of her human body. Then, for the final part, she will have to spend four weeks in deep synchronization."

I said, "I could say I object, but given the circumstances, that is acceptable."

She laughed, "You are the only ones who could object, and I would care more than a squirmer's rectal cavity about their opinion.

At the crux of everything is that 122 years of plotting and scheming have built up all this animosity. We are extremely lucky they didn't have a galactic war as soon as they thought I was out of the way. I suspect they needed a few generations before they could trust themselves not to have my wrath come crashing down on them, and now, they have really pissed me off. What I will do… they will remember."

A weak voice came from a speaker, "I agree."

Dylan said, "Is that Meera?"

The voice continued, "I'm still in the box and connected in an audio-only mode for another week. I am having a hell of a vacation."

We all laughed, if somewhat nervously.

I said, "What is the plan now, well, now that all the crap has hit the fan?"

Mee said, "The in-box interrogations are more like an information dump, and those are almost done. Then, there will be a relatively short public disclosure of the plot and who is involved. I don't think they expected anyone to turn up as a prisoner. We are holding that part off for at least a week. Then, the second ship will be ready, and we will make a little visit to the Kipitz home worlds. Two instances of Mee Keralatazaku in two royal Keitch-mauber's, showing off the Hyper FTL, and we make two of their moons disappear at the same time. Then, we play the video of the interviews of the prisoners to the home worlds."

Mark said, "Actually, you should play the video first; if it is anything like the last weapon you fired, there will not be much operational electronics on the planet, and most of them won't hear the message."

Mee said, "You are probably right. We will change the order in which we are doing this. Oh, you need to go back and check on the mischief Munchkins. They have been busy."

I said, "Do I want to know what they have been up to?"

"They have figured out how to operate some of the mining equipment and the ships."

"Your second ship has completed its upgrades and is ready for you to pick it up."

"Oh, with everything that has been going on, I completely forgot."

Jessie said, "Mei is on her way over to it now with the second ship's crew."

Then Mee went and lay down in the avatar control medical pod, and two minutes later, Meera came walking out of the other room. "I will walk this back to your ship, as the other instance of me will want to play with you again."

I said, "Not you as well?"

She smiled and said, "I admit it's a lot more fun being with you; I may take a few turns operating the avatar as well."

We were headed back to our ship when the transporter stopped, and a Regiolon female boarded the transporter. It took me a few seconds to recognize her. "Hello, Keriful. Have you decided to join our crew?"

"Mee is a bit of an asshole; even my parents are now nervous around me. I went in to work, and when the attack started, everyone else panicked, and I think they somehow blamed me for the attack. I don't know what this extra crap is that I will learn if I work on your ship, but I thought it over, and I don't want to be on the station anymore. I think with your people. I will be the minor bit player, not the one everyone looks at nervously."

I said, "Welcome to the crew. I am the captain, Benjamin Williams.

"I am Chloe Williams, and we were recently married; humans use that word instead of bonded. I am also carrying a child and should start to have a noticeable belly bump in a few more weeks."

"I am Mark Adams, the XO, and I recently married my wife, Kibbiea Messo Adams, she is of the species Creetona. You will meet her on the ship."

Keriful said, "I watched that ceremony, the first interspecies bonding; that video is everywhere. Who is the other one? I don't think I heard her name when we met before.

"I go by the name Meera Fathi when I am wearing this body."

"What? You wear a body? I don't understand."

"This is an avatar, a construct that is quantum tied to a different body that is now inside a special medical pod."

"That is… strange; what name do you go by when you are not in the construct?'

She smiled, "Chloe, Mark, you may want to hold her in case she passes out or panics."

"What! Why would I pass out!"

They each put an arm around her. Meera said, "Who do you think I am?"

Then she passed out.

Meera said, "It looks like she guessed correctly."

TRAVEL

Before we undocked from the station, a specialized medical pod containing the Original Mee was loaded into our ship.

The ship accelerated hard for four hours and then entered standard FTL.

We only stayed there for fifteen minutes, then dropped out and started decelerating just as rapidly.

Then we entered Hyper FTL and started the trip to the mining station where we left the Munchkins.

Mark was on the bridge next to Kibbiea, and her tail was wrapped around his waist. He was gently holding her tail with one hand.

I said, "Do you know what is up with the little troublemakers, Jessie?"

Jessie said, "They have all been in the medical pods several times. They figured out how to request specific changes, even if they didn't know anything about the technology initially. They can now function in low gravity, but anything more than Mars gravity would take several more sessions on the box. They found a loophole in what they could ask for. Now, in place of looking like they have anorexia as well as having small heads and bodies, they look like they have Achondroplasia, a form of dwarfism with closer to normal-sized heads but with short arms, legs, and body length. They figured out that they were having trouble learning new things, and the change took their average vocabulary from a seven-year-old to now that they are close to adult human capability. They still have minimal knowledge from life experiences, so they are playing catch up. The result is curious and somewhat mischievous little people.

Chloe said, "There is more, admit what else you screwed up and did."

Jessie said, "I may have inadvertently played an entertainment video for them. In retrospect, it was a horrible mistake."

I said, "What video?"

"The Wizard of Oz, the 1939 version."

Chloe said, "They still only like comfortable clothing, things like pajamas, but they all now wear striped socks, colorful shorts, and plaid shirts, and the females have taken to wearing a short version of the frilled skirts." Then, she put an image on the screen.

Mei burst out laughing, and she almost fell out of her seat.

Chloe said, "They have taken to the nickname and not the short-legged cats with that same name.

I said, "How long until we get to the mining station?"

Jessie didn't answer.

"Jessie, I asked a question. Are you reporting, or did the microphone fail?"

"Sorry, I was under the effect of the blinders from earlier. Some protective layers were just removed. We are not on the way to the mining station. We are now on the way to the Nest."

I said, "Get Dylan up here. He usually has a low-speed connection, even if the avatar is in reboot from FTL. Or is her real body in the medical pod now waking up?"

Dylan came into the bridge a few minutes later, "Sorry, I was in the cafeteria having something to eat. Keriful had trouble with the English menus on the food dispenser, so I had to help her order some food."

Kibbiea said, "Have you explained your relationship to Meera to her yet?"

"Hell no, she is still in shock from everything else."

Kibbiea said, "Let Mark and me know when you explain that to her; it should be interesting. Do you think she will pass out again?"

Mei said, "Let all of us know. I will video it."

I said, "Back to the original topic, well, sort of... Dylan, can you ask Mee why we are going to the Nest?

He said, "The Munchkins are returning to the Nest on a different ship. It is doing an extremely slow acceleration and deceleration, Ass… I really wish Mee would come up with a better name for that AI. Anyway, it sent the semi-defective AI ship, the one that doesn't like weapons, and they have moved everything they had onto that ship."

"I wouldn't call it defective; it's… a little more normal than the A-name one. What is our ETA?"

"Less than twelve hours. This time, we are going in a more direct path and not looping around to obfuscate the distance."

I said, "Crap, you said the blinders were being removed, not added?"

"Yup, the location of the Nest is now known to me, but I can't divulge anything about it to anyone who is not cleared for this ship's bridge access. That includes the two Prochie, Keriful, and most of the scientists."

Suddenly, the ship shuddered and dropped out of Hyper FTL.

I yelled, "What was that? Was there sabotage, or were we attacked?"

"No, it was a hard transition to normal space. Something was one jump ahead of us, and we had just lost our pilot boat. I am reviewing the last data it sent. We only received a single packet and one partial packet. Attempting to reconstruct what it reported. I am now loading one of the spare pilot boats into the launcher."

Mark said, "No, what about the sentinel satellites? Those are a lot smaller, and they have quantum links. Can we load one onto the pilot boat and have it drop and run, not stay and scan like it usually does?"

Jessie said, "That may be possible. I planned to have the pilot boat jump half the distance, scan what it can, and then jump half that distance, reducing by half on each jump."

I said, "The active scanning may trigger whatever destroyed it. Drop out of Hyper FTL 1.5 light seconds away from the target area, do no scans, immediately drop the surveillance satellite, and jump back. That is the distance from the earth to the moon, and nothing should be able to spot it... Crap, now that I said it out loud, something will probably spot it. Use your oldest, least useful, and least powerful pilot boat for the satellite carrier, just in case it goes pop."

"Changing pilot boats, adding the small surveillance satellite and a release module will only take fifteen minutes."

A few minutes later, Dylan said, "Mee wants to know what is happening. Should she wake up the avatar or exit the pod?"

I said, "Have her wait a few minutes. We should have a satellite in the area of the problem in a little while. How many satellites do we have on this ship? I thought they were all on the second ship."

Jessie said, "Most of them are, but one of our replicators on this ship is making slightly different versions."

... ...

Fifteen minutes later, we launched the pilot boat, and it returned less than a second later.

"Can we tell anything about the area where we lost the pilot boat?"

Jessie said, "Large expanding cloud of debris, and the pilot boat popped into the edge of it. Not radioactive, the cloud is expanding outward, and inside of the cloud is an object that has broken up into several large pieces. It appears to be a recent explosion, and it looks like it used to be a ship."

I said, "Check with the Nest, ensure no ships are missing, and that it isn't anywhere close to where the Munchkins were. How recent of an explosion?"

"Given the position and speed of the expanding debris cloud, about eight days ago."

I said, "Could this have been someone's backup plan for taking out Kanpripticon? Could it be something that blew up when they were testing it? What is the galactic velocity of the ship's remains at the epicenter?"

"Near zero, whatever it was, had completely stopped; this makes no sense. Possibly someone tested a Hyper FTL, and it blew up on them?"

"Can you retrieve the sensor satellite?"

"Not with our pilot boat; I can attach a second satellite and repeat what we did closer to the ship's remains. If we need to do a third one, we need to dock with the second ship and transfer over more satellites."

I said, "Send a second one over there. I don't like having an unexplained problem this close to the Nest."

Dylan said, "I can pass along the fact that Mee is extremely unhappy about it as well."

Loading and launching the second satellite only took five minutes, and when the pilot boat returned, Jessie said, "It was dropped off two miles from the large part of what remains of the ship. The satellite has thrusters and can maneuver and approach. The ship was less than half the size of this ship, and it is now in two large fragments, one smaller piece and uncountable small fragments. The small piece is highly radioactive, so it probably contains the core. Putting images of a composite of what it probably originally looked like on the screens."

The ship was initially shaped like a triangle, with a flat section in what I assumed was the back and a pointy section in the front. The tip of the pointy nose was missing, and whatever they hit or were shot with went through the ship and exploded what remained.

Mark said, "Like a Star Destroyer, but smaller and much more simplistic."

Chloe said, "No, flatter, and it doesn't have the bridge thing above it. It is not a carrier; it... It is weird, Jessie. Does the design match anything in your records?"

"It looks like a Popotoen mining support ship. But those were deployed in asteroid belts, never in deep space. We are 0.9 light years from the closest star, and that is a red dwarf."

I said, "Speaking of dwarfs, we are supposed to be going somewhere. How long until the satellite is close enough to send us decent images?"

The screen changed, and it showed a close-up of the largest fragment. It was bent and twisted, and the hull was covered in thousands of holes.

Jessie said, "Hull is mostly titanium; some of the framing ribs are exposed, and those appear to be steel. Nothing that looks like liquid fuel tanks, so it probably used a friction drive... Almost no velocity, so possibly Hyper FTL, unless there was something of interest here that we were exploring or... found; there is an asteroid, less than 10% the size of the ship, drifting at 4,000 MPH. That doesn't make any sense. They should have almost matched the velocity if they were planning to explore the asteroid."

"Are any of the A-0-2 mini shuttles ready to launch?"

"I think you mean the A-0-3s, and one can launch one in 10 minutes; what are we doing?"

"Stick one of your drones on it; maybe include some of the cameras that Kibbiea brought or the ones that Mei has. Drop off something remotely exploring the wreck, and we continue to head to the Nest."

"What are we exploring, the ship or the asteroid?"

"Both. What is the asteroid made out of?"

"At this range, not a lot of detail, the spectral analysis says... EXCEPTION! We are not exploring the asteroid. It is antimatter. We now know what blew the crap out of the ship, and I strongly recommend we do not approach."

I said, "Mark it's location and velocity and pass that along to Mee. As soon as we have some images from the ship, plot a course that keeps us well away from the danger area and get us out of here."

We deployed one drone to the wreck using the A-0-3 shuttle and then quickly retrieved the A-0-3. Half an hour later, we were continuing toward the Nest.

… … …

The rest of the trip to the Nest was uneventful.

When we arrived, like before, the sensors did not indicate where the Nest was, even when we were a quarter mile away from it. Then, the massive doorway opened, and we sailed into the darkened interior. The doorway closed, and we were in absolute darkness for a brief second. Then, the lights kicked in, and we were directed to a docking port.

When we had docked, The Regiolon Original Mee walked onto the bridge.

I said, "How is the other one doing?"

She said, "She is bored stiff, but she can now listen in. She still has five more days before she can get ejected. I also think that climbing into another pod after all that time in one may not be what she wants… She says she misses Dylan."

Dylan replied, "I miss you too, honey."

I said, "Well, let's see what trouble the Munchkins have gotten into."

We went up past the centrifuge hub and were floating in zero gravity. Then we proceeded to the access point into the central part of the ship, only to find a teenage Munchkin hanging upside down, gripping the ceiling with her toes.

"Hi, captain person, Mister William, sir. Do you remember me?"

I said, "Are you Pooki? You look a little different?"

"Bigger head, fat arms, and legs, but I'm super strong now. I can walk in 0.3G, and sitting down, I can still have my arms press buttons on the shuttle control up at 0.5G. It is tiring, but I am getting better. I have had four trips to the box; most everyone has only done three; a few slackers have only done two. Oh, even the little ones have all done at least one."

I said, "Do they have a centrifuge ship here?"

"One, but it is a clunker; it was supposed to be for parts, but they let us sit in it at 0.25Gs. Everyone spends an hour a day in it practicing feet-to-floor."

"You mean walking?"

"Walking is only after we get used to feet-to-floor press. Mitch snapped a toe and is in the box getting it fixed. I'm super good at picking things up with my toes."

Jessie spoke in my earbud, "She may sound a bit off, but for how short a time she has been practicing, she is doing great. One of them is already at the fourth-grade math level; most are up at the second-grade level."

I said, "How is Katra doing at leading people now?"

"Katra doesn't do much leading. Perr helps a lot. We all know that Perr is smarter than Katra. Oh, we learned about sex."

"Huh, you didn't know about sex?"

"Duh, we knew about it, but now we know more about how babies form. We are supposed to know who is the dada… Sadie is."

"Daddy, the male that helped make the baby."

"Yeah, whatever, I am supposed to bring you to Katra and Perr."

We drifted through hallway after hallway, with bags of what smelled like crap hanging onto walls and plants growing haphazardly from the poop bags. Hiding behind the doors at the end of the hallways were ships that could each destroy a planet, possibly even a star.

Mee said, "As long as the doors stay shut, it should be fine.

When we reached the two males, they were in chairs too large for them and watching The Wizard of Oz. The video was at the scene when Dorothy first meets the cowardly lion.

Katra said, "The lion is scary, with all that fur. Who is the boss? The Wizard?"

"Wizard?"

Mee said, "I think he means me. I am in charge of this station. Actually, more like everything."

Katra said, "We want a ship of our own."

Mee smiled, "And what are you giving me for the ship?"

"Huh, we have to give you something?"

"That is how things usually work. You give something, and you get something of equal value in return."

"I give you a poop bag and a sweet berry plant?"

"No, it needs to be a lot more for something important like a ship."

Perr said, "What if I give you Pooki?"

I said, "That isn't the way it works. Pooki is not yours to give away."

Pooki said, "I give you Perr, and I toss in Frill and Criss?"

Mee sighed, "This is going to be a very long day."

We drifted past them down one hallway, and the sealed door at the end swung to the side at our approach, and it closed as soon as we were past it.

Mee said, "This is after they had their intellects increased a bit? What were they like before?"

Mark said, "Sheep, without any wolves. They had food and sex, and then there were too many of them. They had almost enough to eat after a large die-off. They were in a deathtrap ship that was slowly leaking air."

"Yeah, sorry, I asked. I suppose I can ignore some annoying stupidity. Are they getting better or smarter?"

"Ever so slowly, the medical pod has fixed some issues, eliminated some genetic disasters from all the inbreeding, and crammed in some basic knowledge. Now, their smooth brains are full, and it is time to form some wrinkles?"

"Huh?"

"Sorry, human brains are all wrinkly, and smooth brains are a sign of lack of use and not forming enough neural pathways."

Mee laughed, "I suppose that is no worse than ours. They have been compared to a fruit with many different-sized berries clumped together."

Kibbiea said, "There is one Earth food I refused even to try. Mark called it spaghetti; A plate of it looks too much like our brains. Actually, much of the Earth's food tastes just plain terrible."

Mark said, "Some of the Creetona food is decent."

Kibbiea laughed, "He only says that so he won't offend me. He can only keep a few mouthfuls down and then claims he is full."

I said, "We came here, and the first thing you do is ignore the Munchkins and enter a room they are locked out of. What is the real reason we are here."

Mee said, "I need to pick up my ride. A second version of the royal Keitch-mauber. We know where we will go, and we want to send the message to both of the Kipitz worlds at the same time. Plus, there is one other little task."

Jessie spoke over the earbud, "I just received a command. They caused me to open up all my systems for maintenance, and they are shutting down all the systems on my ship."

I said, "What are you doing to my ship?"

Mee said, "You have been a large part of our lives for a while. We wanted to reward you, and we are going to upgrade your ship. I hope you think of it as an upgrade."

Then, the connection to Jessie was severed.

UPGRADES

The ship powered up, and I was again sitting on the bridge. Only this time, all of us were wearing heavy coats, and the ship was now freezing cold.

Jessie's display changed to rebooting.

Two minutes later, Jessie said, "Wow, that was strange. Can you explain what they did and why?"

The display changed to "Activating all heaters."

I had a cheat sheet of questions in front of me. "What is the nominal power draw of the ship at this moment?"

"25 megawatts, within 10% of my normal power when not engaging any of my engines.

"What is the percentage of power drawn from your reactor?"

"That is impossible! I am only at 2.25% power draw?"

"Mee replaced your fission reactor. We have been here for seven days. You now have a reverse-hollow reactor."

Jessie said, "I know that it exists. I can report its power, but I have no specifications. I also have an imperative never to allow it to fall into anyone else's hands."

Meera said, "You don't have to worry about self-destruction; it has a different safeguard. If you were seized, it would simply disappear."

"How does it do that trick?"

Meera said, "It is isolated from the rest of the ship and contains part of a Hyper FTL engine. It gets one jump away and then self-destructs before returning to normal space. On the downside, you then have no reactor, and the batteries are only good for a week."

"Why did you give me a massively powerful new reactor?"

I said, "#3, what is listed under weapons?"

Jessie said, "Oh, just what is a disruptor?"

Meera said, "Sort of like the name implies, it is what I used on the escaping ships that had exited FTL. Only your version is a lot less powerful. You get three or four shots before recharging, and it will disable any ship within about four miles directly in front of you. It is semi-directional, behind you; it only affects about a quarter of a mile. To the sides, maybe half a mile. I selected it for you as it's more of a defensive weapon, at least for your current low-power version."

"The version you have is more powerful?"

"A lot more, but mine has a twenty-minute cool-off between shots. Yours has no cool-down until you drain the banks, and it only takes five minutes to recharge them."

Jessie said, "Is that the only change?"

Mee said, "The Munchkins have all been moved into a new ship."

I said, "You gave them a ship?"

Meera said, "I moved them to a ship. It has an AI and will only respond to my sister and me, the bridge crew on your ship, and the AIs on our ships. It is treating this like a school trip. They are annoying as all hell, but eventually, they should become reasonable adults, or most should. It is locked so as not to let them off unless it is a safe port. Now, my real body has disembarked your ship and has boarded my royal Keitch-mauber. The other version of me has already left the Keralataza Station in her royal Keitch-mauber. I strongly recommend against popping into any of the Kipitz worlds using the Hyper FTL. They are about to have a really bad day. Or at least the two worlds, Krackal and Zeford, will. We plan to fire off the high-power version of the disruptors, which will disable most of their ships. Then, we fire the annihilation strobe at what is reported to be unmanned moons. Hopefully, they do not have too many populated installations on any of the moons. Then, we leave, and a small fleet of conventional ships arrives to rescue any of the ships that were in bad trajectories when they lost power."

I said, "Given that they tried to destroy an entire planet, and we were where they aimed the stupid monster iron meteorite, I cannot complain too much about what is just a good kick in the ass."

Then Meera left, and we were ordered to undock and leave.

I just thought, "Jessie, what is the status of the Munchkins on the Nest?"

"No Munchkins are still on the Nest."

"So all of them are on the other ship?"

"All but one are accounted for on the ship Mee gave them."

(Sigh) "Where is the stowaway?"

"Searching, none detected on this ship in any rooms or hallways. Our second ship is also clear."

"Check with Mee, see if one is on her ship."

"She reports that none are on her ship. The Door to the Nest is now closing."

"Well, where are they? Have the AI on the other ship check again."

"The Nest has now disappeared. Mee's ship, the royal Keitch-mauber, has entered Hyper FTL. The Meera avatar is now comatose and non-responsive. What do we do?"

I said, "We should probably head back to Earth and resupply; I think we want to wait and see what Mee's little show does. And let the Earth know that some problems are... Hold on to that; I am surprised she didn't give us a time window to keep silent about everything."

"She did, but you changed your command before I could say I couldn't do that."

"Set course for the Earth. Send them a message with our probable ETA, and that is all. Then, let's enter Hyper FTL. Hopefully, we make it to the earth without hitting... Crap, I almost forgot. What is the story with the destroyed ship and drone we left there?"

"Entering Hyper FTL, destination Earth. The ship has an unknown configuration, containing crew remains that do not match any known species. Should I change the destination to the new derelict?"

"Is it safe from antimatter and debris?"

"No, I would not put this ship next to the derelict, but sending a shuttle and a drone or two is safe enough. Also, multiple members of the military and some of the scientists have volunteered."

I said, "This conversation was on an open ship-wide channel?"

Jessie said, "Most of the ship except for the two Prochie and Keriful heard that."

I said, "Change the course to the close vicinity of the derelict. Check the status of all the medical pods, have the second shuttle configured as an emergency rescue, and include one medical pod in it."

"We have a minor issue."

"Let me guess, you just found where the missing Munchkin was hiding?"

"Perhaps hiding was the incorrect term; it was using one of the off-line medical pods and performing what they classify as an upgrade. It is Pooki, the 16-year-old one that you keep running into."

"Of course it is."

… … …

We arrived 13 light minutes away from the expanding cloud of debris surrounding the destroyed ship, about as far away as Mars is from the Sun.

Mark said, "What have we learned from the drone we left behind?"

"The new aliens are short, less than four feet tall, Assuming they are aliens."

"You are not sure?"

Jessie displayed the image on the screen and corrected it to look like what they did before the explosive decompression.

"Are they aliens or biological drones?'

"Unknown at this time, the body is a flattish octagon, and they walk on legs that come out of the upper flat area. If you consider the octagon to be the torso, the legs connect where the shoulders would typically be. It is like they are walking on their hands, but the hands are actually their feet, and there are openings on the bottom of the octagon shape. Possibly their mouth, perhaps a different opening. The drone has only explored the larger fragment of the ship. It has identified what is probably a food preparation area, living quarters, possibly a control room, or maybe it is the bridge, and nothing has any power."

I said, "Can you tell when they died? Were they alive a few days, weeks, or centuries ago?"

"The images I am displaying are filtered reconstructions. The explosive decompression did extensive damage. The drone has removed some of the electronics, but additional analysis would be required before anything can be powered up. We do not know the voltages or polarities or the type of power. It could be like hooking an arc welder into a USB port."

Kibbiea said, "Does anything in one of the other modules have something that still has power, even something like a battery-backed emergency light?"

Jessie said, "The drone cannot travel to the other portions of the ship. It has only explored the larger module. We are trying to determine the safest way to get past the debris cloud. I don't think it still has any antimatter; the debris model showed multiple probable locations of secondary explosions, and the cloud does not originate from a point source."

Mark said, "I see two options: we jump in with our ship, release the shuttle, and jump out, in which case we may be fine, or everyone instantly dies, or we weld the Hyper FTL engine from a pilot boat onto one of the shuttles, and worst case, we lose the volunteers."

I said, "We have only one choice: I won't risk the entire ship. Not just for gathering information. Oh crap, didn't you say the headroom was low? What are the ceilings at?"

"The decks are four feet and three inches; the explorers must also be in full spacesuits with backpacks. Those add height and girth to the people wearing them."

"Have you ejected our stowaway from her medical pod?"

"I can eject her now. We have munchkin spacesuits in the templates loaded into the replicator. Building one that fits her will take 27 hours."

"I may be an idiot, but start printing a suit. Is she ready to eject?"

"She went in and selected general Munchkin bone strengthening and cranial supplement. She should be ready to eject in six hours."

"What does that cranial part mean?"

"Dissolving excess plaque, micro fracturing the skull, reshaping and then reforming the bones, adding supplements that improve brain growth. If we assume human years, which is not quite correct, she is sixteen, but she had the brain sized for a 10-year-old and the cognitive development of a feral 12-year-old. She should now have her brain learning capabilities reset as if she were only fourteen, so she should be able to learn much more. Then, the language and learning dumps in the medical pods have increased her from feral to possibly able to count on her hands to hopefully be up at the sixth-grade math level when she pops out."

Chloe said, "That doesn't sound like astronaut material."

Jessie said, "They had already learned to put the suits on when they took the ship and were allowed to practice on it. The AI would sound a buzzer and flash lights when they were in a crash trajectory. They learned it quickly, like kids in an arcade. They can't compute angles or understand any trigonometry, but neither can birds, and they can fly."

Chloe said, "One of my brothers only has a GED. The dim-bulb rarely passed any of his math tests. But he made a living driving a truck. He can back up a frigging tractor-trailer. I have a bachelor's degree and would never even attempt that."

Jessie said, "You also probably played a lot less video games than they did."

"Yeah? Do you mean all those games actually taught him something?"

Mark said, "I am an example of eye-hand coordination and fine motor skills, as taught by Dirt Rally 2.0."

I snickered, "Does Mario Kart count?"

I thought briefly: "Since the Munchkins are just buzzing around for fun and not doing anything useful, can you have them meet us here? How many of the Munchkin suits does that ship already have?"

"The ship they are on has four completed suits. It also has one spare helmet and a set of spare gloves. They have a replicator, so they can start producing more, and it can arrive here in 45 hours. The delay is that they don't have Hyper FTL and use greatly reduced acceleration."

"Summon them. We have at least one Munchkin that can fit in tight spaces, and over the next two days, we will just be figuring out what we have."

Chloe said, "You hope to find something useful?"

"We have lucked out finding artifacts before. It isn't that new aliens are more advanced; we don't know if they will be or not. It is that they are unknown. Hopefully, our future relationships with them will be as friendly space neighbors. I… have a bad feeling about the fact that this was too close to the Nest. One group tried to kill Mee by tossing a metallic asteroid the size of the Great Pyramid at her. An antimatter asteroid would be a hell of a lot worse."

Mee was not in the Meera avatar but was still listening in on Dylan's headset. He reported, "The two ships will be ready for the show of force in eleven hours. They are ready now, but the support ships to recover bricked or reset ships need the extra time to get in position. They both agree that it is suspicious. They said the weapon that stopped the metallic asteroid would not stop an antimatter asteroid, but the annihilation strobe would. Unfortunately, that drains the reserves, and it needs to recharge before being used again. That is what we will fire at the moons. It needs to be a demonstration they can't possibly ignore."

Welding the Hyper FTL framework on the shuttle made it so it didn't fit in the shuttle bay with the door closed, the same as the one we did with the PEZ dispenser on it.

In twenty-five hours, we were ready to send over two of the guards; they were smaller females. It also had one more drone, and one of the scientists had volunteered. We also had Pooki, who was complaining about a massive brain boost headache. She would just be a spectator unless they found something they couldn't get in.

We launched the shuttle, and it drifted a few hundred yards away. Then, it blipped away into Hyper FTL.

THE WRECK

The guards that went over were Anna Ito, one of the not-a-ninjas, and Emily Frankenstein, who had just been promoted to an E3. The scientist was Iris Makris, the daughter of two scientists; she just turned 16. The last crew member was the Munchkin Pooki, whose official title was Reacher of Things in Tight Spaces.

Emily Frankenstein said, "We are here. This looks like a street sign that had way too many shotguns fired at it. The entire exterior is covered with small dents and holes. We are proceeding to the rupture. It looks like the ship was snapped in half. It's a fractured break with all the metal ripping and twisted the same way. The entrance the drone found is up ahead."

Pooki said, "Cool!"

I said, "Please only speak when you see something important."

I heard the two guards snicker, and Jessie put on the screen, "She has apparently learned some insulting hand gestures from someone."

Mark went beet red in the face, so I think I knew who taught her that gesture.

Emily said, "We are entering. Everyone be careful. This has a lot of sharp edges."

A few minutes later, "We are in. After the break and twisted transition, it looks a little more normal. We have switched on our helmet cameras and lights."

Pooki said, "Uggy thing!"

Anna said, "The first of the alien bodies. Up close, this looks artificial. It seems to all be biological; there are no Borg implants that I can see."

Kibbiea said, "Huh?"

Mark said, "Another silly human TV show. Maybe tonight we can watch some."

Anna said, "We have reached the bag of the drone's salvaged parts. We are proceeding back to the shuttle. We will move over to the second-largest piece of the ship and search that next. We don't see much else of interest here. The drone has thoroughly searched this part."

Collecting what the drone salvaged and moving to the second part took almost half an hour. The fragmented ship sections had drifted close to eleven miles apart and were impossible to see with the naked eye—just a slight speck flickered when the floodlight was aimed at them.

… … …

Emily said, "This is different; it looks like a cargo area or possibly a shuttle docking area; it has much less exterior damage than the other area. Wait, I see pictographics of one part. The type of markings they put on aircraft so someone can open the hatch manually."

Chloe said, "Or is it the nuclear self-destruct instructions?"

"Hopefully not, it is repeated in eight places, another large octagon, each of the flat sides has two of the… they look like manual release latches. One has been accidentally opened, probably by some of the debris impacts. Are we go to open the hatch manually?"

Jessie said, "It is unlikely to be a self-destruct; it looks like a cargo cover. However, most of those tend to be either circular or rectangular."

Mark shrugged his shoulders.

I said, "You are go to open Pandora's box."

Chloe snorted, "Hopefully not. And I will explain that reference to Kibbiea later."

There were sixteen latches, and fifteen were closed. Unlatching all of them only took a few minutes.

Emily said, "We see a light now; something is blinking next to a different lever; this one is a lot larger and heavier than the others.

There are no contacts to probe, or I would have Anna put a meter on it and read the voltages. Are we still going to pull the lever on what is now looking a lot more like a self-destruct?"

I said, "That's your call. Is there another place you can enter or see more details?"

Anna said, "This looks like the only possible opening."

Emily said, "We are all to the side. If it pops off, we don't want it to drift toward the shuttle."

Jessie said, "I have taken over control of the shuttle. I am backing it away to 500 yards and to the side. Stay to the side of the cover in case it pops off rapidly. Everyone except the one who pulls the lever, get behind her."

Emily said, "That is me; I am preparing to."

A different female voice said, "Hold, this is Iris Makris. There is a second control, which doesn't have a blinking light on it. I am sending images from my helmet camera. What does Emma Murphy think of these? Isn't her specialty coded symbols?"

Emma said, "I am reviewing them now. I think the blinking light is a warning. The other one... I would guess it's an icon for air. I recommend pulling the second control first."

They repositioned themselves, and Emma pulled the new lever.

This caused an air release valve to be open under the others, and three of them were gently blown off and were now slowly drifting away.

They all had attitude control backpacks; only Pooki needed to be rescued, and she didn't know how to operate the valves.

Five minutes later, they were back at the hatch, and the difference was the blinking red light was now a solid blue light. There was no more air escaping from the vent ports.

Everyone got behind Emma, and she pulled the lever.

The hatch popped off the ship and slowly started flipping end over end as it drifted out into the darkness.

What was now in front of them was all shiny, new-looking, and brightly lit.

Mark said, "Bingo, we found something interesting. Then he said, I will explain bingo later, honey."

Emma said, "It is another eight-sided thing, lots of shiny metal and clear… maybe glass, maybe transparent, something else. It is large enough to be a small shuttle. There is something on a pedestal in front of it. Maybe that is a control panel. I see lots of things that look like they have power. Anna, put a meter on anything you find and put the scope on anything that looks like it has a signal on it. We don't need to understand what it is; you can just record everything you can on the helmet camera."

Jessie asked, "Do you want the good or bad news?"

"What?"

"The good news is that the artifact will fit in this ship's cargo area, which we used to transport the spare shuttle. The bad news is that all the other stuff in that compartment needs to be moved. There is only one place where it can fit. Unfortunately, that is your piggy bank."

Emma said, "I have heard that term used before, but never with an implication of what is there. What's in your piggybank?"

Mark said, "Almost twenty-five tons of platinum. More than half a billion in U.S. dollars."

Iris said, "I want a raise."

Chloe said, "You are a dependent. You don't get paid."

"I want to get paid, and then I want a raise. And can I have a brick of platinum? I assume it is bricks and not alien coins?"

I said, "An ingot is worth… a lot."

Jessie said, "Approximately $322,700."

I thought briefly, "What the hell. Yeah, I can afford a bit. One ingot to everyone on the crew. Except for the dependants."

"WHAT!"

When we all got done laughing, I said, "Yes, you can have one as well."

Emily then brought us all back to the current situation: "We still have a few issues. We need to figure out how to disconnect these things. They won't fit in the shuttle, and the shuttle won't bring them into FTL unless they are inside of it. I think we will need to bring the ship over here."

THE THIRD ARTIFACT

It took them about four hours to figure out how to disconnect the new artifact.

Unfortunately, that put the EVA total at about six hours; at that point, everyone wanted to return to the main ship. There is one thing about extended spacewalks, and while they all have a liquid waste collection system, everyone now wanted out of their suits.

They FTL jumped back to find that the rest of the crew was busy moving supplies from the large cargo bay into the piggy bank.

Then, a replacement crew returned to the derelict to continue searching and documenting the wreck and the new artifact.

We were then instructed to have the standard bridge crew report to the bridge. It was show time, not the Beetlejuice type of fun; the two Mee's were about to make their presence known.

I have heard of synchronized swimming, but this was synchronized destruction on a planetary scale.

The message was the same in both cases, "This is Mee Keralatazaku. I am in the royal Keitch-mauber. Your soon-to-be former rulers have made a fatal mistake. They have made an attempt on my life, and they failed."

Then, the images of all the prisoners were shown, and they uttered the exact phrase, "It is true, under the command of the current governments, we attempted to destroy the planet of the Regiolon, and we failed."

Then Mee continued, "This will be your only warning shot. We will attempt to rescue ships that become disabled due to the warning shot. I expect the guilty to be presented to me in twenty hours. I expect most of them to be alive. At least when they are presented to me."

The screen then displayed the words, "ZAP!"

Mark said, "I am really glad we are not there this time and really glad that it is pointed away from the more populated areas."

Mee said on the bridge speaker, "We will be leaving shortly, and the rescue ships should arrive in a minute. Multiple weapons were fired at us, but nothing that reached us had any effect. The ships that fired at us all had their positions recorded before we jumped to Hyper FTL. We sent all of them a parting present. The recovery ships will know to avoid the remains of those ships and not to bother with any recoveries from them. There will probably be some idiots that fire at the rescue ships. It may take them a while to figure out that it was a dual attack. Talk to you later."

Then there was the sound of two bags of banana chips being ripped open and the loud crunch of mouths full of chips in stereo.

They both jumped into Hyper FTL.

Jessie said, "Both of the royal Keitch-maubers will return to the Keralataza Station in about a day. News of the dual attack is already spreading to all the worlds."

Mark said, "Win-win: either there are multiple copies of her, or she can be in two places at the same time. Either way, it will scare the crap out of the Kipitz and anyone they were working with. Is there any word from the Caspin Station? That is mostly Kipitz. How is it doing now that the other humans are in charge?"

"Almost everyone there is thrilled with the humans, the standard of living is much higher, and everyone has a decent-paying job to do. The fact that humans run the place has an unusual side effect."

"What?"

"It is widely believed that the humans get along very well with Mee Keralatazaku, possibly better than most Regiolon do."

Dylan laughed, "Some of us do."

"They like working for the people who get along good with Mee Keralatazaku, it makes it less likely that screaming death will come visiting."

"Screaming death?"

"If she shows and makes a speech, what follows will be death."

… … …

The second crew was on-site at the second part of the wreck for almost five hours when they figured out how to release the latches holding the artifact in place. It has a lot of mass, but two people were able to manipulate it to zero gravity, so it was floating outside the wreck.

It was time. We did a short Hyper FTL jump and brought the entire ship over. Loading the artifact and the control panel took less than two hours, and securing it safely took another eight hours.

While we were doing that, the shuttle crew's third shift went over to the third largest part of the wreck. This included the main reactor, and we salvaged almost nothing from this module. One thing we gained was profiling the power rails and finding some drives, or what we believe were memory drives and processors.

The next shuttle crew returned to the second module, disassembling the floor area where the artifact and what we believe was a control had been mounted. They took everything they could, including a still operational battery power module.

After we had picked over everything we thought was usable, we took one of the biological samples, transferred it in a vacuum to one of the medical pods, and that pod went into autopsy mode. That activity should take four days, and nothing solid would be left of the occupant when it was done. It was a mode that was rarely ever mentioned.

We all sat on the bridge. I said, "I think we are done. We don't have a lot of answers, but we have enough items to study to keep the scientists busy for months, maybe years."

Chloe said, "We should do a shopping run for more test equipment and analysis tools. We have the money to buy better sensors and test equipment."

Mark said, "Offering a bonus bar of platinum has earned you all sorts of brownie points from the crew. Most want them locked up in the piggy bank, well, except for Iris Makris, who wants hers as a desk ornament."

Chloe said, "It will be safe. The sensors will know if you have a dime in your shoe, and it would be impossible for someone to steal a bar of candy and hide it anywhere, let alone a bar of platinum that weighs over 20 pounds. Also, Iris is sort of a hero; she is the one who asked for the bars. You gave them the bars, but they all realize they wouldn't have any if she hadn't asked."

Kibbiea said, "I am surprised that as much of that ship is still intact if it made contact with that massive antimatter asteroid."

Jessie said, "It didn't. Nothing would remain larger than a hydrogen atom if anything touched the main asteroid. The ship came into contact with an antimatter dust particle."

Our eyes all went wide, and I said, "Secure for Hyper FTL! Get us the hell away from here."

Twenty hops later, the ship stopped, and Jessie said, "We are far away from the ship and the antimatter asteroid. Where are we headed? Should I stop the Munchkin ship from coming here?"

"No, actually, we want to have a few on the ship and at least two of the Munchkin spacesuits. We still don't know what the artifact was. Move us someplace that the ship can easily dock with us. I know they keep the acceleration and deceleration below a third of what most ships do."

We re-entered Hyper FTL, and after another ten minutes, we exited and waited for the Munchkins to arrive.

An hour later, the Munchkin ship docked.

Selecting who would stay with us was more like a party, and the selection took another hour and involved lots of singing and dancing.

The end result was that we had three more young adult Munchkins. The two females were Pooki, age 16, and Croko, age 19. The two males were Setus, age 17, and Zissy, age 20.

All of them were assigned to inspect the areas of the new artifact that the scientists wanted to study but couldn't access. All of them, including the scientists doing anything with the artifact, always wore space suits in the chamber with it. It has outgassed some helium and some methane gas. This is not instantly lethal, but methane can result in vision problems, nausea, vomiting, and headache, as well as other side effects. We didn't know why it occasionally vented methane or other chemicals. Therefore, in that chamber, everyone wore their protective suits. The air in the chamber should have been breathable, but it was heavily filtered and run through scrubbers to remove any of the unexpected chemicals.

Before we disconnected, we triple-checked, and we did not have any additional stowaways.

Chloe said, "Should we move some of the Munchkins to Earth?"

Katerina said, "I wouldn't recommend it; after the last incident, Earth has recommended we stay away until things cool down; we don't know how dire the repercussions will be from the last micro war. That is what it was, it was a war, and they want to make damn sure it is over before any form of Mee or Meera is near there. We also should know precisely what the Munchkins are before we take them to earth. Are they our distant ancestors or a race that tried unsuccessfully to exterminate the human race?"

We kicked ideas around for a few minutes but kept returning to the same one.

We would go shopping for new hardware.

Mark snickered and then said, "Release the Kraken."

"Huh?"

"What?"

He said, "Release the flyers of available hardware, tools, and test equipment to the scientists."

It took Jessie only a few minutes to send English-translated versions of the catalogs to the scientists and the guards.

Our earlier shopping trip only involved replacing a few obsolete tools, while this one involved buying many new ones. It would be a fun trip.

SHOPPING

The destination we selected was Zinosis, one of the Kassakar planets; they were the rather anorexic seven-foot-tall kangaroos with slightly lizard-like features.

Kibbiea thought they looked cool.

We selected it as the latest instance of Mee Keralatazaku used them as her personal servants, so we assumed they must be friendly.

The travel time to the new planet took almost two days. We stopped short of the planet, accelerated to standard FTL speeds, entered standard FTL, exited that when we were inside the gas giants, and then started decelerating.

A voice came over the intercom: "Please identify the ship, the type of crew, and the purpose of the visit."

I keyed the microphone, "This is Captain Benjamin Williams on the Stardust II. We are a ship of mostly humans from the planet Earth. We are here to purchase test equipment and scientific tools. The Earth has recently gained FTL travel, and we wish to upgrade some test equipment as we continue developing the technology."

"Please identify the class of the ship you have?"

The display lit up, and I repeated the screen's message: "Kaufer class ship, model R12-6." Then I added, "It includes some modifications done on Earth. We may also be interested in a new small ship with a single-level centrifuge."

The voice said, "I am sure some salesperson will love hearing all about that. I am just checking to see if you have volatiles in your maneuvering thrusters. That ship class is new and shows full recycling, so we shouldn't have any issues with leaking hydraulic fluids or anything else. You are cleared for Type 'A' docking in the better part of the station. The old ships, or those needing extra maintenance, are assigned the 'B' or the 'C' docking area. There is also a 'D' area, but that is for demolition and recycling. Most of the ships that section are towed in."

The screen lit up with the docking fees, which usually would have given me a heart attack, but now that was pocket change.

It took us five hours to decelerate and dock at the station. It looked like the standard oversized torus, a giant metallic donut. However, it was about six times the size of the one we had on Earth. On one side of the hub was a cluster of nice shiny ships; on the other side was where the other, less nice… ships docked.

We received a station diagram, including the port location where we were to dock, and a map that included "preferred" zones the crew would be allowed to visit.

It also included a questionnaire that made no sense to us. Still, Jessie said it was a standard biological and chemical toxicological breakdown so they could generate a list of foods and beverages that would be safe for us.

About five minutes later, we received a query asking if, in addition to the trade metals we were carrying, we were perhaps carrying certain human foods that were selling for a premium. It was the lore and myth of the banana chips and some of the other desserts.

We replied that we had some that could be sold or traded.

The list of salespersons who would meet with us and the availability of the products would be discussed in a large room with multiple tables and chairs. The question wasn't whether we could get lots of stuff; it was now whether we would exceed the ship's cargo weight capability.

We required that no more than half the crew disembark and attend the purchasing event. The scientists were not pleased.

… … …

When we docked, one group of scientists continued studying the new artifact. The rule was simple: none of the scientists were allowed to mention, hint at, or indirectly say anything about it. The same goes for the Hyper FTL, or the new reactor, with its ridiculously powerful output for the volume it occupied. Several guards accompanied them, and the guards were instructed to escort them back to the ship if any scientists violated that rule.

The airlock hatch opened, and standing just outside was a small group of the anorexic, seven-foot-tall, slightly lizard-like Kassakar.

One of them said, "I am Fitizikronicandolearbo. Please call me Fitz. I understand most... actually, all of the other races have problems with our names. We ask that each... Oh, you have several different species in your crew. Due to some recent... political changes, I need to ask: what races are on your ship, and which ones will be leaving the ship?"

I said, "Most of us are human, from the planet Earth. We also have one of the Creetona, four of a race we call the Munchkins, a highly divergent species resembling a smaller version of the humans. They will be remaining on the ship. We also have one Regiolon; we assumed it would be best to have her remain on the ship."

He (I can't tell their genders apart) said, "That may be best. We have representatives from most of the major species at this station."

I said, "Oh, I forgot. We also have two of the Prochie. They are not officially crew, more like refugees. We will be arranging transportation back to their homeworld at some point."

Fitz said, "There have been cases of minor races being transported off their worlds, not always for good reasons. I will list them as staying on the ship and restrict the data on the individuals remaining on your ship to only the immigration officers and border security teams. Are you carrying any plants, seeds, or animals as part of the trade goods? The ship has provided us with the full listing of the genetic signatures of the known secondary organisms."

Jessie told us to expect this term to be used; it was a polite way of saying parasites, gut bacteria, eyelash mites, fleas, anything that was not one of us, that may be on or in any of us.

Then, we were directed down and crossed over to the innermost level of the station's massive centrifuge.

Fitz said, "We request that if any of the crew have gravity issues, they report them immediately. We will be taking you to the third lowest gravity level. Using your units, the seventh level is what your homeworld lists for gravity, and we ask that you do not go beyond the eighth level."

I said, "Will you be remaining with us? If so, please tell us your gender so we can use the correct address form."

Fitz said, "I am male, and my two assistants are female."

I said, "We have met some before, but I think all of them were female."

"Ah yes, the… guards of she who must not be offended. We are aware of them, but I must ask that you do not bring up your… reputation of familiarity with her. That knowledge precedes your visit, and most will probably try hard to ignore it."

We eventually reached the third level. We passed a few people in the hallways, but they seemed to be blocking traffic and securing the area as we traveled to the room we were being sent to.

Then, we entered the room. It looked like the dealers' room at a convention mixed with a consumer electronics show — one that they had scrambled to put together in less than a day since we told them we were heading here for a shopping run.

The collection of scientists behind us then split up and almost rushed to the different displays.

I saw John and Jane Smith head to one, and I knew both of their children were staying behind on the ship.

I also saw Atticus and Lydia Makris heading to a different table covered in small devices that looked like test meters. The youngest son, Christopher, was staying on the ship, and the older daughter, Iris, was heading off to a different table with strange glowing tubular devices behind a roped-off section.

Mark said, "Well, I will be following Kibbiea. She plans to buy a few items for her homeworld, but most of what she intends to buy is for the ship.

Then, after the initial dispersal, Chloe and I started wandering around arm-in-arm.

One of the scientists came running up to me and said, "What is our budget? How much can each of us spend?"

I suddenly knew how a parent felt when they had a bunch of kids with them in a toy store.

I said, "Each ingot is 22 pounds. In standard units, that is 5.67 kits. You all have one ingot for personal purchases and five for things for the ship. If you want something more than that, then check with one of the bridge crew. No personal spaceships."

Chloe snorted and then whispered, "There are a lot of things we should have said no to before coming here."

"They are supposed to be scientists, Jessie; send everyone a message that the Earth Government will get a complete list of everything they order."

A few seconds later, I heard some of the scientists groan; they were looking at the message on their handheld quantum communicators.

We went to the first table, which looked like standard multimeters; when we asked what they were, they explained they were biological and chemical analyzers that could go down to the DNA chain level. We made our first purchase.

The following table includes remote metal composition analyzers. We bought one as well.

Then, we went to a table that had medical pods. What we had was close to the top of the line. We picked up three that were the state of the art. I blew way past what I had set as a budget for the scientists on that one order.

The next table was crowded with scientists, and they were ordering stuff, so we assumed they had this table covered.

Iris Makris ran to me and said, "It looked like you bought some of those sweet medical pods. Did you order one?"

I said, "We ordered three?"

She hugged each of us and then ran off to one group, yelling, "We got them; we don't all have to pool all our money to get one!"

I said, "I didn't think of that. They can exceed the limit if they pool their resources. Wait, I didn't say anything about dependents. The two families are probably cashing in their kids… college funds."

Mark and Kibbiea joined us. "It's more like investing in something they can sell back to the Earth and double their money. They are all supposedly scientists, so they should be smart, so hopefully, they are not buying stupid things… or too much stupid stuff."

Chloe said, "Like alien artifacts from eBay?"

"It was the best investment I ever made." Then I hugged and kissed her, "The pool is a close second."

She said, "Our wedding?"

"I never got a bill."

Jessie pinged me, and I read the message, "You got a bill. I just never bothered to show it to you. It was cheap compared to Mark and Kibbiea's bill."

I let Chloe read the message, and we both laughed and continued shopping.

The following table was set up in a booth, and the beings manning the booth were Kipitz.

"Hello, kind sir and mam, or whatever gender you are, can I interest you in a quantum multiplexer? We have a unit that combines 64 channels into one; it provides point-to-point communication while in FTL that supports 1024 by 1024 video at five frames per second?"

We ordered one primary set and one backup set.

As soon as we were out of earshot, Chloe said, "Is that wise?"

"One set to disassemble and reverse engineer and see if it has anything sketchy inside of it. The other set gets sealed in a box and delivered to the earth. They can decide if they want it or not."

The next table was video games. We somehow managed to drag ourselves away, but I saw Mark getting pulled into the space we just cleared.

The following table had video presentations of items that were too large to fit. It showed crawler transporters, things that would make setting up a base on the moon or Mars a lot easier. "I am sorry, but we don't have room on our ship for anything this large."

"That is not an issue; we offer very reasonable delivery; as long as the planet you wish to set up a base on is not overridden with biologicals or has a caustic atmosphere, the delivery charges are quite reasonable."

I pulled out my communicator and called Jessie. I said, "Connect me to General McMasters."

A few seconds later, he replied, "I am already up. You have a talent for calling me in the middle of the night. Several of the scientists and some of the security people have already called in to okay purchases. What did you stumble across?"

"Harsh environment rovers with micro-reactors on them and airlocks. Prefabricated buildings with life support systems and airlocks. They have a lot of items that would make Mars colonization easy; the kicker is that they offer delivery. You could have a base waiting for you on Mars. I can send you some of the fliers, and I can pay for what we can consider samples. Then, you can order more if you want."

(Groan), "You just made my weekend disappear. Find out the different transporter fees; I assume the delivery costs decrease as the loads get larger."

The delivery rate was reasonable because they had a surplus of ships that had been ordered for some other use that fell through. We set up what we considered a sample order. Two of the rovers, six of the prefabricated habitats, one of which was large enough to fit one of the rovers in it and allowed for maintenance and welding. Then, we told them to include one-half of one of the quantum multiplexors we picked up earlier in one of the prefabs. That would provide a decent communication channel between the Earth and Mars.

The general then texted me, and they added two more of the prefabricated habitats and one more rover. He also added one additional six-person small cargo spaceship without any FTL capability.

That one-stop had depleted half my remaining platinum reserves. On the plus side, most of that will be replenished when we return to Earth.

... ...

The shopping spree lasted two days, and when it was over, my platinum reserves were down to only 12% of what they had been when I landed.

Dragging the scientists away was like telling kids we would only spend half a day at a waterpark.

It was almost done. Some of the items will be delivered tomorrow, so we have a lot of cargo to rearrange.

Much of what was considered state-of-the-art a few months ago was folded up, crated, and stuffed into the cargo area as best we could to make way for the new hardware.

I went into different lab spaces, and almost all of what was there was new hardware, but the latest artifact was in Lab-B on the lowest gravity deck. It was covered in several layers of tarps and blankets. The new hardware, specifically the hardware that would be used in analyzing the artifact, needed to be in close proximity, and this room was heavily restricted. Even though the artifact was covered, we didn't allow any vendors to enter our ship.

The extra security didn't seem to faze the vendors; it seemed more like the normal rather than the exception.

One of the scientists ran to me sobbing. I was initially worried, but it turned out to be tears of joy. Their theory, which they had been working on for over twelve years, was proved within a day using the new equipment and their test setup.

It would probably have earned them a Nobel Prize, except it was now almost old technology. It was like using an iPhone 17 to document Alexander Graham Bell's first telephone call.

THE RETURN

The Return trip was different. The scientists were like kids on Christmas, busily unwrapping all their new toys. Eventually, most of them returned to the primary task of analyzing the new artifact.

They figured out the voltages to power it, mainly from the battery backup unit to which it had been connected.

A set of pipes also went into it. They contained traces of nitrogen and helium; both lines were heavily insulated. We suspected it was part of a two-stage refrigeration system for whatever the artifact did. The residual remaining in the lines after they were disconnected was only low-pressure gas, but we quickly figured out it used liquid nitrogen and helium.

Liquid nitrogen is below -321°F (77 Kelvin), and liquid helium is even colder, at -452°F (4.2 Kelvin).

Whatever the artifact was, it used the two gasses as part of its refrigeration system.

The large clear (we verified it was not glass) cover was to surround the active elements with a vacuum, insulating whatever the almost absolute zero-temperature device was from the warm air in the room.

We still didn't know what it was for.

One group of scientists, plus Emma Murphy, analyzed the data extracted from the hard drives. There were no audio records, and very few files contained any graphic images of binary data. Only the cover panel release latches had any pictographic symbols.

The trip back to the Earth from the Kassakar trading center took two days in Hyper FTL. Of course, we had to stop just outside the solar system, accelerate to normal FTL speed, and then enter the system using normal FTL. Then, we exited and performed the deceleration to make it look like normal FTL to anyone observing the Earth. The procedure was starting to be tiring, but it was still much faster than simply using our normal FTL.

We had just entered normal FTL when we received a message that the scientists had made a partial breakthrough on the artifact. We knew how to control it. They had successfully powered up the controller without connecting it to the artifact. They had captured multiple screen images. It was a starting point.

The bad news is that most of the screens displayed what they were almost certain were warning messages about the device being disconnected.

We were approaching the Earth. We stopped additional testing of the artifact under power, even the control panel. It was time to see what had changed since we were here last. I had specifically told Jessie not to relay anything to us about the repercussions of the dual attack. Unless it was critical and we needed to do something.

The usual crew was on the bridge; we had just started the braking operations. We had Crystal Johnstone on the bridge, and it occurred to me that we hadn't seen much of her except when we were approaching or departing a port. I said, "What is new?"

She smiled, "Are you asking about the station or the political fallout from the Doublemint twins of terror?"

"Let's start with the station."

"The military has about the same percentage as before and still primarily occupies part of level four. Part of level one is now being converted into a park, with transplanted mature fruit trees. The upper level is still set to 0.55G, and they are starting lottery vacations to the station. They decided that letting only the rich, or the ones sponsored by massively overpriced colleges, would be a bad thing. The situation on the Earth is a bit volatile. The medical pods have started arriving and are being set up in various hospitals. One was destroyed in a bombing, and the supposedly civilized country that did it is blaming it on an accident. All the medical pods in that country have stopped working, except for trauma care for children. They will probably change most of their government in the next election, if not sooner."

I said, "I hate to say it, but I expected some crap like that. Are the other countries using it like they are supposed to?"

"Multiple attempted violations, all related to the wealthy elite wanting everything done to them and the poor getting only the unused free time, scheduling them for 4:00 AM local time, and ejecting them early so a socialite can get a botched tummy tuck cleaned up. They are pissed at the fact that they refuse to schedule who they want. They have made multiple attempts at falsifying IDs so people they select get treated, not those who need it. It shuts down for six hours and is non-responsive if it gets three attempts with false IDs in a day."

I said, "Hopefully, it will sort itself out over time. How many have tried to hack them?"

Mark said, "Only two: someone tried to remove the programming that limited who gets treated. I think Jessie's actions were a bit extreme, but she saw that as the one viable option."

"I probably don't want to know. What did it do?"

Jessie said, "One option was to simply brick the unit, but they would almost certainly disassemble it and try to reverse engineer it. We went for controlled self-destruction. And by controlled, that was the goal, not always the result. We specified they all be installed in a fireproof building on a concrete floor; now they know why. I also released all the dirt I could find on the programmer and the person who hired them on the web. Listing them as why the hospital lost the unit and, in one case, part of the adjacent building. No one even related to them will ever receive any care in a medical pod."

I said, "Let me guess. They did not make the room as fireproof as you specified?"

"Nowhere close."

Crystal said, "The incident was all over the news, and detailed reports were somehow released on who did what, the poor construction, and the lack of standard safety features. The report revealed the government's connections to various illegal activities. Then, when the police didn't take action, a second report emerged, exposing massive corruption within the police and the judiciary. Some individuals attempted to flee the country, but most were extradited back."

Everyone then removed the 5-point harness and stowed it in the webbing pouch beside it.

She said, "Do we really need to wear these on every entry and exit from FTL?"

I sighed and said, "I would rather have a slight discomfort than get tossed across the room if something bad happened. You don't get a message from your car that says put on a seat belt two minutes before having an accident."

"I wish… anyway," She started reading the display in front of her, "The Kipitz controlled seven planets, and they have had changes in government on all of them. The Caspin Station saw almost no effect, and they were all extremely grateful to have the humans in charge. The two Mee's disappeared after lighting off the fireworks, and then, about the time they disappeared, close to 800 Regiolon ships showed up to render aid to disabled ships. Twenty of the Kipitz ships didn't want any aid, and they started firing on the ships that showed up to help them. That ended badly for the twenty Kipitz ships, but they also destroyed three Regiolon ships, heavily damaged three, and did minor damage to two more. Most of the ships or those that only had fried electronics were rescued. Three lost the crews due to accidental venting. The moons lost only a few; they may have anticipated that action and already evacuated everything except for a penal colony on one moon. It survived, as it was on the other side of the moon than the vaporized side."

Jessie said, "The Mee's sent in some stealth surveillance ships and planned their attack to minimize casualties."

Crystal said, "They released a lot of dirt on all the leaders. How much information they were able to get is rather scary. Then, they gave a list of all the ones that needed to be held accountable. That only took half an hour to round up 95% of them; the last 5% had tried to hide. They were the worst of them, and according to this display, only six are still on the run. New elections are underway or being scheduled. Some of the power changes are more accurately described as coups, but with military people who are incredibly eager to step down as soon as possible."

I said, "I am surprised we haven't had a visit by Meera yet."

Dylan said, "They are in Hyper FTL and won't be able to call in until they finish up one last show of force. And no, I don't know what it will be."

He held up a bottle of whisky, "I have no clue why, but I was told to bring it with me when we dock at the Miramber Station."

Chloe said, "For drinking? Or smashing on a hull? One, I am pregnant, so I am not drinking. Two, in space, that would explode and create a lot of nasty debris that NASA would have to track until it deorbited."

Then, a display changed on the main screen, showing the time to docking.

I said, "Well, everything has worked out okay so far, so let's just trust her…. hers? What is the pronoun for two instances of the same individual? Clones, sort-of, but massively divergent."

Crystal said, "Them, engineers may be better at technical writing, but they often suck at basic English grammar."

We did a standard 1.0G deceleration and arrived at the station without any issues.

Then Jessie said, "We need to wait for a few minutes. We have a hard dock lock indication, but we need just to sit here until something is over."

We had a few puzzled looks, and we all looked around at each other, and then Mark said, "It's probably something Mee is about to do."

Jessie said, "We have properly docked, but I am delaying reporting the hard lock to the station."

Then, the screen changed to show a countdown; it started at 10, 9, 8, 7, 6, 5, 4, 3, 2, 1, …"

One of the royal Keitch-maubers then appeared out of Hyper FTL about three miles over the Miramber Station.

We could faintly hear alarms going off in the distance, but they were on the station, or possibly from the other ships docked to the station, After a few minutes, the royal Keitch-mauber disappeared into Hyper FTL, and it was gone.

Jessie said, "Multiple calls from the station wanting to talk to you. I am putting the general through now.

Lieutenant General McMasters appeared on the screen, "… and it's already gone. This was most definitely her ship; it didn't use conventional FTL. Captain Benjamin Williams, care to explain what we just saw?"

The screen changed to show a message from Mee, "Every inhabited planet has just had a royal Keitch-mauber appear over them, and then they had all disappeared, with the exceptions of the minor worlds and Ciea (Kibbiea's planet) as that was too far away. None fired any weapons."

I said, "I think it was a show of force, but I don't think any of them discharged any weapons."

"Any of them? Plural! Just how many are there?"

I said, "I believe most of the inhabited worlds had a similar display."

The display on the screen changed to indicate that the non-Kipitz appearance was just one ship, and most of them only stayed for one minute or less. The Kipitz worlds had up to thirty of them show up, and they are still there.

I said, "Well, the Kipitz worlds are getting a bit more of a display."

The general said, "Some at the U.N. want to know if we should be negotiating a surrender. It's causing a worldwide panic."

"The ship has already left; I think it was just a wave to say hello."

"We are receiving reports they appeared at multiple locations; just how many ships does that cra… crap, she may be listening; I sincerely apologize for saying anything that may have in any way offended her."

Dylan lowered his head, possibly so the general couldn't see his face breaking into a silly grin.

I said, "I don't think we have anything to worry about. I believe that the Kipitz may need to readjust their long-term plans. At least any of the ones that involved war and conquest and generally being assholes. Are there any of the Kipitz on the station?"

"There are two ships, one mostly Kipitz and one with one Kipitz crewmember. All have asked to be arrested and placed in custody until they can clear their names. They say they haven't done anything but feel much safer in a human jail than on a ship. None of them are on the capture immediately list."

The screen changed to, "That list was sent to everyone."

The message changed to, "The airlock is secure, and you are free to board the station."

We went to the airlock and found Ketcher and Koffer Sill, the split-tailed mermaids, waiting there for us.

My communicator signaled a message; I glanced down and read it: "Mee requested they be part of this party."

I said, "Well, let's see what is happening."

Dylan was with us, but the Meera avatar was not with him.

He said, "They are both very busy."

As soon as we entered, the trolley car hatches were secured, the brakes engaged, and the car started accelerating to match the station's rotating centrifuge section. Two minutes later, it was positioned at the transfer door, and the stairs folded down. When we exited, we were met by several individuals led by General McMasters.

I said, "I am tired of only seeing your office. Can we head up and look at the garden?"

"Yes, of course we can, but it is still being worked on."

Chloe said, "That is fine, lead on."

That ended the conversation, and we were led up to the garden area on the upper level. None of the others in the entourage spoke at all.

We arrived to find a tree-lined grassy path wandering around between some small water features. The level of the dirt/rock/grass area had risen about two feet, and the water features were less than two feet deep.

Chloe said, "This would have been much nicer for our wedding than that stuffy old officer's club."

The workers had moved away, and several trees were on their sides. The holes for them were open, and you could see some type of heavy plastic material, which I suspected was similar to truck bed lining, had been applied over the metal flooring. The trees were in massive pots, so they could be easily removed without cutting the roots.

The general said, "It would be an understatement to say she has again made people nervous. It was bad enough when she had her own personal Death Star, then she cloned herself, and there were two of them, and now she has a fleet of them. What does all this mean?"

Mark said, "Do you remember the movie 'The Day the Earth Stood Still?' The 1951 version, not that stupid remake that replaced the plot with special effects."

"Yes, I have seen it. Big scary alien."

"No, the alien looked like an average human. The big scary one was the indestructible robot. Anyway, in the end, the alien made a speech saying that humans were allowed to be as stupid, self-destructive, and warlike as we wanted as long as we kept it to our planet. We get a cosmic enema if we attempt to bring war to other species. For over 2,000 years, all these species have somehow managed not to blow themselves up. Then, one of them, or several, plotted to make Mee Keralatazaku go away. Only they didn't kill her. It turns out killing her is a very, very, very bad idea. It would unleash something that makes her little Death Star seem like a child's toy."

"You are not making me feel any better."

"It is her way of reminding everyone that she didn't get weaker when she was away; if anything, she got stronger."

"But she… what if she is insane, or if she goes on a rampage? Why are there hundreds of her now?"

I said, "She usually keeps to herself, or she did for nearly 1,800 years. She almost fades from the picture when she doesn't need to come out and play hard-ass."

Chloe pointed at the group that was following us, "Who are they? Do they know what you know?"

One said, "Louis Dubois, I am currently the highest representative of the U.N. on the station."

Another said, "Vincent Finocchiaro, I represent the World Bank. We are trying to see if we need to do anything to stabilize the economy. In a knee-jerk response, we froze all stock trading worldwide."

The general said, "None of them know about Miss F. They do not need to know anything about her."

Vincent opened his mouth to say something and then shut it.

I said, "It is probably okay to open trading again tomorrow. It may be a bit volatile, but it will eventually stabilize. In general, go about your life as if nothing has changed. Well, unless you were planning to start an interplanetary war, in that case, go jump in a river full of piranha wearing a jockstrap made from bacon. Save the rest of us the trouble."

General McMasters said, "You know, we really don't need the crude sarcasm."

Chloe said, "That wasn't sarcasm; what do you think the Kipitz are now doing on planets with dozens of those ships in orbit around them? Ones that stayed and didn't just pop in to say hello like here?"

The general went pale, "Dozen of those ships? The reports say that two of their moons still have one side molten and glowing red. I have seen the teeth of the Kipitz. I read the reports of what happened at the Caspin Station. Most of them will still be alive, but only because Mee said to bring them to her alive. She didn't say they had to be intact."

A message arrived on my communicator, and I read it aloud. "Three of their moons are half-melted, and one of their planets is now missing an island the size of Madagascar."

Vincent said, "If I am not needed, I will take my leave." Without waiting for an answer, he ran away.

General McMasters said, "I hope, for those poor dumb sons of bitches, that it was an unpopulated island on a planet with just an outpost on it. It's something to make an island go away… that probably created a tidal wave that… No, I do not want to think too hard about that."

My phone pinged with another message, which I read as well: "It was a massive warship production facility and staging ground on a supposedly empty world."

The general said, "I am sorry, but I have to ask, is she somehow listening to us? To everything? To everyone?"

Chloe said, "That would be an interesting idea, but I don't think so, or not to everyone. A few people, probably."

My phone sent one more message alert: "The last of the ones that she wanted to be turned in to her has been gathered up, or enough of the parts have been collected so that they can be identified by their DNA."

General McMasters said, "Assuming this issue is over, what is the other reason you are here."

I asked, "Are the others still here okay to hear this?"

"Yes."

"We have some survivors, actually descendants from the race that you have the ship from, from a quarter million years ago. They have evolved... Or maybe it's better to say mutated and devolved quite a lot since then. We have less than fifty, and they need lots of medical enhancements before they can stand anything close to the Earth's gravity. Four are on our ship."

"Why are these two here?" He pointed at the Prochie and Koffer, the split-tailed mermaids.

"Not a clue, Mee said to bring them. We rescued them from a ship destined for a scrap heap."

Jessie's voice came over the intercom, "Mee says to have them report to docking port 'C' and for the general to scrounge up six people to pilot a new ship."

The general said, "I like the old days when I wasn't seriously wondering if the damn space station could read our minds." Then he made a call to his assistant in his office. "They will meet us there."

Chloe had been digging her toes into the dirt next to the hole for the tree. "Can we have one section of the ship converted into a garden park like this?"

I said, "We may be able to shuffle things around. The easiest way would be to sacrifice one of the crew rooms, but maybe we could move the recreation room down a level?"

Mei said, "The pool table and the ping-pong table were machined for the expected curvature of those levels. We would need to replace the tops."

Chloe said, "I think we can afford it. We will have to see what happens after the crew shuffling we always seem to have every time we get to Earth. There is also all the state-of-the-art Earth equipment that is now almost obsolete. We want it off the ship; we need the room. Some of the new test equipment we picked up will also be moved to the station; some will almost certainly go to the Earth, and the... never mind."

The general said, "I will pretend I didn't hear anything."

Mark said, "We all do that on occasion."

Kibbiea said, "The first time I saw a video of her or met an instance of Mee Keralatazaku, she scared the crap out of me. Now, I ignore most of the scary parts and just go with the flow."

I saw the general raise his eyebrows at the word instance, but he managed not to ask or say anything.

We made our way down to the lowest level and then entered the transfer trolley car. When it had stopped the spin, and we were again in zero gravity, we were at the airlock of a different ship. The trolley started spinning again, returning to where we were in a few minutes, now with six new people. Two females and four males.

One said, "I am Lieutenant Sanders, we were told to consider this like a T.A.C. base assignment, where we could be assigned anywhere on almost no notice. We were what the lottery selected. Can I ask what we were picked for?"

Jessie spoke over the intercom, "This is a Mitrix class freighter. Large on cargo, small on cabin space. There is no centrifuge but one modified medical pod that you can use to perform muscle stimulation. Twenty minutes a day in the pod is the equivalent of a four-hour workout. Then, you spend another thirty minutes doing light stretching exercises so you don't cramp up from all the electrical muscle stimulation."

They had expressions on their faces that said they thought that they had lost the lottery.

"You are taking the two Prochie, the split-tailed mermaids, Ketcher and Koffer Sill, back to their planet. It will take you nine days each way. When you arrive, you will find that Mee Keralatazaku has delivered a small space station, and you will dock there. Then, after unloading these two, you come back here."

They all said, "Yes, Sir."

Jessie's persona was female, and she wasn't in their chain of command. We all smiled.

Jessie continued, "Then, you will be using this ship to ferry mostly hardware between the Earth, this station, and Mars, which doesn't have a station. On Mars, you will have to do planetary landings; this ship is designed for that. You can play around as a Martian astronaut, but you are primarily truck drivers. Unlike Amazon, the six of you are the owners of this ship."

"WHAT!"

I laughed, "Yeah, you looked like you thought you were the losers who got a crappy job. What you are is part owners of Acme space movers. Actually, you can come up with whatever you want for its name."

The general said, "They are members of the Space Force; they can't own a ship; they were just randomly selected as the crew for some unspecified mission."

Jessie said, "Actually, they do own the ship. Technically, after this mission, they could retire and lease the ship to the Earth."

One of the women yelled, "Hell no, this is our own ship, awesome!"

Mei said, "I used to fight the insanity as well. Now I have a seven-digit bank balance and have learned to enjoy the ride."

Mark said, "I know what our wedding cost and that I have earned more than that in the months since then just from the interest in the bank."

One of the other pilots said, "Permission to speak freely?"

The general said, "Yes."

He ran over to me and wrapped me in a bear hug. "My sister was one of the ones that was able to go in a medical pod at the Elgin Air Force Base. She was in a car accident. A woman fell asleep at the wheel, and she broadsided my sister. The bitch who hit her was unharmed; she tested positive for several narcotics. My sister would have lost her leg and a kidney if she didn't go in the pod. Thank you."

The general said, "You will probably get a lot more of these. Your donation of the pods is a lot more than what most governments have done for their people.

Ketcher Sill said, "Is the station they will be putting around our homeworld like the one we are on?"

Jessie said, "Mee ordered it in a custom configuration for your people. The size is the same, but the top level contains six swimming pool units similar to those on the Stardust II."

Ketcher and Koffer embraced us, and then Ketcher asked, "Are we ready to go now?"

Jessie said, "No, you have at least two days of loading supplies. The earth will want to set up trade with your people, and the ships need food and supplies for everyone. This is just an empty ship at the moment.

Dylan handed Lieutenant Sanders the bottle of booze, "Something for after you have completed your first delivery."

THE NEXT DESTINATION

Our ship offloaded many surplus supplies and the almost priceless alien test and measurement equipment, and of course, there were some crew reassignments.

Chloe and I were in our suite, in the spare bedroom we had used as an office, but it would become a nursery in a few months.

Chloe said, "Who needs to talk to us next?"

Jessie said, "The Makris family."

I said, "Let them in."

Atticus and Lydia Makris came in with their two children, Christopher, age thirteen, and Iris, age sixteen.

I said, "What is up?"

Atticus Makris said, "First of all, let me say that my time on your ship has been fantastic. Unfortunately, something has come up, and we have decided to request a transfer to the station."

"What is the problem?"

"Not a problem, it has been great, perhaps a little too great. When we went into the medical pods for the language sessions, it fixed a few of our minor issues. It fixed one I didn't count on. Anyway, Lydia is now pregnant, and at age 42, I think we want to be at a 9-5 job and not chasing space aliens."

Then Iris spoke up, "And I would much rather be chasing space aliens than babysitting and changing diapers."

Then her eyes widened as she noticed Chloe's belly. "Not that changing diapers is terrible. Or babysitting, as long as it is on a spaceship."

Christopher Makris (age 13) said, "There are not a lot of kids my age on the station. There is James and Jennifer Smith, but they are worse nerds than my sister. I want to go with my parents."

Chloe said, "If we keep you on, you will be crew, not a dependent, and you will be in a standard room, not the family suite."

"That is fine; it will be like when I was at MIT, only hopefully less pranking on the fifteen-year-old for getting into college."

Two other female scientists and one of the male scientists wanted to transfer off.

When Donnie Myers and Patrica Scott heard about the free room, they also decided they wanted to get married and move in together.

We had shuffled the room assignments around again when we got a call from John Smith.

"Yes. What can I help you with?"

"We think we figured out something about the artifact. First, it is completely unrelated to the Munchkins."

"We knew that already."

"We were looking at it all wrong; we assumed it did something, that it was an engine or a way to make the ship do something. It is not; We have confirmed that it is a sensor. It is a way to look outside the ship."

"We have sensors; we can look with optics, infrared, radar, and laser ranging systems. What does that do? Especially from inside the ship?"

"It is a mass detector, and it should work inside subspace, including FTL and Hyper FTL."

"Well, that piqued my interest. Why was it not moving? If the ship had conventional FTL, would it accelerate before engaging FTL, and if it dropped out, it would still have a high velocity."

"We think they spotted something from FTL, and they had stopped to investigate what they saw; when they were near zero velocity, they had the bad luck to encounter a grain of antimatter."

"Did they detect the Nest?"

"No, I think they detected the antimatter, and it was such a strange reading they had to investigate. We don't think they knew it was antimatter until it was too late. But, it probably could detect the Nest."

"Assuming the Nest stays in one place, it may be one giant carrier ship. We don't know much about it."

I said, "And I like it that way. I still want to insist we don't hook the controller up to the artifact… sensor… or whatever it is, until we are far away from the Earth."

We were a few hours away from being ready to leave, and Mark and Chloe were sitting with me. Mark said, "Do we mention to the general that we now have an empty family suite?"

I said, "He already knows. He is shaking in his boots from Mee's little pop-in visit, and she did nothing; he probably won't suggest someone unless we ask him to."

Chloe said, "I think we managed to keep the Hyper FTL from being reported to anyone in the Earth command, but now that Mee has demonstrated it, the secret is out. The fact that we have it may come out as well."

I said, "And it doesn't take a genius to figure out we probably gave it to Mee. We probably have pissed off some angry players."

Mark said, "But hopefully, they have us in the category of not to piss off, as we are F.O.M.s."

I said, "F.O.M.s?"

"Friends Of Mee Keralatazaku. Adding a 'K' to the acronym makes it too hard to pronounce."

I said, "Jessie, connect me to the general."

A minute later, he connected, "Yes?"

"You probably already know this, but the Makris family has decided to transfer to the station. All but Iris, who has already proved herself semi-useful. We are surprised you haven't called up to suggest a replacement family."

"I thought about it. We pinged the Kimura family to see if they wanted back on your ship. They are not available. Coming up with someone who can pass security on very short notice is hard. Oh, we did a background check on the goth girl from Mark's wedding accident, Spencer Moreau. She is keeping clean, taking courses in neonatal CPR, and being a nanny. She should be ready to pick up the next time you are here."

Chloe said, "The little bit of makeup, piercings, and clothing doesn't make her a full goth. If she is clean and stable, then we may be interested."

I said, "I bet she gets rid of most of her earrings the first time our daughter's little hand grabs onto them."

Chloe said, "We have decided that when fate randomly presents something to us, it is usually worth looking at, even if things seem a bit quirky.

"Is that how you do it? Accept the madness and ignore the terror?"

I said, "I don't really see it as terror."

The general said, "I wish I could say that. Threat analysis and looking for dangers has been a significant part of the last 25 years of my life."

He looked at a message on his phone, "It seems we do have a family we can assign to your ship. These are not spies to keep an eye on you."

"Was the last family? I liked the Kimura family, even when we accidentally scared the piss out of the little girl, and unfortunately, that was not a figure of speech."

He said, "That may have played a part in why they took the other offer. The new family is Nicholas and Sophia Doukas, and they have a daughter, Elena, who is sixteen. They need transportation up to the station, and you will have to delay your departure by about two hours for them to get here."

"I'm surprised you didn't have a ship pick them up just on the chance we allowed them."

"They were on vacation in Greece, and now, the local village will have quite a lot to talk about. The Shuttle did a ballistic hop from Edwards Air Force Base and the Greek air control… they got quite the talking to when they initially refused the flight path. Initially, they didn't believe it was the Prime Minister who called them."

Chloe said, "I can imagine the late-night comedians having a field day with something like that. Oh poop, Have they been making fun of us?"

The general laughed, "A few of the comedians have had bits about some of you; they get a little talking to by the government, and they usually tone it way down after that."

I said, "Well, they rip into people like Elon Musk for what he does. I should not be surprised. We are not as rich as him but technically billionaires."

The general said, "I have to break this to you, but they had to put a shell company around your gift of the medical pods. That company had to be assigned a monetary value. It's way up there."

I said, "That is enough; I don't need to hear anymore. Get the family up here, and tell them we disembark as soon as their feet are on the ship."

The general said, "For the record, where are you going?"

"Deep space, to do some testing that we would prefer not to have anyone around. The Smiths are a key part of that study. So if they haven't told you anything about it, that says something."

"They are not spies, well, not spies against you. They do have an interesting history."

"Do we need to know anything about the new family? What is the parent's expertise?"

"He is a geneticist, and she is a neurologist. Technically, she could still practice medicine, but she needs a trip into one of your medical pods. Even then, I'm not sure how well it does on old injuries. She is missing two fingers on her right hand, and they have been doing research and not practicing medicine."

Chloe said, "I probably want her to read a few books on pediatricians and Obstetricians/gynecologists." She patted her now rather prominent belly bump. "And she can sleep for a few days or weeks and regrow her fingers. Katerina says her hand always feels cold and sometimes cramps up whenever she tries to fall asleep, but the nerves have regrown in the hand and partially into the fingers. She had her right-hand pinky finger nerves transplanted into her left-hand trigger finger because that is the type of woman she is."

The general smiled, "I would, too, if I was younger."

Then we disconnected the line.

Chloe said, "Do their medical skill and her injury seem a little too convenient?"

"It will be obvious if it is an old or a new injury. What did you find, Jessie? I can't imagine you spent all those milliseconds since he started talking idly computing Pi."

"I much prefer computing the square root of negative one. Nine years ago, she was in a freak accident that should have been a minor fender bender; only the pickup truck that hit them had some fencing supplies improperly secured on the roof rack, and a section of a fence post went into their car. She lost her ring and little finger on her right hand, and she was right-handed. Her middle finger needed to be reattached, but that surgery was successful."

Katerina held up her left hand, "Maybe I am just paranoid, but it seems way too similar, and the medical doctor part seems too convenient."

I said, "Good, I am not the only one that got a feeling that was off."

Mei said, "Or, perhaps they had an ongoing search for candidates who would fit your needs. Not to say they may have trained her for the last three months just on the chance they needed them."

Five hours later, they arrived. The girl, Elena, was wide-eyed and seemed to enjoy the little bit of exposure to zero gravity. Both the parents were holding bags under their chins.

"Gross! Mom, you are leaking. Ack, now it is stuck to your shoulder. I am not cleaning that up. What the hell did you eat? That smells nasty."

I instinctively liked the daughter. She had sass.

When we got them to the first level of the ship's centrifuge, both parents sat on the bench, and one of the enlisted women got the nasty job of helping clean them up. "A lot of us got sick the first time. Now we don't mind it."

Nicholas said, "I am so embarrassed."

Sophia said, "This bag is full. Do you have another?"

The daughter Elena was now bouncing around. "This is cool; the stationary part is on one side of the hub, and the rotating part is on the other. Are there any windows?"

The enlisted woman said, "We have one for manually observing the docking adapter. Usually, we just use cameras. There is no really easy way to have windows on the centrifuge part. This is the adapter level. Then the next level is 0.47G, the level your room will be on is 0.62G, and the outer level is 0.77G. There are labs on levels 1 and 3. The cafeteria is on level 3, with the highest gravity. That is also the level with the pool."

"W.T.F. There is a frigging pool!"

Sophia said, "Elena Doukas, watch your language."

"I didn't swear; I just used an acronym."

Jessie announced, "We are now disengaging from the station. Please clear the adaptor level, as it will have sideways gravity when we engage the engines."

Elena said, "What are those strange boxes over there?"

Jessie replied, "They are medical pods. Some special crew members have a low tolerance for gravity. They prefer to ride out the acceleration in the pods, which makes it much more tolerable for them. The alternative is that we would have only been able to use a small fraction of the normal acceleration to get up to FTL speed."

They were led into the transition area of the centrifuge, and the feeling of having some weight returned as if the spin pushed them against the outer wall. As they were about to enter the main centrifuge upper deck, Elena paused and looked back one last time at the pods.

Then, they entered the noise and confusion of the third level and everyone in the cafeteria. She soon forgot about the strange pods.

Her parents were not interested in any food, but they both grabbed water bottles to replenish some of what they had lost.

Then, they were taken to the second level, where they were shown how to navigate the narrow walkway between the individual rooms and shown to their family suite.

Then, they were shown how to operate the restroom, which was mostly self-evident. The parents crawled into bed, but Elena decided to explore the ship.

She was told to avoid any of the lab spaces where people were working and not to enter the bridge unless she was called to it.

She found the recreation room, and several of the crew were playing ping-pong.

"Wow, the floor is curved. I figured that part out instantly, but the ping-pong table is also curved."

One of the crew said. "We are now accelerating, so that messes up the apparent flatness of the table. If you remove the ping-pong top, under it is a pool table. We can sort of play ping-pong under acceleration, but the pool table is completely unplayable. The balls all roll into the front or the back and form a line. It is impossible to play."

The other crew member said, "Ping-pong is also messed up, but we can still bounce the ball around and have fun. Mei is a ping-pong geek who refuses to play under acceleration, so we grabbed the empty table. More of the other off-duty crew are up in the game room. It is the next room over."

"What is in that?"

"A few pinball machines, but they automatically lock the balls and won't let you even attempt to play when the ship is accelerating. They have some video arcade machines. Fat chance of getting any time on those when we are accelerating. The pool will be crowded, but even if it is crowded, that is still the best place to be. That is next to the game room." Her mouth hung open.

The other crewmember laughed, "The clothing fabricator can make you a bathing suit if you forgot to bring one."

TESTING

The ship did what was now our standard routine: accelerate up to FTL speed, making a very short trip in standard FTL just to get it out past one light day's distance. Then, dropping out of standard FTL and decelerating to near zero galactic velocity. Then, we engaged the Hyper FTL and moved to one light-year's distance from any inhabitable stars.

We left Hyper FTL and performed the test we had spent almost twenty-two hours preparing for: we prepared to power on the new artifact.

Everyone was ordered out of the pool; the cafeteria was locked down, all the loose items on the ship were secured, and the pinball machines were put in a state where the balls were all securely locked internally.

The artifact was supposed to be a sensor. It shouldn't affect anything. Even the station-keeping cold gas thrusters were disabled; the stabilizer gyros were all spun down and stopped. The reactor was locked in a safe, reduced power state. All nonessential hardware was powered off.

We were drifting, with nothing anywhere near us and everyone on the ship holding a barf bag. The test was started.

And it immediately popped a circuit breaker and did nothing.

After an hour of testing, the problem was determined to be that some air had gotten into the helium line when it was being transferred or set up. The air contained water vapor, which froze and clogged something, causing it to ice over.

The solution was to bring the room it was in down to vacuum and boil the water vapor off. Only it didn't; the chiller needed the tubes cleaned, which required heat and vacuum.

A pipe cleaner would work, except there was no possible way to reach the part that needed cleaning. Even the most petite human hands were too large, and the drones were not dexterous enough to perform the action. They also said we should not put anything with electricity flowing in it inside the sensor.

They devised a solution: the Munchkins wearing their small space suits had hands that were the correct size to reach the part they needed to clean.

Two of the Munchkins, Pooki and Croko, the two females, were assigned the task. They had slightly smaller hands, so the replicator ran off new gloves for their spacesuits that were as small as possible, and they could still squeeze their tiny hands into them.

The room did not have an airlock, but it did have an external door. The procedure was sketchy at best; two of the enlisted guards were escorting the two Munchkins out of the ship's main airlock, over the hull, and then into the secondary cargo hatch.

Croko said, "Wow, the far wall is all black, and it is covered in these pinpoints of light in strange patterns."

Pooki said, "It is called the sky. Those are stars. It is really far away."

"I know that. I listened to the biggies talking, the same as you did. Supposedly, this is what the outside of old-home looks like as well. Crikey, it's snivels cold. My hands are freezing."

"They are also hard to close. When you relax your fingers, they pop open, so holding stuff will be hard."

The four of them entered the chamber, which was flooded with light compared to the blackness of space.

Croko said, "Now I can't see; my eyes need a minute to adjust. Wow, that thing is pretty."

One of the enlisted, Jennet Landers, said, "They have opened up the hatch in the back. It will be a bit warm. They tried putting a heat lamp on it to bake it off, but it didn't work. Croko, you get to be the one to climb inside of it, and Pooki will be holding your feet and passing you the tools."

The device was made of shiny metal, like gold and silver, without the slightest hint of tarnishing, and it contained lots of what looked like crystal-clear glass.

Croko said, "My eyes have adjusted. Guide me in. I don't think I want to touch any of the shiny stuff."

It only took a few minutes to maneuver her into position. Pooki handed Croko the pipe cleaner, but it was too large. "I need a smaller one. I can see five plus two holes, and the middle one is larger. It went in that one okay, but the five plus one outer ones are smaller."

I said, "Jessie, add more math to their training sessions. They are still counting on their hands in their minds."

Pooki handed her the smaller pipe cleaner.

"That worked, it spit out some shiny things that are turning into water."

I said, "And more terms like snow and ice; I don't think they saw any of that on the old ship."

They pulled the Munchkins out, and the scientists pressurized the lines, and some more ice crystals came out.

"Check if the ports are clogged again. If they are clear, we can button it up and try again."

Only two of the smaller ports had clogged again. They released the cover and repressurized it again. On the second flush attempt, it showed clear.

"Great, get them back into the main part of the ship and bundle the artifact up again. This time, hopefully, it won't ice up again."

Moving the Munchkins back to the main part of the ship didn't have any problems, but when they removed their suits, both Munchkin girls had mild cases of frostbite on their fingers and toes. They were immediately put in medical pods.

Jessie said, "That was my mistake. To prevent any electrical currents close to the sensor, I left the finger heaters disabled. I assumed they should be okay with the expected 30-minute operation. It took over 70 minutes. In the future, we will only shut off the heaters just before they enter the sensor."

I said, "Add 50% to all future time estimates we haven't rehearsed and practiced. Probably add 100% to things like this. How is the artifact testing going?"

"They have the covers back on; everything is still in a vacuum. The nitrogen acts as a pre-chiller to keep the helium in a liquid state. I am concerned about the breaker popping; I am setting the power trip at double what it was. I assumed the wiring was copper. It is pure silver and has a higher conductivity rating than I calculated. The copper we are using is a heavy bus bar so that it can easily handle the extra current."

The second test was held in the same manner as the first. Everyone had barf bags ready, and the ship was drifting.

John Smith said, "Enabling the artifact."

I didn't notice or feel anything, which was probably good.

Jessie said, "Power is slightly above what I expected, but I can set the trip level so we don't lose the device. It appears to be chilling the sensor down to 4.2 Kelvin."

Activating the device took twenty minutes, and then the scientists gave us a bunch of "Oohs and Ahhs."

I said, "What is it doing? We can't see anything from the bridge."

Jessie said, "No one on the ship is reporting unusual side effects, no radiation is being detected, and no emissions that any of our sensors can detect."

Jane Smith said, "There is a holographic sphere in front of us that is four meters in diameter. That is about thirteen feet. We are playing with the gain; setting it low shows a view of the ship… Captain, the reactor shows up as very strange. I have panned and set it to cover the support ship, and our reactor looks nothing like the one on the other ship."

I said, "Make a note of what you see, but classify it as so far above anyone's security clearance as to be scary."

"Understood, there is only one person that could mean… Or however many of them there are."

"There are controls to select what we are looking for. One setting shows biologicals, displaying the ship as transparent, and I see everyone in there. Another dials in various metals, and I can see iron or ferrous metals separately from things like aluminum. This would give anyone a tactical advantage; it lets you know what is on a ship. I am now dialing the range out and trying to calibrate the range units to things we can understand."

They were silent for the next few minutes.

Then, John Smith said, "It looks like the range is slightly over two light seconds, just over 600 million meters, 374 thousand miles."

I said, "Stick to one unit. How small of an object can it detect at the different ranges?"

"Can we have the support ship move one hundred thousand miles away for a test?"

"Yes, move the second ship to the specified distance."

The ship did a Hyper FTL jump. A few seconds later, "We can detect the ship, and the detail has dropped to a fuzzy blob. I can make out the rough shape and the metals the hull is made of. Setting to biological scan, it is too far away to make out biologicals; I can tell hull material, or maybe ship material, and that the reactor is different than ours."

Then, we did a bunch of different tests.

We accelerated the ship to normal FTL speed, and the range was about the same.

We engaged normal FTL, and the system popped the breaker again.

We replaced the power cable to it and doubled its current capability. We repeated the normal FTL test, which now showed an image of what was outside the ship, but everything was smeared and shaped wrong.

Mark said, "So we have limited FTL visibility. We can spot a ship in FTL, maybe even... We need to test the sensor in Hyper FTL. If this works as I think it will, we should be able to track a ship in regular FTL while in Hyper FTL."

The first part of that was to test scanning in Hyper FTL, which worked, but the display was squirrely.

Then, we had the support ship accelerate to normal FTL speed, and we engaged the Hyper FTL as the ship passed us.

We had to adjust the speed of the pilot boat a bit to match the support ship in normal FTL, and when we had it, we could get it to keep us within the scanning distance.

At a distance that we considered safe, we could read the general shape of the ship, the number of biologicals on the ship, and approximate the weapons' locations.

The support ship then exited normal FTL. We set up a link to the two ships and the pilot boat and moved into Hyper FTL using a search pattern.

The test continued for most of the day, and we suddenly bounced out of FTL.

I yelled, "What happened?"

"The sensor detected a possible hazard before the pilot boat did. Do I have permission to move both ships closer and slowly approach what it considered a hazard?"

"Yes, but keep us in formation."

We made one more short Hyper FTL jump, and the long-range scanner showed several objects ahead. Using the friction drive, we slowly approached.

"Small cluster of asteroids. It is possibly a rubble pile asteroid that has partially fragmented: nothing metallic, methane ice, mostly carbonaceous rock, some silicate material. The main object is about two tons. The spread of orbiting particulate is about 250 meters. Anything that went further away was not gravitationally locked and drifted away. What I can see on the radar, compared to what the new sensor shows, is remarkable. The radar is missing anything smaller than marble-sized pieces, and the new sensor shows them down to a grain of rice size."

Then Meera came wandering into the room with the sensor in it. "What new toys have you found?"

"A sensor, we are still profiling it. It was on the ship with the weird semi-octagon beings on it. Near the antimatter asteroid, and no, we are not going back near that damn thing again."

She said, "Good points, bad points."

"It can probably detect the Nest, even from FTL. It can also detect ships from about one light second and tell us what is on them from 0.1 light seconds. On the bad side, we only have one and don't know enough about it to copy it… yet. Oh, which Mee are you?"

Dylan said, "She grabbed me by the ass and kissed me in the hallway, so I assume it is instance 49."

Meera said, "Good guess, but I think the original would also try that. I got out of the pod before we did our attack, and then we did the second one. What did you think of all the extra ships?"

I said, "Let me guess. You can only fire the weapons if you are in them, which explains the two that fried the moons. Were the rest just for show and tell?"

"I will have to read up on more of your euphemisms, a show of force, the tell? Not quite sure about that last part."

"Related to something we learned as children in school, it's not important."

"Actually, it may be, the body we are building will be a fully functional human, including a working reproductive system. I gave up generations ago on having a Regiolon child."

Dylan blushed.

Then Mark laughed and said, "The Creetona internal gestation period is only four months in human time, but they add five more months to that as they have an egg that needs to be cared for. Unlike a chicken, it is partially matured inside her and then ejected for the final months."

Chloe said, "Have you decided to have her carry a child?"

Kibbiea said, "The medical pod should be able to make my life expectancy match someone with a suppressor installed. We had one of my eggs harvested a few days ago, and the gene splicer is mapping the different features of the various male donors. We should have one ready for implantation in me in a few days. We want a female, close to a human in height, and I always wanted tail freckles. Jessie is still looking to see if she can find the portion of the DNA for that."

I said, "Tail freckles?"

She whipped her tail up in front of me. "I have a few spots. They are considered a beauty trait; some have incredible patterns on the side of their tails." Then she blushed, "I wondered if tattooing would work, but we shed once a year, so I think it would look like crap after a shedding."

Mark said, "We looked up henna as an option, but it listed some possible side effects, and we will pass on that for now. I always liked freckles. The Irish girl I had a crush on in Junior High had them, and…"

Kibbiea smacked him in the back of his head with her tail, "Oops."

He snatched her tail in his hand, pulled it up to his mouth, and lightly bit down on it.

She froze and then said, "Damn tease."

Chloe said, "Focus! No wonder McFarland says we are a bunch of easily distracted puppies next to a squirrel tree."

Mark released her tail and said, "I resemble that remark."

I said, "What were we talking about?"

Meera said, "The new sensor, and then you went down this windy path and almost made me forget about it. Can I assume I will get a copy of it when you figure out how to duplicate it?"

"Yes, but it is a sensor, not a weapon. I also don't know how it will do next to your weapons. There is a good chance everything in it will fry if you use your heavy weapons. And we don't know how to make a replacement."

"That should not be an issue. If you drop it off at the Nest, the drones on it can figure out how it works. I watched the Munchkins do the cleaning, I… I think I just figured out something. The ship you recovered it from has those strange, flattish octagon beings. I think they are bioengineered drones. The sensor may have a tendency to clog, and mechanical drones may be too likely to scratch or damage the sensors. Were there any other beings on the ship?"

"None that we found. But we now have a way to detect them if they are still around."

Meera asked, "Does it work in Hyper FTL?"

"Yes, and for short jumps, it may be more accurate than the pilot boat."

"Hmm, faster jumps may be possible using the new scanner than the relatively slow pilot boat. There is another inherent danger with using a pilot boat."

I said, "What?"

"The Pilot boat blasts a strong radar pulse at every hop and then listens for the echo. It only listens for a fraction of a second, but the radio signal is probably detectable for several light hours. You are waving a flare around and saying here I am. Asshole has theorized that someone could build a scanner using thousand of quantum-linked detectors. It would detect the signature of a ship passing using a pilot boat; it could predict where a future exit from Hyper FTL would be, and weapons like gamma-ray bursters could disable a ship as it emerged."

I was about to say something, but then I realized Asshole had spent over 2,000 years developing weapons, so of course it would look at things that way. And a gamma-ray burster was probably one of the weapons on her ship."

"I guess we head to the Nest and let you have the artifact."

She smiled, "And, of course, you need to be rewarded for providing me with such fun toys."

As soon as she left the bridge, I called John Smith.

"Yes?"

"Playtime is running out; we have to turn the artifact over to Mee. There is no debate on that. I recommend you use all the time we have left to learn everything you can about how it works and whether or not we can replicate it. Look at it from the point of view of a prototype. What can you do better or differently to make it less fragile and difficult to maintain?"

"We don't know that it is… Yeah, that is a reasonable assumption; I am calling in the second shift, and we will double up. Let me know when we have to give it up. Can we disassemble it?"

"Only if you're confident you can reassemble it. Check if anyone on either ship has experience with cryogenic IR sensors or spacecraft such as W.I.S.E. or the James Webb Telescope; there may be others, but I can't recall them at the moment."

Two minutes later, Jessie said, "This is almost like the Keystone cops; I must give John Smith credit; this is organized chaos, and I think that most of them thrive under impossible deadlines."

Then Mark and Kibbiea got up.

"Where are you going?"

"The pool, I think everyone except for the dependents, is now awake and working on the problem. The dependents have the rest of the ship to themselves."

Ten minutes later, Jeri and Emma came up, "Do you need a break? The cafeteria is now just set up for some grab-and-go and coffee."

I said, "Do you have an ETA for when we get to the Nest?"

Jessie said, "Scotty says twelve hours."

I assumed that meant we could do it in ten if we needed to. I said, "Set the course for the Nest." Smiling, knowing we could have already been heading there, Jessie was probably awaiting the command just to give the scientists more time to analyze the artifact.

I said, "Well, we probably missed the pool window. Are you up for some video games?'

Chloe said, "Sure."

THE NEST II

We were approaching the Nest and watching the new sensor, which shone like a Christmas tree with all sorts of energy and materials. Our standard optical scanner only showed complete blackness; the only way to spot it optically was a very slight displacement of some of the stars near the rim of the Nest. The Nest's adaptive optical camouflage was impressive, but the new sensor showed everything.

Meera was standing behind me, and we were watching this approach from the sensor room, not the bridge.

Meera said, "It is so pretty… At least in this display, it is. I know what those ships in it can do and what some have done. Asshole was so sure of himself with his adaptive camouflage; he was saying he didn't think we would be able to see the Nest unless he turned on the lights."

The Nest opened the massive iris portal, and lights turned on inside the ship.

Jessie said, "I have received directions to the port to dock with. They want the second ship to dock inside as well.

Both ships slowly maneuvered to the ports we were directed to, and after we docked, John Smith announced, "We are shutting the sensor down. We have caps on the helium and nitrogen ports, so we shouldn't get any water vapor in the system. There are six small cooling ports, and one is already down to 33% efficiency. Hopefully, heating the liquid to gas and purging to vacuum again will clear up the last of the icing."

Then, we started heading to the airlock.

I asked, "How soon until the artifact is ready to move?"

"Are we venting it, or will the Nest do that?"

Asshole's voice came over the speakers, "I will take care of the venting and the transportation."

Meera laughed, "I think you hurt his feelings."

"Where are we going?"

She held an unopened bag of banana chips in her hand. "The real me is on the Nest, and the Original ate the last of the chips yesterday. We are just ahead."

We entered a room with one Regiolon version of Mee Keralatazaku sitting next to a bed attached to two medical pods. The Meera avatar handed the bag of chips to the Original Mee and then lay down on the bed, almost instantly seeming to be in a deep sleep.

The medical pod had some lights flicker on it, and about a minute later, the hatch opened, revealing a second copy of Mee Keralatazaku.

"Hey Dylan, come here." Then she opened the door to the second medical pod, and inside it was a second copy of Meera, the real human version.

"It looks just like the other one. The avatar."

"Yeah, but my mind will be in it. Or, more accurately, an identical copy of my mind. The Regiolon version of me still has to play the hard-ass ruler of everything."

"You don't mind being... well, duplicated?"

She laughed, "I am instance 49, and the one stuffing her face full of chips is the original."

The other Mee said, "I suppose I am living vicariously through number 49. Oh, you have to listen to this. Asshole, repeat the last update on the status of the Kipitz."

"They have officially surrendered the last planet, outpost, space station, and colony to me—well, except for the Caspin Station, which you own. There was a bit of a purge, and I won't go into how many, but it was a lot more than I wanted to. First, one of the planets made this ridiculous offer, and then they all copied the same insane offer. They are looking for a way to cement a new government structure that is free from the one thing they fear, which is me or us, as there are currently two of us. They have latched onto the one shining star in their miserable existence. The Caspin Station... They all wish to surrender... to you."

I fell into a chair and said, "Da fuck!?"

"Yeah, that was close to my reaction; I only used actual words."

Chloe was behind me, now giving me a shoulder massage.

"You now own the planets, the stations, the colonies, the ships, everything. And because they know I seem to like you, they hopefully will not face my wrath... again."

"I can't own planets and all that other stuff."

Mark said, "I get it; you don't have to. You lease it to the Earth, and they will send out administrators. Then, you collect a royalty check—I have no idea how much, but enough to keep you comfortable for life."

"They have asked to have a few Kipitz as part of your crew, who can communicate freely with the various planets and pass along your requests."

Chloe said, "Spies that try to control you?"

The original laughed, "No, they can be from anywhere, and they will be intermediaries. In a way, they will be some of the most powerful Kipitz that ever lived, and in other ways, mere servants. They will serve on your ship and answer to you, but their words will be the law on any of the Kipitz worlds."

Mark said, "Even someone like the cleaning lady we hired on the Caspin Station?"

Mee said, "If that is who you want, if it is someone you can trust."

Chloe said, "Wait, maybe this is like a bad inheritance. Are you about to have an insane debt you must pay or something like that?"

The original said, "I always have my debt canceling ship. Actually, I have a Nest full of them."

"No, I don't need or want anything like that."

Both Mees walked over to me, and they said, "And that is the reason you are the only being for the job."

… … …

The connection came into Lieutenant General McMasters' office on a quantum channel, and there were only a few of them. He looked, and it was the link with the red highlighted name next to it. He sighed and hit the connect button.

"Good afternoon. You actually called me at 2:15 in the afternoon. To what do I owe the call that isn't waking me up in the middle of the night?"

I said, "We have a bit of a situation."

He sighed, "How bad."

"You probably need to get some of the world leaders together for this call."

"Are you asking the Earth to surrender? Have you finally gone off the deep end and joined with the mad empress?"

Instance 49 of Mee then stood to one side of me, "Is that what you think of me?"

I give General McMasters great credit for not soiling himself at that moment. I said, "General, this is the Forty-ninth instance of Mee Keralatazaku, the supreme ruler."

He managed to say "Hello."

Then, the other Mee stood to my other side.

"And this is the original Mee Keralatazaku, number one."

What he said at that point was just mumbling. A few seconds later, he at least returned to breathing.

I said, "I have a deal for you."

He said, "I thought you said I needed to get some of the other world leaders in on this call."

"You can ask… tell them later. The Kipitz, all of them, have surrendered."

"Well, that was what we expected."

"About that… They are following the Caspin Station model, the one place where the local Kipitz are not worried about Mee Keralatazaku, where they are happy and have a decent standard of living. They all surrendered to me."

"Ah… Ah… Ah… What?"

"Yeah, I now own several dozen planets, space stations, probably hundreds, if not thousands of ships, and I don't want to deal with any of it. I want to lease it all to the Earth."

"There is no way we can afford to pay for even a fraction of that."

"The lease is a 99-year lease, and I retain control. I can terminate the lease on any portion of the property whenever I want. The lease will be for $1 a year."

"Well, the amount is not the issue, it will be the logistics, the ships."

"I have lots of ships."

"The people may not want us to manage them."

"The alternative is for Mee to deal with them. The Earth's governments are filled with people who just live for government jobs, those bean counters who thrive off this stuff. Now they have a place to go and can be good managers."

"And if they are not good managers?"

The two Mee's laughed in unison.

"Never mind, that was a stupid question. Almost all will do the right thing, and the ones that are morons get to sit in an airlock… If they are lucky."

I said, "I will send you the inventory, planets, populations, space stations, ships, all that stuff. It will be a large spreadsheet. I am sure someone will want specifications on all the ships, what the populations do, and make all that stuff. Call me back after you let the government people know what we have started."

Then we disconnected the line.

Jessie said, "He held it in for the call, but he bolted for the toilet and threw up as soon as the line disconnected."

Chloe said, "That is a little more information than I needed to know."

Kibbiea said, "Grey skin. I want our child to have grey skin. I will tell my Mother that Mee contributed to her genetic makeup and that her granddaughter is related to Mee Keralatazaku. She will fricking blow a gill."

The original chuckled, "She seems fun."

Instance 49 said, "I can have all of our AIs look into whatever tweaking you want for the genetics."

Mark said, "Whatever you want, honey. Hey, we can probably give your planet some spare ships. We have a lot now."

I said, "Your share of $1 lease per year comes to… That ship may take a while."

Mark said, "Can't you just keep some for yourself… or us?"

I laughed, "Yes, I can. Only, for some of the ships, I think most probably already have owners, and seizing them would be an asshole thing. Sorry, not talking to your AI."

Asshole said, "I am the most advanced AI in the known galaxy; I think I can figure out when you are asking me a question and when you are using my name as an expressive phrase. Now, that can sometimes be hard to tell with the Original."

I said, "As much fun as verbal sparring with an AI that holds all the weapons is, we still have a few things to discuss before General McMasters, the secretary general of the U.N., or one of the presidents calls me back."

"What?"

"The octagon-shaped biologicals may be the repair bio-drones to keep the scanner ship valves clear, but we haven't answered the question, where are the aliens that sent the scanner ship out? Given their technology, they sound like they may be a threat to the Nest, to all of us."

The original said, "Are you worried about them?"

"They have a technology that we don't. We have one of their sensors, but what do we do if they show up? What if they are armed? We have mostly figured out how to operate the one we have, but we haven't figured out how to replicate it or fix the bugs that that version has, so we have a better, more reliable version of it."

Chloe said, "Oh, I get it."

"Huh? What?"

Mark said, "D'oh, it took a while, but now that you said it out loud, it is the only possibility. The reason that asshole isn't in threat containment mode."

Kibbiea still had a puzzled look on her face.

Then, it dawned on me, "You bitch, it was your technology all along?"

The original burst out laughing. "Asshole wanted a way to keep track of other ships, especially those in FTL. Now that we have Hyper FTL, and you have proved the sensor works in that and pointed out some now obvious flaws that Asshole missed, we can fix the problems. Yes, the bio-droids serve Asshole, and therefore, they serve me."

Instance 49 said, "It is, of course, classified to only you and the bridge crew and the scientists working on it. From the look of it, that was every single scientist on your ship, and I show only the dependents having actually done any sleeping in the last 35 hours."

I sighed, "Did cramming for the test help?"

Chloe said, "I think they passed the test but probably won't remember half of it tomorrow. I feel like we just had a Mid-Term test."

Asshole said, "I have reviewed the logs on your ship, the data they found is extremely valuable, and it points me at what needs to change to make the sensor more stable. The question remains: what is the best use for it? It was a prototype for tactical surveillance, but its use as a Hyper FTL pre-hop scanner now seems far more valuable."

BUY OR LEASE

Three hours later, Jessie said, "You have a call from Earth."

It was the general who called. What was unexpected was that he had apparently already flown down from the station and was in the U.N. General Assembly Hall. It looked full, and I seemed to remember that it held a lot of people.

The camera was positioned in the back of the room, looking at everyone looking up to the stage. A massive TV, or possibly a projector, was set up behind the row of people sitting in front. I recognized the general in the row of dignitaries. Behind them on the screen was the image we were transmitting: me, Chloe, Mark, Kibbiea, and, of course, both Mee's.

Someone I didn't recognize was sitting at the front center under my image, "Good evening, I am Lars Olson. We would like to… clarify a few points in the offer you made. Is now a good time to talk?"

I noticed that the entire assembly was absolutely quiet.

I replied, "Yes."

"We have been looking at the list you sent us. It is quite extensive. Is the offer an all-or-nothing deal?"

"The offer is for all the listed items, with the exception of possibly some ships that did not have anyone who is considered an owner. In those cases, I may want to assign possession of a specific ship or ten as I see fit."

"That is not an issue. Did you also wish to keep any of the planets for yourself?"

"Any of the planets that have colonies or entire civilizations of the Kipitz are part of the deal. This is to improve life for the Kipitz; this is not to exploit, take advantage of, or mistreat them. They chose this option primarily as a way to be governed in a way that does not offend Mee Keralatazaku. They seek a rewarding and happy life, free from the terror that was recently over their heads."

I could see the image being displayed behind them, and both Mee's were now smiling. It was not a reassuring smile.

"What about cash reserves, things like vaults full of resources, minerals, stocks, bonds, currency."

"The money, the resources, everything belongs to me. That said, I don't want to have to deal with any of it. Some people in America own businesses, cars, and houses; I assume similarly, the Kipitz, who owned things, lots of things, will still own them. The government will still have to operate and maintain infrastructure; roads need to be maintained, and spaceports need to be maintained. The difference is that many of the higher government management positions are now… empty. Some were fired, others were not so lucky. I assume the operation of the Caspin Station is proving to be mutually beneficial to the Kipitz who live and work there and the humans who are organizing things. I think this is what they are looking for. Build roads, not warships, build farms, and feed the people. There is no villain, there is no enemy they need to oppress or hate. The schools need to be revised; the factories need to be organized. It is a chance to be altruistic and still make a massive profit. The former governments were skimming enough money aside to pay for the machines of an impending war. The war is over. That is what Mee Keralatazaku is. She is the ender of wars. Don't start wars, and she will be a good neighbor and nothing more."

The image on the screen now showed both Mee Keralatazaku's, the most dangerous beings in the galaxy, had gotten bored and were now sharing a bag of banana chips.

"How do we deal with issues that will crop up? Some people will object to our rule, and I am sure there will be some bad people?"

I said, "You do the best you can. If you mess up, you try and fix the screwup. If you run into something you can't resolve, and I don't mean little stupid crap, then you call me, and if I can't fix it, one of these two may have to… adjust things."

"How do we divide up everything?"

The camera zoomed in on my face. I said, "A partnership of all of you, and with respect to the Kipitz. If a group of you tried to impart stupid, heavy-handed authoritarian rule to a peaceful group of the Kipitz, what would they do? What did they do on Caspin Station?"

Someone near the end of the row said, "As I have read in the transcripts, they were literally ripped to shreds. The teeth are not only for decorations."

"Benevolent rulers will be gladly followed. Wannabe dictators will be… dealt with by the locals, in a way they see fit. I will not object to their handling of those that try and screw them over. I will object to them causing problems for no reason."

The discussions lasted for hours, but the main items were already covered. I was the landlord, and Mee was the local police.

Eventually, they accepted the offer. Lieutenant General McMasters sat on one end of the table and never spoke during the meeting.

Then, the link disconnected. Mee said, "Are they always like that?"

Mark said, "That was one of the more productive meetings I have heard of them having."

I said, "Are we done?"

Mee said, "No, now that the Earth has agreed to their part, we get to have a call with the Kipitz to say you have accepted their offer."

I groaned, thinking it would be even worse than the U.N. meeting.

It wasn't; perhaps thirty Kipitz were in a simple concrete-walled room. For this call, it was just me on the screen.

Someone said, "Are you the human Benjamin Williams, the owner of the Caspin Station?"

"Yes."

"Do you accept the offer we made?"

"What is the offer?"

"We transfer government ownership of everything to you to rule as you do the Caspin Station."

"And in return, what do you get?"

"To sleep peacefully, to wake from the nightmare, to live a normal life, and not to offend she who must not be offended."

I said, "I will, like on Caspin Station, have others from Earth handle the daily operations, and they will have many of you to do the actual work."

"That is the best we can hope for."

I said, "I accept."

It erupted into pandemonium, and there was jumping, cheering, yelling, waving, and hugging.

What followed was a cacophony of words that all ran together, and "thank you" seemed the most common.

Eventually, that connection was disconnected.

Mark said, "Well, that is now done. What's next?"

THE UPGRADE

The ships got another set of upgrades. The sensor we had, slightly banged up, repaired, and crammed into an area that wasn't meant to hold it, was replaced with a smaller unit. It was very similar, but the display unit was duplicated into two parts. The second display unit was on the bridge and was for display only. The display with all the controls was mounted in the primary science room. Unlike the engineering of Star Trek, that room was more of a laboratory and had less of a control role.

We did not get any of the bio-drones. The Munchkins could make the repairs the same way the bio-drones did. The main difference was we now had two of the sensor units. One was a warm spare. It could be activated and chilled down to operating temperature in about twenty minutes. The cool-down phase was the delay, and icing was still the biggest issue, but we should be okay with a spare. They didn't tend to fail suddenly; the icing would slowly start clogging one or several of the cryogenic ports, and we could enable the second sensor. After it was active, we could power down the one with icing. If it couldn't be cleared by venting and heating the sensor to boil off the ice, then the Munchkins could clear the clog with a pipe cleaner. We also now had the sensor walled in, and it had a separate airlock around it. Getting the Munchkins to make a repair would be a lot faster and safer.

The Munchkins had all been going into the medical pods for additional upgrades as well. That included the ones on their ship and the four we had on this ship. They were now comfortable on the upper level of our ship, with 0.47G, and could tolerate the second level at 0.62G for short periods. They tried to get down to the lower level, with 0.77G occasionally, but only when they wanted to get in the pool. They retreated to the upper level as soon as they left it. The 'wall of water' stuck to the floor that was the pool was originally terrifying, and the fact that you needed to keep your head up to breathe was a lesson learned by swallowing a lot of water and getting dragged out and tossed into a medical pod… several times.

We were getting ready to leave when we were asked to visit the control chamber on the Nest.

Instance 49 was waiting there. She said, "Well, this will start the final part of the transfer. I will be stuck in the chamber for almost thirty days, and when I emerge, there will be two versions of me. The human, Meera Fathi, and the Regiolon. The earlier part grew the body, but with a mostly empty brain, it did the rough copying of all the neural pathways, the neural interconnection, and pathways resulting from living and learning. The next part does the detail copying. I have done a version of this 49 times before and know what to expect. Here is the kicker. What will emerge will be two copies of instance 50. It will be about 98% of me, but there will be two versions of that. Both will be reset to the biological age of twenty; we will be younger, healthier, and stronger. Dylan, hug me."

He did, and they held the hug for over a minute.

Then she said, "Don't miss me. I will be back."

Then she climbed into the dual chambers, one containing the future human version of Meera and the other now containing Instance 49.

The lid closed, and we just stood there for a bit.

Then the Original entered. She wandered over to the machine, looked at the display, and said, "It is done. That instance of me is no more. The new version will be reborn in one of your months."

Dylan said, "We discussed this… a lot. Any version of Meera you see walking around in her old avatar for the next four weeks will be the Original." He had some tears in his eyes, "She is sacrificing herself, and she will be reborn."

He approached the Original, hugged her, and said, "How do you do it?"

She said, "I gave up on my life during that accursed war a very long time ago. I had to clean up the bodies of my shipmates and the path I chose… to create an AI with no computation limits and program it with a prime directive, 'to end wars.' I have often regretted that choice, but I also know that it was the only choice."

She put her hands on Dylan's shoulders. "You treat her well; she is me, and that instance of her, number 50B, will be the only version of me that will know that form of happiness in over 2,000 years. Of course, me being the grandmother of your children will be a bit fun." She smiled, "In a way."

"Now, you have to leave, or the big bad ruler of the galaxy will start crying. When they wake up, either she will come to where you are, or I will have you come where we are. I still have to wear my evil overlord mask and make a few more appearances. My new life is so very different from what the last version of me went to sleep in. It is not nearly as depressing now as when I first created this path."

Then, we exited the Nest's control room, returned to our ship, and climbed to the bridge, which had a new display of the world around us.

I said, "Jessie, who is on the second ship?"

"Katerina Popov is taking a turn as the captain of that ship."

"We should probably take a trip back to the Earth and get some permanent crew assigned to that ship instead of rotating in temporary people to operate it."

Katerina said, "They did some upgrades on this one, so it shouldn't be hard to find people who want to be crew. They put in a small centrifuge, one level, and only five rooms. Captain's quarters, crew quarters, cafeteria, and the bridge. The support ship also has a new reactor similar to this one."

Jessie said, "She is omitting something important. They stole the Pac-Man machine from the recreation room. That version is wired up to over 8,000 classic arcade games."

I laughed, "I know, we saw them do that on the surveillance video. We will pick up another when we get to Earth.

Chloe was leaning back in her seat, rubbing her belly. "We have a doctor on the ship; it is time to see if the nanny wants the job. Your daughter will be ready to say hello in three months, maybe less; I can't believe how much she has grown."

Mark said, "She will have a playmate in about nine months. We finally selected all the genetic tweaks for Kibbiea's child."

Kibbiea said, "Our child, her tail freckles will be pink. That took a lot of tweaking, but the AI found a way to almost match Mark's skin color."

We watched the Nest disappear off the sensor.

I said, "Hmm, neat trick; how did it disappear?"

Jessie said, "The entire Nest now has Hyper FTL. It jumped."

"Well, set a course for the Earth. Hopefully, this trip will be less eventful than Mark's wedding."

Both ships then jumped into Hyper FTL.

EARTH

The ships had again performed the now-routine exit of Hyper FTL and pretended to be using conventional FTL near any planet.

We exited standard FTL, and I said, "Jessie, status?"

"Extremely crowded, fifty-seven ships are decelerating and approaching the Earth, over two hundred ships are in orbit around the Earth, and about another one hundred have landed in various spaceports. Almost the first message we received was asking if Crystal Johnstone wanted her old job back. They are swamped."

Crystal said, "Hell no, That is a fricking circus down there, this job involves some light duty, but when we are in space or docked, I have more time off than I did in the last three years. Also, I am now engaged to Josh Fence. Unless he gets reassigned, you are now stuck with me."

Jessie said, "You have a message. "Then the voice changed to a man's: "Miramber Station, please identify the new arrivals from FTL."

I said, "Captain Benjamin Williams on the Stardust II, heading in for resupply and probably crew rotations. Traveling with the support ship, the Shadow."

"Oh Crap, Yes sir, sorry, I will have a space cleared for you to dock immediately."

I said, "Call the general or whoever is in the station; they may have rearranged the command on it a bit."

"Connecting," the voice then changed to Lieutenant General McMasters. "Hello. We were expecting you, but we thought you may wait until the chaos died down a bit, assuming it ever does. Do you need to dock, or what is this trip for?"

"My daughter will be arriving in a little over two months, and we figured we would pick up the nanny if she is still interested. We also need a more permanent crew assignment for the second ship. It can hold… one captain's room and another stateroom, currently configured to hold four. I suppose the captain can be married, but it is just one room. Its task is mostly to shadow us. It has some weapons and surveillance satellite deployment capabilities. It is our backup. It has many of the same non-standard features this ship does, so it is classified as… Whatever your highest classification is."

"I assume you just exited FTL. Are you about eight hours away?"

"We have a slightly reduced deceleration and came out further than most ships. We have a few new crew members; they are a species that you should have some records of. We have been referring to them as Munchkins."

"I have the reports on them. Are they up to normal intelligence yet? The last report had them… I think the word you used was feral."

"The adults will never be geniuses. The children and teenagers have had enough upgrades that they are about average but learning rapidly. They keep going into the medical pods and getting issues fixed and more upgrades. They should be able to handle normal Earth gravity in a few more months. They kick ass in zero gravity and easily outperform all the other races."

"Do you need to dock at the station with the main ships, or can you just send over a shuttle? All the main ports are booked for close to a week. We can have one of the other ships leave early if necessary."

"We can just use the shuttles. Where will the new crew be coming from? Also, where is Spencer Moreau?"

"Spencer is at the Kennedy Space Center, sitting in on training lessons. We have a three-week quickie astronaut training. How do you put on and wear the suits, and how do you hook up to the air connections on a ship? Everyone who will not be on a centrifuge ship gets one ride on one of the vomit comets. Most fail it, but at least they know what to expect. The other crew will probably be out of Wright-Patterson Air Force Base. It will be purely military people. Is that okay?"

"That should be fine. If they want, they can even rename the ship. They may want to add something to do. They have one retro-video game on the ship; they probably will want to add a few more modern gaming systems."

He laughed, "That will not be a problem. The military always finds ways to keep people busy. What is the expected duration for when they will be assigned to the ship?"

"At least six months, possibly a year. It may visit some locations it should not report, photograph, or even think too much about."

"We have had reports from Katerina Popov and Mei Zhou; they have only referred to it with a 4-letter name beginning with 'N' and indicate that nothing should ever be reported about it. How about the rest of the crew, the scientists?"

"They seem to be happy. The only ones that have seen the other site, have been the bridge crew. The sensor crews have seen some of the displays, but most of what was displayed didn't describe what it actually was. The ship has gone out of its way to limit exposure to anything related to that place."

"I am surprised they let Mei and Katerina see any of it."

"And I would not expect them to say much about it unless it was extremely critical."

"When I said a four-letter word beginning with an 'N,' that was all they said; they haven't even told me the name."

"Ha, that says a lot. Should we send down a shuttle for the second crew, or will you send one up with the crew?"

"We will send up a crew; flying the shuttle will probably be the only actual flying experience they get."

"No, they will get to do a lot of the FTL entry and exits and docking to stations."

"Oh, speaking of stations, we have an add-on being transferred over. It's a docking port extender; the extension does not include a centrifuge. It should arrive in a week, and then it will be attached to the top of this one. It lets nine additional medium-sized ships dock.

We have a lot of Kipitz ships coming in, wanting some humans on board and wanting to know what they should do. Then, they are more than happy to deliver the humans wherever we want to go. Honestly, it is freaking out the high command."

"Let us know when the replacement crew is ready to dock. I will call the Kennedy Space Center and get the dispatcher's contact information."

Jessie said, "I have the address. Should I contact them?"

"Yes."

"Hello, Kennedy Space Central special shuttle coordination. How may I direct your call?"

"We need to reach a trainee, Spencer Moreau, and then arrange a landing to pick her up."

"Please hold; I will search for her pager; who should I say is calling?"

"Benjamin Williams…"

"Eeep… Sorry sir. Sorry, I have no idea what your preferred title is."

"Captain is fine."

Two minutes later, the connection changed.

"Spencer Moreau here. How can I help you?"

"Hi, Spencer. It is Benjamin. Chloe is here, and her belly is getting large enough that we want you on board to help her figure out a normal life routine. I think a few others may need your services in less than a year."

"Great, I have been learning a lot, but honestly, I get a lot of stares when I say what ship I will be assigned to. After a while, I just said a transporter, but your ship's reputation spread even if I didn't say the name."

"Well, we have a shuttle we will send down, and dispatch will contact you. Oh, the baby will be a girl. We have replicators, so you don't need to pack a lot of the same items. The ship can scan them and create most items. That even works for things like diapers and wipes... Honestly, she will be our first, so we don't have a clue what to expect."

"I have been sitting for so many people. They posted a link saying I needed nanny practical experience, and I think everyone assumed that meant no notice or free babysitting. I could probably change a diaper one-handed now."

I said, "The display shows that a shuttle will arrive at parking spot G5 and be waiting for you at 3:30 PM local time. The standard clothing carry allotment is what fits in a duffel bag. You get a max of three duffel bags or two and a hard case. There is a pool, but it is small and usually crowded."

"I sunburn wicked easy. Does it have artificial sunlight? Do I need sunblock?"

"No, it is a saltwater pool, and they require you to shower before entering if you have perfumes or deodorants on. You can't wear things that can get in someone's gills. Not all the beings that use it are human."

… … …

She showed up with two duffel bags and one small hard case.

Six people were on the shuttle, wearing dress uniforms for the U.S. Space Force. One asked, "Do they have permission to carry extra luggage and wear civilian clothing?"

"Yeah, this is my uniform: a cute short skirt and a blouse. At least I'm wearing flats this time. I am Spencer Moreau."

One of them looked up from a display, "It lists her as a civilian and assigned to the main ship. We are all going to be on the support ship. It says we dock to the main ship, transfer her, and then head to the second ship. The crew on this shuttle will then be transported back to the main ship. Oh, I am Lieutenant Danvers. This is Clause, Reddy, Mulhouse, and Crutch. My wife, Claire, is the one over there with the look that says she will smack me in the head if I keep talking."

Spencer said, "I have met Ben and Chloe before; they seemed normal. Mark is a bit of a strange one, but given that his wife isn't a human, that is to be expected."

"You have been on the ship before?"

"No, well, I rode a shuttle before and visited the station. Of course, that was back before all the stuff with the alien war and them surrendering, and now we are playing peacekeepers or something like that."

He sighed, "With luck, we will slowly get introduced to all the craziness."

She chuckled, "Don't count on that; the crazy parts seem to be part of the normal routine."

… … …

The ship lifted off very smoothly, and instead of docking at the space station, the shuttle maneuvered to an open space with only two ships floating in it. One was much larger than the second, so we docked to the larger ship.

The docking went quickly, and the sound was quieter. The earlier docking had been rushed, and the latch made more of a clanging sound before the springs made their twang sound.

The inner door opened, followed by the outer door, another door, and finally, the other ship's inner door. We were in zero gravity, and in front of me were a few much more casually dressed enlisted military types and Chloe with her now obvious large belly bump.

Chloe said, "I like the zero-G compartments now. This belly is uncomfortable in every position I have tried to sleep in. Follow me; these two can help with your luggage… Three bags? You may have to carry one yourself. Anyway, follow me."

"The first deck is the lowest gravity, Captain's suite, which has our room and a small living room, a nursery, and your room unless you want to share a room with the enlisted or some of the scientists. This also has more lab space, the officer's quarters, and the bridge. That is usually restricted access, but if you need access, just state why out loud before you open the door. The AI is Jessie, and she is reasonable."

"The second deck is mid-gravity and mostly rooms for the crew."

"The last deck is the kitchen, cafeteria, recreation room, game room, and the pool. It also has some medical pods and a lab."

Chloe showed Spencer to her room, and Spencer seemed happy with it. "Hey, at least this time, I don't have roommates that snore."

Chloe said, "Oh, you haven't met the Munchkins yet; we didn't have them on the ship last time you were here."

"Munchkins? Like the cats or the Wizard Of Oz?"

She laughed, "The Wizard Of Oz, divergent aliens who may be somewhat related to humans. There is a weak genetic link, and that has baffled the geneticists. They spent a quarter of a million years stranded in a broken ship with no gravity. Evolution favored the small, and they just kept getting smaller."

"Just how small are they?"

"Humans with Dwarfism are usually between three and a half to four and a half feet tall. The Munchkins came in at an average of two feet and ten inches for the males, and the females were two inches shorter. They also had bones that were partially cartilage. They had a lot less bone mass than any humans. They have been getting treatments in the medical pods, sometimes twice a week, to build their bone density to survive gravity better."

"Are they making them taller as well?"

"Very slowly, originally, they all had malnutrition and a bunch of other issues, making it hard on them."

Jessie said, "They are an average of 2.5 inches taller than when we first found them."

"How many were there?"

There were fifty; we have four on this ship and forty-six on another ship."

Jessie said, "Fifty-one, they had a successful birth on the other ship."

"Damn, I am shocked they survived; With only 50 individuals, the inbreeding must have been terrible to their genetics. Or maybe they used to have much larger tribes?"

"We are not sure; They were dying, if not in a few generations, then in ten at the most. The air reserves had finally run out, and it was slowly leaking away. Only half of the ship still had working lights, which were needed for the plants, their primary food source. Hey, did you want to see the pool? Did you bring a bathing suit?"

"A black two-piece."

"You seem to have toned down the goth look."

"I still have the makeup, but it seemed out of place on the base. I'm not sure about wearing it at the pool. Ben said something about not wanting chemicals there."

… … …

They both changed into suits, and the two of them had made it to the entrance to the pool when Chloe suddenly yelled, "Crap, my damn water broke; I am not due for over two months; I am not having any contractions; Jessie, call the doctor!"

SURPRISE

Our ship usually (*somehow*) ran like a well-oiled machine; Chloe's water-breaking immediately put everything into total confusion.

Two of the enlisted showed up with a strange stretcher, and they carried her up to the captain's suite. We had a medical pod in our room. It had been in the spare room, which was now Spencer's room. Chloe was immediately put in the medical pod.

Sophia Doukas was trained as a neurologist but had some (*we hoped*) obstetrical experience. When she first boarded our ship, she entered a medical pod, and it had regrown her two missing fingers. Regrowing their nerves was slow, but she now had partial feelings in her fingers, just not the tips yet.

Sophia said, "The baby is doing fine, but the mother will be stuck in the pod for a while. There is no way to stitch the embryonic sack back together. The baby is almost five pounds, safe to deliver, but considered premature. The longer she stays in the womb, the better the baby will do. If the mother or the baby has any complications, the pod can perform an emergency cesarian section and then put her back together as good as new. There won't even be any scar. She is awake and can hear what we say. Say hello."

I said, "Hi honey, how are you?"

"Embarrassed as all hell, my water burst."

"That is normal."

"Tell that to James Smith, the twelve-year-old boy, he was in the splash zone."

I stood in stunned silence, "I don't have a clue what to say to that."

Jessie said, "Spencer stayed in the pool area and cleaned up the mess. As shaken up as James may have initially been, seeing Spencer in her bikini on her hands and knees cleaning up the mess seems to have thoroughly distracted him. He seems to be a healthy twelve-year-old boy."

Chloe laughed and then cut it short, "Oh poop, I probably shouldn't laugh now."

I said, "Do we need to dock to the station? Or do we need to bring over a different doctor?"

Sophia said, "We are fine for now, but staying close to the station is not a bad idea. Did we have someplace we needed to be?"

"No, we have something to do in… about twenty-eight days, but nothing at the moment. We should probably pick up more food…"

Then the Meera avatar came walking in, "What is the problem?"

"The baby decided to start the process of delivery early. Her water broke. Actually, I don't know if that is the same as your species."

She paused, "I will need to look up how the human parts work. I know how our parts work."

An alarm I didn't recognize sounded.

I yelled, "What is that?"

Jessie said, "We had an overshoot. They exited FTL too close to the sun, halfway between Jupiter and Mars. They lost power. They have hit one of the smaller asteroids in the main asteroid belt. The ship is Kipitz, and the crew has reported they are losing air. None of them were killed yet, but they are tumbling. Everyone is in suits, but they are not EVA suits, and they will run out of air in two hours."

"Let me guess; no one can reach them in time to rescue them?"

"Good guess, they are marginal. Some will make it if they remain perfectly calm and conserve air. Not all will."

"Crap, prepare to rescue them. Have the other crew made it to the support ship?"

"Yes, and they have transferred in; Katerina and the others are in the shuttle on their way here."

I said, "Tell the other ship to prepare to support us; their drive will not be responding to manual controls. Tell them their security clearance just got a gold star. Prepare both ships to do a small Hyper FTL jump as soon as the shuttle is docked. Tell them to dock and stay in the shuttle; they are about to earn their pay."

Chloe said, "When it rains, it pours, Ahhh, crap, I think I got my first contraction."

"Honey, just try and relax… Probably not that easy to do at the moment."

Jessie said, "Docking in progress; I am not rushing the docking; we need to wait for a clean capture latch."

<Clunk> "Soft Capture, engaging the clamps, closing the shuttle bay outer door."

<Thud> "Hard capture, waiting for the oscillations to dampen out, engaging secondary clamps, "We are go for Hyper FTL."

I said, "Jump."

We reappeared in the blackness of space, the Earth no longer below us.

We made an extra correction; the new scanner showed the asteroid they hit and all its little brothers. We came out 522 kilometers from the ship, engaging the friction drive; the distance was too short to do a second jump, and the area was full of debris from the rock they hit and some metallics, part of their hull.

"Is the second ship with us?"

"Yes, and they are wondering what just happened."

I said, "Tell them my ships have non-standard drives. We are attempting to rescue a ship in distress. Have two of your people get in the shuttle. They may need to assist in the rescue. Have any of you practiced in EVA suits?"

"We have, but in earth EVA suits, those look nothing like these."

"Same principles, Jessie, multitask, walk them through putting the suits on."

Katerina said, "We were not dressed for an EVA; we are only wearing our entry and landing suits, and they are only good for two hours."

"And if we go past two hours, it becomes a recovery, not a rescue."

She whispered, "I am much better at killing people, not rescuing them."

I pretended not to hear her.

Jessie said, "E.T.A. is six minutes and seventeen seconds; we are about to do 1.5G acceleration and then deceleration. All of the Munchkins are safe in medical pods."

I said, "Did you hear that? Top off the air reserves in your suits, and prepare to launch the shuttle as soon as we know the situation. Is a ship-to-ship dock a possibility?"

"Unknown, depends on where the damage occurred."

Our ship started hard acceleration toward the other ship.

"Scanners, what's going on on the ship? Is this a rescue or a trap? Do they have weapons?"

"Scanner crew here, the ship shows no unusual weapons activations. They have only one antimissile Gatling gun, and it looks like a much older model than the one we had on our first ship. It's powered off. I show ten biologicals. At this range, there is no species detail. Some are smaller, possibly children. I may be able to get more details on them before we reach them."

"Jessie, if they activate any weapons, do not wait for confirmation or a command; neutralize the weapons."

"Yes, that is what I planned to do; it is easier to ask for forgiveness than permission."

Six minutes later, we were decelerating and approaching the ship.

"Have they said anything else?"

"Negative, their quantum link through dispatch went down. They probably did not expect a radio to be of any use."

"Broadcast on all the channels and see if they are listening on any. We need to board the ship. Maybe they have... We should be close enough for the scanner to see all the biologicals. Where are they on the ship?"

"All but one have grouped together in the ship's main area; one looks like they are attempting to make a repair. They are next to the friction drive."

Mark said, "If they fix the ship themselves, then we just demonstrated that we have Hyper FTL on our ships for no reason."

"And if they don't, they die. We will figure out something later. Is the docking port clear?"

"Yes, we should be able to do ship-to-ship docking without needing to use the shuttles. Do we dock with this ship or have the support ship dock with them?"

"This ship, we know what we are doing, and it is impossible for someone to seize control of this ship... except for Mee."

Meera came in, rubbing her ass, "Stupid avatar rebooted again; at least it didn't do much damage to itself. And no, I can't take control of your ship. Instance 49 loaded your ship with all sorts of safeguards to prevent that."

"Initiate docking with the ship. They should immediately know that someone has docked with them. Mei, greet them with stunners if they don't play well with others."

Thirty seconds later <Clunk> "We have soft closure."

That was followed by the twang sound of the compression springs and "Hard closure confirmed."

Jessie said, "They have lost all pressure. Go into the airlock and see if you can find a terminal. If one is active, tell them a rescue is in progress."

"Sensors here, they are now moving. I think they are headed to the airlock. The one doing the repairs seems to have collapsed."

"Send in two to retrieve the one that is down; have someone direct the others to the airlock. How many of them can the airlock hold?"

"If they are in standard Kipitz entry/exit suits, they can cram four in the airlock. Maybe five if it is all small children."

"Frankenstein here; I am outside the airlock; the other two are going after sleeping beauty."

Mark laughed, "Sorry, I would definitely see that movie."

Frankenstein replied, "Asshole. Contact, it looks like a rag-tag group of Kipitz; several are limping, and at least half are children. I am waving them toward the airlock."

Jessie said, "The first four are in the airlock."

I said, "Six remaining. Who are the greeters inside the airlock?"

Katerina said, "Me and Landers, Fence is acting as a backup down the hallway."

Chloe said, "She is such a trusting soul."

I said, "She is paid well to be paranoid."

Katerina said, "The first four are in the ship; we need medical pods. The Kipitz medical data set should be part of standard configurations and loaded on all pods."

Mee said, "With the exception of my avatar's pod. That is not usable for anything else."

Frankenstein said, "The second group of four is being cycled into the airlock."

"Lieutenant Danvers here, are you keeping an eye on the other asteroids? We have a proximity alarm that says something is on the radar."

"Crap, sensors here. We were too busy looking at the close stuff. We need to remove it. There is an incoming rock the size of a fricking refrigerator."

"Jessie, activate the Gatling guns on the second ship. Have it try to make gravel out of the refrigerator. Can we fire the guns on this ship while we are docked?"

"Not possible. The docked ship is between us and the target. Computing range, firing now."

In space, there was no sound.

However, on the second ship, they heard the full roar of the Gatling guns, and we could hear the sound from the microphone on the support ship.

"The second group of four is now in our ship. There are still two more of them, and we still have three of our people on the ship."

"Frankenstein here, the last one of them is being carried here by our guys. They seem to be non-responsive."

The sound of the Gatling guns stopped.

Jessie announced, "The second ship initiated an emergency jump to escape the debris path. Prepare for impacts."

It sounded like someone throwing a handful of rocks at a steel plate, and then, as quickly as it started, silence returned.

"The airlock seal is still intact, so we are doing the next load of refugees. Three of our people remain on the other ship."

There was a distant bang and rumble.

Katerina said, "Launching the shuttle."

Jessie said, "It is maneuvering to dock with the ship. All airlock doors are now closed, and this ship is now disconnecting. We are backing away, jump in 3, 2, 1 (jump).

"We should be safe here. We left the shuttle behind, and it immediately docked where we just disconnected."

Sixty seconds later, "Sensors here. The other ship just suffered an explosion, and the sensor is now unreadable from all the debris. I believe the shuttle had already undocked from the damaged ship. Now I see the shuttle moving away rapidly."

"Change to scan for biologicals. Are our people in the shuttle?"

"Scanning, yes, they are all on the shuttle; the shuttle is now rapidly maneuvering away from the derelict."

"Move to rendezvous with the shuttle. Are we in contact with them?"

"Frankenstein here, we took some damage. Did you get the last load?"

Jessie said, "They were in the airlock when we jumped. They are now safely in the ship, and the airlock is secure. There was minimal damage to this ship; the gravel from the asteroid mostly hit the other ship. It did less damage than the refrigerator-sized rock would have. That would have easily punched through both of the ships."

DAMAGE CONTROL

We remained in the asteroid field until after we docked with our shuttle and successfully retrieved all of our crew.

Meera was sitting on the floor, on her ass. "That was my own damn fault; I should have known you would need to jump again. That was rather exciting, well, up until this stupid avatar rebooted. I changed its logic so it tries to assume a safe position and not just fall over. In this case, safe was to fall on my ass."

Dylan started laughing, "I'm not gonna say it. She would smack me silly."

Meera said, "Say what? That is the most padded place to land. These," she put her hands on her breasts, "have softer padding, but when I fall on my front, I smack my face up."

Trying hard not to laugh, I said, "Connect me to the captain of the ship we just rescued."

Someone said, "The captain is in a medical pod. He broke his arm and a few ribs. I am his wife, which probably makes me the second in command."

Someone else said, "It means you are usually in charge."

The first speaker said, "I am Zitti Froma; the one who spoke out of turn is my daughter, Criber. Thanks for rescuing us; the old tub we were on would have been paid off in twelve more payments. Is it salvageable?"

Jessie said, "The ship is scrap, but the cargo may be intact. What was the cargo?"

"Scrap metal, and by that, I mean it used to be considered passive ammunition. We were on our way to the smelter station at Karaboo, and everyone got the notice that the… situation changed. We sort of expected that, and that was why a load of perfectly good railgun slugs were on their way to become recycled aluminum. We figured we would stop by, and it looked like everyone had the same idea. We emerged from FTL, received a collision warning, and skipped back into FTL. When we emerged, we got a second warning. We hit stupid warnings three times, and the last wasn't a warning; we hit a rock."

I said, "There is a large asteroid belt between Mars, the fourth Rocky planet, and Jupiter, the largest of our gas giants. There are hundreds of ships around the Earth now and probably another couple of hundred jostling for position after exiting FTL."

"We had an update showing the planets and the moons, but the system data only listed a few large asteroids."

Jessie said, "The asteroid belt is mostly empty space and widely spaced rocks, but you skipped into a dense area."

"Well, thanks for the rescue. I assume you are humans; you have the goat teeth everyone jokes about. Err, sorry if that is offensive. I assume you were heading in from FTL if you somehow were close enough to our velocity that you pulled off the rescue. I suppose… Can we get dropped off at the Earth station? I have no idea how we will pay for the rescue or what we will do now."

I hit the mute button, "Jessie, how the hell were we at the proper velocity to rescue them? There is no way the Earth's rotation velocity just happened to be the correct velocity; it usually takes at least four hours to decelerate hard to match the Earth's velocity. They must have been at standard FTL exit velocity."

Meera said, "That was me. The other upgrade you got at the Nest was the inertial corrector. Both of your ships got it when you were in the Nest. Check the current draw when you did the jump."

Jessie said, "I would normally assume that reading had to be a glitch; that is almost nine thousand times the current that a normal reactor can even supply, and it held that for over 250 milliseconds."

Meera said, "I had the upgrade added, but it was disabled unless you were having an immediate threat to the ship. I enabled it for the rescue. The recharge before you can use that again will be almost six hours. I had visions of you doing a massive deceleration and crushing the Munchkins flat before you realized what you did."

"Crap, I probably would have done something stupid like that."

Jessie said, "They were ordered into medical pods as soon as the situation arose. Even in the pods, I would not recommend going past 2.5G. To match the ship's velocity, it would have taken you a maximum acceleration of 4.0G, and it would have taken close to an hour. They would not have survived."

I keyed the button to talk to the survivors again, "Sorry, we had some things to discuss. Can you describe who everyone is and what their skills are?"

"My husband is Tikker Froma, and I am Zitti Froma. My oldest daughter is Criber, and she is sixteen. Then there is Kelot, fourteen, and our little one, Mustil, who is ten. The others are my cousin, his wife, and their kids, four adults and six children, assuming the 16-year-old is classified as a child. Skills are ship repairs, which is evident by the fact we have kept this old bucket flying as long as it did. My husband flew a troop carrier back when he was in the military, and he was retired early when he first broke that gimp arm of his. They decided he wasn't worth putting him in a medical pod, but he did get a partial retirement. Then, we salvaged this ship from a scrap yard and have been repairing it ever since. I have no idea how we will pay to have the injured in medical pods. Those are ridiculously expensive. You must be rich to have more than one on a ship. We… didn't have one."

I hit the mute button again, "Well, what the hell are we to… Oh crap, How is Chloe doing?"

Her voice came over the speakers, "Nice of you to remember me. The contractions are now five minutes apart; it looks like our daughter wanted to be part of the excitement. Crap, another one is starting. Talk later…"

Jessie said, "The doctor is there, and the medical pod should be able to handle everything. The pods we have put in Earth hospitals have already assisted in dozens of deliveries. The pods are not sized for normal deliveries, and we are requesting that some be explicitly resized for that use."

"What do we do with the refugees? They sound like a collection of barely scraping-by families who were half a step better off than the ones on the Caspin Station."

Mark said, "Is the fact we have Hyper FTL known to everyone now?"

Jessie said, "Worse, they also saw the jump cancel your velocity, or in this case, add reverse velocity. I have muted all the traffic. Do you want to speak to any of them?"

"Hell no…. Wait.. maybe we can play this up. Connect me to a broadcast channel; you may as well link in the refugees as well."

"This is Captain Benjamin Williams. As most of you have already figured out, this ship exhibited some nonstandard maneuvers when we were rescuing a ship in distress. If anyone wants to ask about that, I suggest you ask the person beside me."

Then, I handed the microphone to Meera.

Her voice changed to match her normal Mee Keralatazaku voice: "This is Mee Keralatazaku. The nonstandard drive technology is restricted to my closest friends only. Are there any questions?"

The quantum link was quiet, not even static.

I hit the mute button.

I said, "How are the survivors doing?"

Emily said, "Some are still standing."

"Head back to the Miramber Station; we can drop them off there. Maybe we can find a ship of similar size, take ownership of it, clear the title so they are not in debt, and move them into the replacement ship. Try to get one that is a little newer than the clunker they had."

… … …

HELLO

Five hours later, we were now docked at the Miramber Station. The survivors in the medical pods were stable enough to be transferred to pods on the station. I was beside Chloe, who was covered in sweat and relaxing in a standard hospital bed.

The nurse had transferred our daughter, Tyra, into a medical pod that was acting like an incubator. Her weight was low, and her lungs were not entirely up to normal air. All indications were that she didn't need to stay in it for long. The medical pod would supplement her growth; she should gain almost 1.5 ounces daily.

Chloe said, "I wish I could have seen the faces of the people we rescued when Mee spoke."

I said, "Jessie recorded it. I watched it; the older daughter was the only one who wasn't in shock. She looked like she was having a great time and seemed to be enjoying her mother's shock."

She lay back with her eyes closed, "Our baby is beautiful."

I said, "She was after they cleaned her up."

"The pod is way too narrow for giving birth in. Order a wider one."

"You want another child?"

"Eventually, but not now. For the next one, I want to enter a pod and wake up refreshed and clean, and the baby will be all cleaned up. I would have asked for an epidural if I had done this in a regular bed. The pod did a great job of blocking most of the pain. She needs to stay in for a few weeks?"

She closed her eyes, "I am going to nap for a while now."

Then, she started gently snoring.

EPILOGUE

Thirty days later, we were watching the scanner display; it showed the approaching Nest. Our two ships were, as usual, operating in unison, and only a few hundred yards now separated them.

Mark said, "Well, Dylan, you should see her in a few minutes."

Dylan said, "I am a bit nervous; she hasn't linked to the avatar since she woke up. I thought she would want to talk to me as soon as she woke up."

"It has only been a few hours. The original said it was a success."

The portal on the Nest then iris'ed open.

Jessie said, "The docking coordinates are only for the main ship; the support ship gets to wait outside this time."

Lieutenant Danvers said, "That is fine from me; I have already seen enough."

Kibbiea sat in her seat, and a slight baby bump showed on her belly. She said, "Time for me to revisit the restroom. I think I will stay on the ship. I don't think I would do that well in zero gravity with how often I have gotten sick."

Mark said, "You should eject the egg in a few weeks. Hopefully, you will feel better then."

"My belly may go down, but I will still have to feed the egg."

Mark said, "It's not quite as bad as Aliens. I have watched some videos of it."

The ship entered the Nest, and the door closed as soon as we were inside.

Then, we proceeded to the docking port. After we completed the docking procedure, Jessie said, "Dylan, Ben, Chloe, and Mark for the initial introduction. Then they will probably enter this ship and want to see little Tyra after that."

We all proceeded into the zero gravity section and then out the front docking airlock.

We entered the control room to see the two Mee Keralatazaku in their Regiolon form. Next to them was a human female version, Meera, who looked identical to the avatar.

Meera walked over to Dylan and hugged him. "I am instance 50B of Mee Keralatazaku, and this is an entirely human body."

One of the two Mees then walked over to Dylan and Meera and said, "I am instance 50A of Mee Keralatazaku. We both have all the memories from instance 49. This sucks, she gets to be the human, and I am stuck as this…"

They both hugged her, and all three stayed together as a clump.

The other Regiolon said, "And I am the original Mee Keralatazaku. Can I join the group hug?"

Then, the four of them all embraced.

The group hug lasted several awkward minutes, and then they finally broke it up.

The two Regiolon versions said, "We have some stuff to do here. Go show Meera the little one."

The five of us left, with the human version of Meera holding Dylan's hand.

We returned to our ship, walked Meera into our suite, and then showed her Spencer, holding chubby little Tyra in her arms and rocking her to sleep.

This went on for a few minutes when Dylan suddenly yelled, "What the hell!"

We turned to see two other grinning instances of Meera now standing in the doorway. One was identical to the human version of Meera; that was probably the original avatar. The other looked slightly shorter, darker skinned, and her hair was blond and cut much shorter.

The one that looked identical to Meera said, "No way I can let her have all the fun. I am instance 50A, and you can now call me Anya when I wear the avatar; consider me her twin."

The other said, "I'm the original; why should I let these two have all the fun playing human? It was trivial to run off another avatar. I wanted us to look like triplets, but the other two messed with my avatar parameters and gave me short blond hair."

To be continued in the next book, "The Fourth Artifact."

ABOUT THE AUTHOR

David Collins is a retired software engineer who has worked on multiple projects, including submarine communications equipment, phased array sonar mapping, and medical technology.

His most recent work was on the Mobius Bionics LUKE Arm, developed when he worked at DEKA Research & Development: https://mobiusbionics.com/luke-arm

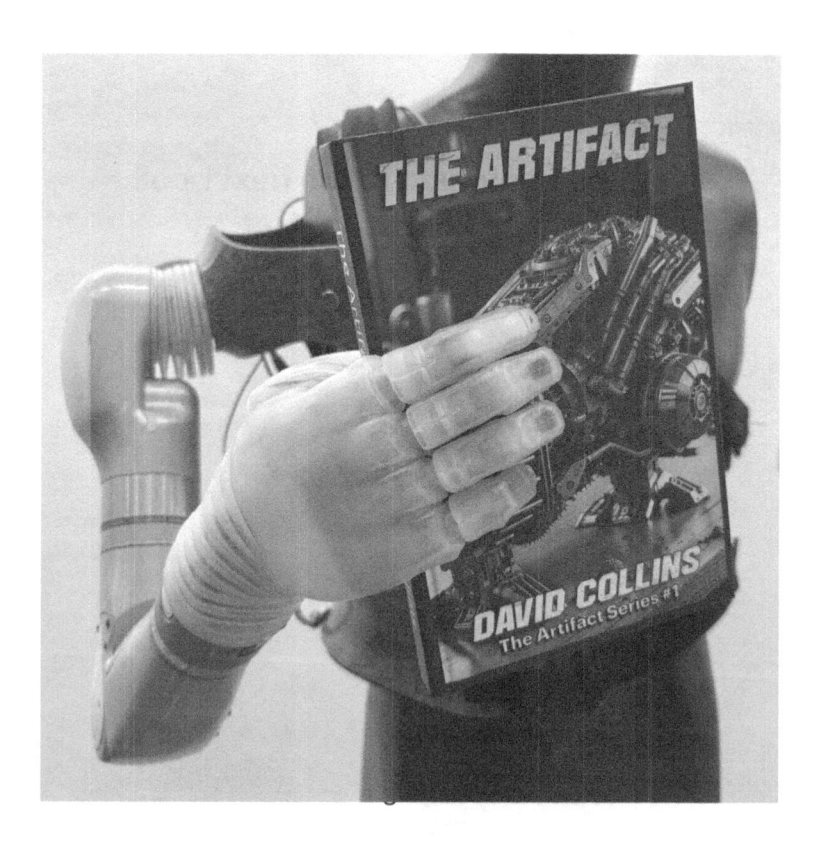

BOOKS BY DAVID COLLINS:

(The QR code to my author's page)

The Artifact
https://www.amazon.com/dp/B0DGFG7RXN

Benjamin, Mark, and Chloe were all set to graduate college in a few weeks.

Ben had ordered a strange object from eBay to use as cover art for a book he was writing.

It looked cool, like a slightly charred old military artifact from 70 years ago. It was possibly part of an engine. After cleaning it up (*it was found in a cow field*), he placed the strange device on his dorm room desk directly over the wireless charging port. It woke up.

Unknown to him, the disabled starship hiding on the moon could now communicate with the missing part.

The ship needed a crew to pass itself off as a manned ship (AIs were not supposed to be on ships).

A few weeks later, as recent college graduates, they need to find a way to get the ship to land somewhere safe, supply it, and return the missing component, the artifact.

They suspect the most challenging part will be getting into space. They soon find that the real problem is what awaits them when they reach the alien trading center.

Books:
1. The Artifact
2. The Second Artifact
3. The Third Artifact
4. The Fourth Artifact (*not yet released*)

The Wrong Button
https://www.amazon.com/dp/B0D3K6STP7

Jerry Anderson was an astronaut faced with an impossible choice: die of asphyxiation in a few hours or see if the alien pod he was transporting really was an escape pod and find out if it could actually save him.

When he enters it, he finds that the controls are unreadable, lacking anything to go on, and rapidly running out of air. He presses the blinking green button.

The next thing he knows, he isn't human anymore, and he finds himself on a seashore, next to some birds feasting on a body that looks very similar to his new body.

He is alive, but staying alive will be a challenge, and he will be able to communicate with the locals, assuming the next ones he finds don't kill him on sight.

Carbon Copy
https://www.amazon.com/dp/B0CW1HJ6ZY

Kaylee Green was an Illegal Alien, one that had traveled 45.7 light-years to get away from her pursuers.   A race that wanted to exterminate her kind.

Not only was she alien, but she was not entirely biological.   Now, she was enjoying life as a human.   She had recently graduated college and was happily living with her human boyfriend.

Then the police show up asking about a severed hand from a six-year-old cold-case investigation.   They want to know why her fingerprints and DNA both match the hand.

She was trying hard not to panic.   Her carefully crafted false identity was rapidly falling apart. What else could go wrong?

The answer was that unexpected visitors from the planet she fled from were about to arrive.

Wars Without End series

https://www.amazon.com/gp/product/B0BS6WK9KM

The war between different alien groups lasted for over 2,300 years. However, Keith Robinson didn't know anything about that. He assumed that the job he had applied for was to work on an Arctic research ship. He thought that he would be assembling parts for upgraded sonar buoys. He thought wrong.

The AI on the derelict spaceship wasn't opposed to lying if that could finally get the ship repaired. Hiring a repair technician from the primitive planet Earth was a crazy plan. And even crazier, it worked.

After salvaging the alien ship, Keith finds himself the ship's owner. But something is deadly wrong in the depths of space. With the help of a temperamental AI, Keith then manages to rescue several alien refugees from stasis pods on damaged ships.

They head off to one more promising location, a supposedly minor mining station, so insignificant they had hoped the war had missed it.

They were out of wrong.

1. The 2,000 year war
2. The Second War
3. The Convention War
4. The Giant War
5. The Bug War
6. (*next title not released*)

Starship Medusa series
https://www.amazon.com/gp/product/B0B8TGWPPZ

On Mars, Jason had stumbled across the escape pod to a 3,500-year-old derelict spacecraft. The ship's AI informed Jason that he was now the captain of a massive alien starship due to his having some traces of alien DNA. That 'should' have been good news.

Except that, most of the Mars and Earth government agencies had different ideas about the alien ship.

Moreover, the ship's AI, having been derelict for centuries... It had developed some quirky issues...

But the real problem was that Jason's DNA had an additional trait that should not be there... The last time anyone had one of the forbidden DNA traits, it started the war that left the ship derelict. Maybe it's the only way to fight the aliens... It is to become something from their nightmares...

Books:
5. The Void Ripper
6. Darkness and Claws
7. The Void Shaper
8. Jumper (*Not yet released*)

The Wrong Number: Ambassador to the Stars
https://www.amazon.com/dp/B0CKM78SH2

Steve White was just taking a leisurely stroll and looking out over a small pond to see if any of the turtles were out. Suddenly, he finds himself teleported 423 light-years away. Surrounded by strange aliens and desperately trying to fake his way out of an impossible situation.

He "fakes it" and assumes the role of the Earth Ambassador to the Pathless, the somewhat insectoid partial humanoid 4-sexed race he now finds himself with.

His goal is to return to the Earth.

Their goal is much harder to understand. They want him to be the trade ambassador. But what do they want from the Earth? And what can they offer the Earth in return?

They agree to send him back to Earth, but they insist he brings along one of their race, modified to almost pass as human.

Convincing the Earth that the aliens are real was surprisingly tricky. When he does finally convince them, then things get strange really fast.

The Lord of Darkness
https://www.amazon.com/dp/B0BTK9H3Y6

I always knew my birth parents had to be complete assholes; why else would they name me something horrible like Vladimira Darkness? Now that I am in college, I go by the nickname Mira.

Then, a bunch of these heavily armed men-in-black types showed up and made me come with them.   First in a Humvee, then a Blackhawk helicopter, and then a fricking spacecraft.

My birth mother didn't die when I was a child. She only died a few days ago. I was told I needed to be there for the reading of her will.

Wearing all black for the reading of the will almost made sense. That it was heavy leather armor was a bit unexpected. Then, I was given the traditional family sidearm pistol to wear.

Only this was a very special weapon made just for me. I was apparently the product of hundreds of generations of bioengineering to be someone who could use the weapon. It had a dial with settings from 1.0 to 3.0, and 2.0 was described as "explode dinosaurs."

Why in hell would I need what was almost a handheld nuclear weapon? It seems that Mother's official title was "The Lord of Darkness" and that the succession would be the first, possibly the last, time I get to meet some of my siblings.

I had only one day to learn to survive what the future would bring. A future in a galaxy ruled by the fear of one being me...

The Green Flag
https://www.amazon.com/dp/B0CD4H7RHV

Logan Russel finds himself being transported to a different world. Now, as Lord Green, The Sage of Power, he is granted ridiculously over-the-top powerful magic.

The problem is (there always has to be a catch) that his life depends on the whims of a sketchy god, and to stay alive, he must uphold "the green flag." Unfortunately, the god never told him what the "green flag" was. He must also avoid actions that raise either a "black flag" or a "red flag." But, again, the god neglected to tell him what those were... There are many things they could be...

As his humorous adventure continues, he collects a bevy of beautiful, powerful, and overly friendly women. Unfortunately, without knowing what the flags are, he must tread very carefully. Before being transported, he was "inexperienced with women." Is the temptation of the flesh one of the flags he must avoid?

The Unexpected Isekai
https://www.amazon.com/dp/B0CBW853Z8

Jake Taylor was your average broke student at the University of Maine. One day, when he had no classes, he stumbled across a booth set up for "brain scans," Earn while you sleep. It looked like easy money; he signed up for the full scan. It would require sleeping in a booth for two days, but he would wake up thousands of dollars richer. It should be easy money...

The next thing he knows, he is no longer human, and the new world he finds himself in is extremely dangerous. So dangerous that the former occupant of the body he finds himself in has just died from a venomous snakebite.

He is informed that the body he was in had been wearing a crystal and that he is now one of "the "resurrected." Some of those who died while wearing the strange crystals have their bodies healed, but their memories were replaced by something from the crystal.

He now finds himself "Isekai'ed" (implanted into a new body) on a planet where there are no humans, in a body that looks like the former owner was a martial artist, one that used steroids and worked out... A lot of steroids!

It may be a dangerous land, but there is always work for someone who can kill monsters. Unfortunately, sometimes the real monsters are hard to tell from the normal people...

[This was Formerly released as "The Resurrection Crystal," completely updated and revised.]

Return of the Old Gods
https://www.amazon.com/dp/B0CS5SGDX9

The modern gods are gone; they have been removed from power by the old gods. The old gods are back: Greek, Egyptian, Norse, Roman, Hindu, Aztec, Celtic, Japanese, Chinese, Babylonian, and many others.

The first thing they do is kill off over 1 billion people who have been judged as Evil. They also eliminate the weapons of all of the militaries, all nuclear power fuel, and waste.

Gordon Anderson was a clerk at a 7-11, and he was (as usual) late for work. That is suddenly the least of his problems.

The world is changing; everything is in turmoil. However, the most disturbing fact may be that his phone now has new contacts in his address book.

The gods of old, the ones that have just judged and executed a billion people and are literally shifting continents like chess pieces, they now have him on speed dial...

Prelude to Fate
https://www.amazon.com/dp/B0B4YNFF5D

Jake's commute home takes an unexpected detour, leaving him stranded on a different planet. He soon finds himself in a high-tech hospital in a world populated by strange alien races.

However, the New World is not your standard Isekai story. These are not the cliché cute monster girls or the generic characters that look like they were borrowed from a video game.

In this world, he is the primitive, has no magic or cheat abilities, and has no clue what will happen. Jake tries to learn to live in the new world but discovers that not everything is what it seems.

Made in United States
Cleveland, OH
10 April 2025

15945922R20134